ADVENTURE AWAITS

VOLUME ONE

EDITED
BY
DAVID GREEN

COVER IMAGE BY

AMANDA JANSDOTTER BISSETT

First Edition
Published by
Breaking Rules Publishing Europe, 2021.
This is a work of fiction. Similarities to real people,
places,or events are entirely coincidental.

Adventure Awaits vol 1
978-91-986841-2-4

Adventures

SADIE DEVEREAUX– ESCAPE FROM ROMILEY ISLAND

CHARLOTTE LANGTREE

Sadie Devereaux pounded her fists against the door and shouted. It had closed behind her only seconds ago, but already a trickle of water covered the hard stone floor. Her gut clenched. She never should have taken this job.

"Dammit, Romiley! Open the door!"

Silence was the only reply. Cursing under her breath, Sadie turned back to look at the room. She'd have to find another way out.

Her boots splashing in the water, she checked for windows, found none, and looked up at the ceiling; there were no vents or windows she could see. Why the hell had she agreed to take this job?

She knew why, of course. *Max Garrett*. Just thinking his name made her blood boil.

She wouldn't have risked dealing with Charles Romiley IV for any other reason. He was a real piece of work. From what she'd heard, he got his kicks out of tormenting people.

Sadie tilted her head. That madman was probably watching her and having a good chuckle at her expense. A quick glance above the door confirmed her suspicions; a compact CCTV camera was aimed in her direction and followed her as she moved. She waved at the screen and flashed a wide grin before throwing a rag over the device to block his view.

Romiley liked to watch people struggle. He wouldn't have created a room with no chance of escape; it wasn't his style. No, he'd make it difficult, but there would be a way. There'd be no point to it all if she had no hope of actually getting out.

The room was filled with old objects designed to look like antiques, but Sadie's trained eye recognised the tell-tale signs of modern knockoffs. Imitations of famous paintings hung on the walls, and a pair of urns bookended the doorway. Why had Romiley created a room like this just to fill it with water?

Sadie closed her eyes and groaned when realisation hit her; he wanted it to look like an escape room.

"Moron."

With that in mind, she searched the room again, reaching beneath low tables and above high ornaments. Hidden on the floor of a birdcage, she found a key. It was large and ornate, with decorative curling patterns, and clearly too big for the main door. Glancing around, she spotted a wooden chest and used the key to unlock it. The lid was heavy as she lifted it.

Inside, three padlocks guarded three smaller boxes. Each needed three numbers to unlock it.

Sadie grimaced as the water passed her ankles.

Time was running out. She pulled the pictures off the walls, checking the backs and beneath the paper backing for clues. Behind an impressive copy of the Mona Lisa, she found a number puzzle. Her mind immediately began working it out. If she could figure out the correct order for the numbers, they would form three codes that would no doubt unlock the padlocks in the chest.

It didn't take Sadie long to solve; years of doing puzzles with her grandmother had sharpened her brain. Still, each second more water poured into the room.

Hurrying back to the chest, she put the codes into the padlocks and opened each box. The first contained a Jack of Hearts card. The second held a small board of wood. The third was filled with compact dirt, with a small hole in the centre of it.

It took her a minute.

"Black," she said. *Black*jack. *Black*board. *Black* hole. "What the hell is that supposed to mean?"

Heart racing as the water reached her knees, she swept several trinkets off a tabletop and pulled a rug up off the floor. Nothing.

Her eyes caught sight of a high shelf filled with

various bottles and jars. Pulling a chair across to climb up, she reached onto the shelf and took the glass containers down, one at a time. Some were empty, some held coloured liquid, but three of them hid more clues; a black spot, a miniature building-block scene of a salon, and a tiny, exquisite painting of a sleeping girl.

"Salon… Hair salon?" Sadie mumbled to herself. "Spot… light? No."

She closed her eyes and took a deep breath.

"Beauty." *Beauty* spot. *Beauty* salon. Sleeping *beauty*. "*Black Beauty*."

Eyes widening, she turned to the bookshelf and scanned through several titles before she found the right one.

Wading through waist-high water to reach it, she pulled on the spine of *Black Beauty*.

A loud groaning sound reverberated through the room. Sadie backed away from the wall and tripped over the trinkets she'd pushed onto the floor. Sinking under the water, she held her breath until she clambered back to her feet, then pushed the wet hair back off her face.

She was going to kick Romiley's arse for this.

With painful slowness, the wall with the fireplace opened out to reveal a narrow passageway. With the seal broken, water gushed along the dark path until it was no higher than the ankles of Sadie's boots. She reached back to wring the water from her hair and did the same to her soaked t-shirt. She daren't look at the state of her boots, but the squelching of her socks was not a good sign.

Her mouth clenched into a tight line, Sadie stuck her middle finger up at the covered camera before she headed into the pitch-black passage.

Until her eyes accustomed to the darkness, she kept her left hand against the wall and her right hand out in front of her face. Her fingers caught on thick cobwebs, and she shuddered.

She walked for what felt like an age, guessing at left or right turns, and backtracking when she hit a dead end. If this was the kind of thing Romiley had set up for trespassers, she hated to think what might have happened to Max. The silly fool should never have come here; but then, neither should she. Was he really the fool, or was she the fool to have followed him? Was all of this really worth it for the sake of an ancient stick of wood?

She wanted to sit down and rest, but stubborn pride kept her moving. After a few more feet, a faint breath of air teased at the damp fabric clinging to her skin, and she shivered. She had to be near the exit! Moving faster, she scraped her arm against the wall but ignored the pain to race along the corridor.

Gradually, the passageway grew lighter and lighter until she could see the space ahead of her. Just around a sharp corner, a heavy oak door nestled in a smooth stone wall. Sadie pushed the handle down, surprised when the door opened, letting sunlight stream into the darkness.

"What the…?"

Stepping out into verdant countryside, she took

a deep breath of the fresh summer air and looked for clues to where she was.

Romiley owned the whole island, which was pretty impressive when you considered the fact that it was only marginally smaller than Tuvalu. Research had told Sadie that Romiley was the only occupant, though why he needed so much space to himself was anybody's guess. When she'd beached her small boat earlier that day, she hadn't intended to venture any further than the sole building, only two miles from where she'd landed. The large complex seemed the likeliest place to keep the staff, and that was all she was interested in.

Brow creasing, Sadie realised she had no idea where she was now, and no idea how to get back to her boat to get off the island.

"Dammit."

At least she was out of that room.

Straightening her shoulders, she stepped out onto the grass and made her way down the hill towards a wide patch of trees. Huge shrubs dotted the landscape, and hills rolled like waves into the horizon. With a bit of luck, she'd at least be able to find something to eat.

She'd been walking about an hour when the sky turned a dusky pink and she knew she'd have to find shelter for the night. Wandering through the dense wood, her boots crunched on twigs and pressed soft leaves into the dirt as she walked.

Her stomach grumbled, so she foraged along the woodland floor until she found a patch of wild garlic and some wild strawberries hidden in the shade. She would have preferred to wash them, but they made a nice feast after almost twenty-four hours on no food. When she stumbled across a small stream, she followed it to its source at the top of a hill and enjoyed a cool drink to wet her parched throat.

When something lumbered out of the trees at the bottom of the hill, Sadie blinked and wondered if there'd been something funky about the wild garlic.

The beast looked to be around twelve feet tall. It was a drab grey-green colour, with brighter feathers atop its head and across its long tail. Walking on strong hind legs, its forearms were short and stubby, and its huge jaw opened wide to reveal dozens of razor-sharp teeth. A deep-throated, booming sound echoed through the valley as it sniffed and looked up the hill to Sadie.

Sadie's mouth gaped open. When the beast began to shuffle up the hill, she jumped to her feet and legged it down the other side towards another section of forest. The back of her throat burned as she forced ragged breaths into her lungs, putting everything she had into running from the creature. Her calf muscles screamed, and a stitch stabbed at her side; still, she ran.

Just inside the treeline, a large hand grabbed her and pulled her down a steep incline into a large pool of mud.

She writhed against him, fighting to escape, until a familiar voice hissed in her ear.

"It's me! Be quiet until it's gone."

"Max?"

He pressed a finger to her lip, and she lay still, staring into his ice-blue eyes. The wet mud soaked into her clothes until she shivered. An earthy scent filled her nostrils. Her elbows sunk in the mud as Max's weight held her body down.

The booming call of the beast hovered along the treeline for several minutes before it faded away as the creature gave up and went elsewhere.

Max waited a little longer before climbing to his feet and offering Sadie a hand to help her up.

Ignoring him, she stood on her own and looked him up and down. He'd lost weight; the lines of his cheekbones were prominent beneath heavily shadowed eyes. What had been slight stubble on his jaw had now grown into a beard, and a fresh scar marred his forehead. His clothes were covered in mud, like hers.

"What are you doing here?" Max asked.

Sadie arched her brow. "Looking for you."

The lines next to his eyes grew deeper.

"Shaun hired me to find the staff and look for you while I'm here." She looked away. "You kind of missed an important event, you know."

He shuffled his feet in the dirt and ran a dirty hand through dirtier hair. "I should have been in and out, Sadie. I would've been back in time, but Romiley…"

"Yeah. He's a crazy son-of-a-bitch. Speaking of…" She put her hands on her hips. "What the fuck was that thing chasing me? Tell me it wasn't what it

12

looked like."

"Can't do that, darlin'. It was exactly what it looked like."

"You're telling me I just saw a fucking T-Rex on an island in the twenty-first century?"

He nodded. "Romiley has a lot of… unique things here. T-Rex is probably the biggest of them, but he has a host of other dinosaurs roaming the land. He likes to collect rare things."

"Rare. Sure. Dinosaurs aren't rare; they're fucking extinct!"

"Not anymore. Romiley apparently hired a team of people, then killed 'em off when they'd done what he wanted."

Sadie shook her head as she sat on a tuft of grass and picked clumps of dirt off her legs. "This is a nightmare."

Max sat next to her, stretching his legs out and leaning back on his elbows. "My boat was trashed. Do you have one stashed somewhere?"

"Yes. It's out of the way, so it should be okay. I'm not sure where we are in relation to it, though. And we can't leave without the staff."

"Honey, our lives are more important than a piece of wood."

"It belongs in a museum, Max. I'm not leaving it with Romiley."

He sighed. "The sun is almost set, Sadie; let's rest. We really don't want to be outside in the dark. We'll pick this up again in the morning."

Max walked ahead, leading Sadie deeper into

the forest until he pointed out a small shelter made with sticks and packed with mud and leaves. It was well hidden, and Sadie wouldn't have spotted it without his help. Pulling a section aside, he gestured for her to enter. Once they were both inside, he pulled it closed again.

Sadie looked around. There was just enough room for them to lie down side by side, but it would be a cosy fit. It seemed sturdy enough; not much would be able to get at them, unless it was strong enough to ram the whole structure down. She nodded her approval.

"You've been dodging dinosaurs and living in this for three weeks?"

"Two and a half." He corrected her. "It took me a couple days to break out of Romiley's compound."

She snorted. "A couple of days? I got out of his escape room in a couple of hours."

"That's great," he said with a laugh. "But I wasn't in an escape room. I was in some sort of dungeon. I occasionally saw guards when they brought me food, but I was mostly left alone. I have no idea what he planned to do with me."

"How did you get out then?"

"Managed to overpower a guard and grab his keys."

She pursed her lips. "Risky move."

Max shrugged. "It worked. Didn't help me out here, though. Almost three weeks, and I haven't been able to get the staff or get home."

She shivered as the night grew colder and pulled

her knees up to her chest so she could wrap her arms around them. "Yeah. About that."

Lying down on the ground, he stretched out and pulled Sadie down to lie beside him. Once there, he wrapped his arms around her and held her until she stopped shivering. Outside the shelter, nocturnal animals snuffled along the forest floor, and an owl screeched.

"I had to cancel it all, Max," Sadie said in a soft voice. "The chapel, the reception, the honeymoon. It was too late to get our money back."

"I'm so sorry, Sadie." His whisper warmed her ear.

"Why did you come here, Max? You should have said no; it was too close to our wedding. Now it's all ruined."

"I really thought I'd be back in plenty of time. I'm an idiot. I swear I'll make it up to you. We'll rearrange the wedding as soon as we get home, and I promise I won't be going anywhere until we get back from a month-long honeymoon in Mexico."

Her eyes stung and she snuggled closer into him. "I'm holding you to that."

Max pressed a kiss against her brow, and they settled down to rest. Within seconds, Max's breathing grew heavier.

Sadie sighed. "I'm glad you're alive, you idiot."

A bustle of noise woke them before the sun rose. Paws stampeded across the forest floor, followed by a strange honking sound.

Sadie opened her mouth to ask, but Max squeezed her arm to silence her and shook his head. Only when the noise had died down did he release her.

She looked at him, head tilted to one side.

"Raptors," he said grimly.

Her eyes widened. "Can't they smell us?"

"The mud helps with that." He gestured at their filthy clothes and faces. "I've also got garlic and mint, and other smelly plants worked into the shelter to help block our scent."

"I knew you were more than a pretty face." She grinned.

He leaned in to kiss her. "I'm really happy to see you, Sadie. Let's get this show on the road so we can go home and get on with our lives."

"Do you have a plan?"

He winced. "Not really. I can get us back to the compound, but beyond that I have no idea."

"I guess we'll have to wing it."

They moved with caution, hiding within the woods for as long as they could. When they had to venture into the open, they zigzagged between hiding places and kept watch for dinosaurs.

In a wide valley, they saw several herbivore species grazing in the long grass. Sadie stopped to watch for a moment, marvelling at the sight before her. A huge triceratops stood beside a stegosaurus at the edge of a small lake, and a diplodocus reached up to munch on leaves while a young ankylosaurus frolicked with its parents close by.

"This is amazing," she said.

Max put his arm around her shoulders and looked at her. "It sure is."

They moved on with some reluctance, knowing time was of the essence. As the sun reached its highest point, they saw the top of the compound rising above the crest of the next hill.

"I wonder what else Romiley has in store for us," Max said.

Sadie clenched her fist. "I know what I have in store for him."

A deep-throated boom sounded behind them.

"That's not good." Sadie gulped.

She glanced over her shoulder and saw the tyrannosaurus rex lumbering towards them, picking up speed as he walked.

"Run!"

Max and Sadie raced over uneven ground, pushing their bodies to the limits of human endurance. Still, the T-Rex gained on them.

"They can walk at speeds of twenty-five miles per hour!" Max yelled. "How the fuck can we beat that?"

"Shut up!"

She stumbled, and Max yanked her back onto her feet. They crested the hill and half-ran, half-rolled down the other side. At the bottom, Romiley's compound towered into the sky. The wall was way too high for them to climb. The T-Rex boomed again, closer this time, and the earth rumbled with each thunderous step it took.

Sadie spotted a tree further along the wall. "Boost me up!"

Heart pounding, she climbed onto Max's shoulders to get onto the lowest branch, then moved to a better position so she could help him up. Once they were both in the tree, they climbed higher. The T-Rex reached them, reaching up with powerful jaws and narrowly missing Max's foot as he clambered away.

Level with the wall, Sadie edged along a branch until she could swing down and stretch her legs out to reach the top. It was precarious, and she almost fell, but thoughts of the sharp teeth waiting below spurred her on. As soon as she was safe, Max followed.

Balancing on hands and knees, she looked over the edge of the wall into the compound. "That's a long way down."

"And no trees to help us."

"There's water at the bottom though; look! It's like a moat or something. Seems about right for Romiley."

"We can probably make that." Max agreed.

Sadie sighed. "I'm going to get wet again."

Without hesitation, she jumped off the wall and into the cool water below. Holding her breath, she swam back to the surface and pulled herself onto the grassy bank at the other side. Max was close behind her. She opened her mouth to speak, then swore.

"He has a fucking crocodile!"

Running on fumes, they zigzagged away from

another huge-jawed reptile until they scrambled through an open gate and slammed it shut behind them. Gasping for breath, they sank to the ground and rested for a moment in what appeared to be an ornamental garden.

"This guy needs help," Sadie said when she could breathe again. "What the hell else are we going to find here?"

The sound of voices carried through the air. Scrambling for cover, Max and Sadie hid behind a small potting shed as Romiley and another man walked into the garden.

"Sir, there are now two people wandering around on the island," the man said. "We need to do something about it."

Romiley waved his hand dismissively. "Arnold, there are dozens of dinosaurs running wild beyond my gates; I'm sure those two miscreants will have been eaten by now."

"I looked them up, Sir. They seem to be resourceful people. I don't think we can afford to underestimate them."

"I suppose you can send a team to find them." Romiley sighed. "It was quite entertaining having guests for a while. I was looking forward to watching as they were eaten; they've spoiled all my fun."

Sadie and Max looked at each other.

"Sir," Arnold continued. "I think we should reinforce security around the viewing room. These people deal with antiquities; they'll no doubt be after the staff."

"As you wish. Let me know when they've been found, will you? And have Paulette bring me some coffee in the sun lounge."

The voices faded as the men moved away.

"The viewing room?" Sadie said.

"I say we follow them," Max suggested. "It sounds like Arnold could lead us where we want to go."

She nodded her agreement, and they moved with caution in the direction the two men had gone. It was easy to follow them; they had no suspicion that Sadie and Max were inside the compound. The men went inside the main building. Romiley turned left, and Arnold turned right. As the door was left unlocked, Sadie and Max slipped inside and followed Arnold.

The grey-haired man walked through several rooms until he reached a large oak door in what Sadie assumed was the centre of the compound.

"Double the security here," Arnold ordered the group of three men guarding the door. "We might have some trouble."

"Aye, Sir."

The guard spoke into a radio to request more men, and Arnold nodded before leaving the room by a different route.

Sadie grinned.

Max narrowed his eyes and shook his head.

She nodded, planting a kiss on his mouth before stumbling into the room with a quick giggle. The guards looked up and tightened their grips on their guns.

"This isn't the bathroom," Sadie said with a hiccup. She tilted to one side, and over-corrected to veer back the other way.

The guards glanced at each other.

"I've never known Romiley to have guests before," one said.

"He has good whisky!" Sadie commented, adding another hiccup for good measure. She stepped closer. "I was only gonna have one, but he showed me a dinosaur! Did you know he had dinosaurs?"

She edged closer again, placing a hand on one man's shoulder.

"A fucking dinosaur! Had to celebrate that. Did I tell you he has good whisky?"

A guard with a grizzled face cleared his throat. "Listen, lady…"

Sadie didn't give him a chance to finish. Straightening up, she grabbed the closest guard's gun in a two-handed grip and rammed the butt up beneath his chin. He fell to the ground unconscious as she swung round to smash the weapon against a second man's head. As she turned to the third guard, she found herself looking down the barrel of his gun.

He opened his mouth to speak, then his eyes rolled back into his head. He crumpled to the floor, revealing a scowling Max behind, an empty vase in his hands.

"You hit him with a vase?" Sadie asked.

Max shrugged. "It was handy."

Adrenaline pumping, she grabbed a set of keys

from one guard's pocket. They worked quickly to pull the men into a nearby cupboard, then wedged a chair beneath the door handle in case they woke up too soon.

"They already called for more men," she told Max. "We don't have a lot of time."

Using the keys to unlock the door, they dashed inside and gaped at the spacious room before them. With high ceilings and no windows, the only light came from carefully directed lamps aimed at various display tables. The sound of Sadie's boots on the marble floor echoed through the room as she walked around to take a closer look. The paintings on the wall were definitely original pieces of art, and each carefully placed stand held precious trinkets and artefacts that were no doubt worth millions of pounds.

"It's like a museum," she said, eyes wide.

Max snorted. "A museum that nobody is ever allowed to visit. What's the point of all this stuff being hidden away? There are pieces of history here. Look there; that's an original Kapelhoff. If I'm correct, this piece here dates back to pre-Roman times."

"I think this sword belonged to William Marshal," Sadie added, her voice high and light as she marvelled at the wonders before her. "Max, none of this should be here; it belongs in a real museum."

"The staff is over here, look. What the hell did Romiley do to get his hands on all of this? He must have sold his soul to the devil."

A throat cleared behind them, and they turned to see Romiley and several armed men in the doorway.

"Not quite the devil," Romiley said with a smirk. "Although I do believe several people have all but sold their souls to me. You'd be amazed at what people will do for money."

Sadie moved to stand beside Max. "People know we're here, Romiley. This will go a lot better for you if you let us go."

He ran a hand through his thick head of grey hair and laughed. "But then who would I feed to my sharks?"

She looked at Max as the guards moved closer and pointed guns in their direction. "He's joking, right?"

Max grimaced. "So far we've seen dinosaurs and crocodiles; I doubt he'd be afraid to keep a couple of sharks."

Sadie's mind churned as she and Max were handcuffed together, back-to-back, before being shoved inside a small cupboard. They stumbled, tripping over each other and falling at an awkward angle. Max's chin thudded against the floor, and Sadie's arms twisted behind her as she landed on top of Max.

"I won't keep you waiting long, my dears," Romiley said before slamming the door shut. "My sharks are hungry."

Rolling until they were able to sit up, Max curled his fingers around Sadie's and squeezed.

"Damn it!" She cursed.

"It'll be okay. We'll find a way out of this."

"How? We're handcuffed and about to be fed to

sharks by a madman. Do you have an idea?"

He sighed. "Not yet, but I'm sure we've been in worse scrapes."

Sadie arched her brow. "When I get free, Romiley is gonna feel my boot so far up his arse, he'll be able to taste it."

"That's my girl."

They sat in silence for a while, each pondering their situation. There was only one faint bulb flickering in the ceiling; the shadows were deep and dark. A scurrying noise in the back corner made them shudder.

"Max?" Sadie began.

"Hmm?"

"You remember South Africa?"

He tried to twist his neck to look at her and winced. "Sure. What does that…? No! You said that hurt like a mother!"

"It did, but I don't see another way out of this. I've done it before; it'll be easier this time."

Max swallowed. "Sadie, you can have the highland cow at the wedding."

She blinked. "What?"

"Honey, if you do what I think you're about to do, you deserve something wonderful when we get back home. I know you wanted the cow, and we said we couldn't afford it, but let's have the damn cow. Hell, we can have our own farm full of 'em if we get out of here."

"Max Garret, I could kiss you!"

He chuckled.

Sadie took a deep breath. There was a sharp crack, and she grunted before blowing air out between her teeth. "Son of a bitch, that hurt."

"You dislocated your thumb; I'm not surprised it hurt."

She slipped her left hand free of the cuffs, leaving her right hand still cuffed to Max's left. He turned and planted a firm kiss on her lips as she popped the thumb back into place.

"Get us out of here and I'll make good on that promise," he said.

"Oh, I will. I'm not sticking around to be shark food."

A guard hammered on the door. "What's going on in there?"

One corner of Max's mouth tilted up. "You've got to get in here! She's having a seizure!"

"I'm not falling for that," the man growled. "But I will come in there and gag you if you don't shut up."

Sadie and Max shouted and screamed as loud as they could.

When the guard entered, Max floored him with a powerful right hook. The man behind him was kicked in the groin by Sadie. The third man, peering cautiously into the room at his fallen colleagues, was knocked off guard when Sadie grabbed the barrel of his gun and stripped it from him with a move so fast, he was unable to counter it. She aimed the weapon and instructed Max to search pockets for keys to their cuffs.

Within seconds, they were free of the handcuffs. With Sadie still pointing the gun at the downed men, Max used the cuffs to secure the three of them together. Despite looking, there was nothing within the room to attach the cuffs to so no doubt the men would be able to move once all of them were conscious, but Sadie was satisfied they would be out of her hair for a while.

Max closed the door and locked the men in the room, ignoring the shouts of the two who were still awake.

"Let's just get back to the boat," Sadie said. "Shaun can send a whole team to sort Romiley out. I want to go home and get married with a highland cow in my wedding party."

Following her back along the corridor, Max narrowed his eyes. "I thought the cow was just going to be in a couple of photos."

"If we're having one, it might as well be involved in the whole thing," she replied. "Oh, it could be the ringbearer! That would be adorable."

He muttered something unintelligible under his breath, and wisely said nothing else.

When they entered a room with wide double doors leading out into the garden, they paused.

"I think this is the way I came in," Sadie said. "Nowhere near the dinosaurs."

"Yeah, this should lead to Romiley's beach, where I assume you landed. He wouldn't want any dangers around where he could be seen in a pair of swimming trunks."

26

Sadie shuddered. "Don't put that image in my head."

The room was a large open space, with a section filled with white sofas, presumably for entertaining guests—though if Romiley ever had guests, Sadie would go back outside and kiss that T-Rex. On the other side, a home bar housed several bottles of alcohol behind a marble-topped counter; a jar of colourful cocktail umbrellas sat beside an old-fashioned ashtray and a bowl of peanuts.

"Have we gone back in time?" Max asked.

Sadie snorted.

The wall beside the bar was mounted with weapons, while the opposite wall sported bright paintings of jungle scenes and portraits of women in various stages of undress.

"He's a real charmer, isn't he," Sadie said.

They walked warily towards the doors, eyes darting around the room to monitor each of three possible exits. They were almost out when two men appeared ahead of them. Backing up, they saw armed guards coming through both of the other doors, followed by a smirking Romiley.

"You two are like a bad penny," he said. "I think my sharks may just have to go hungry. I'm growing bored of your shenanigans. Any final words?"

Sadie looked at Max and waggled her eyebrows towards the bar over her shoulder; it was the only clear direction they could head in. He nodded.

"I have something to say," Max said.

As Romiley waited for him to continue, Sadie

and Max launched themselves backwards and rolled over the bar mere seconds before bullets shattered the bottles and glasses on the wall behind them.

"Get me some alcohol," Sadie hissed as she tore a strip off the bottom of her shirt.

Max grabbed a can of beer. "Are you hit?"

"No, you idiot." She huffed, pushed him out of the way, and grabbed a full bottle of vodka that had survived the first round of bullets. "This looks like strong stuff."

"Come out now and we'll kill you quickly," Romiley called out.

Sadie soaked the strip of her shirt in the alcohol and shoved the rag into the bottle neck. "Matches!" She forced the lid back onto the bottle, trapping the rag in place.

Looking around, Max spotted a pack of matches on the edge of the bar and slid it across the floor to Sadie.

Hands steady, she lit a match and used it to light the end of the rag. Without pause, she threw the bottle over the bar and ducked back behind the counter, covering her ears with her hands. Max did the same.

The loud smash of breaking glass was immediately followed by the whoosh of flames and the pained screams of burning men.

"Run!" she yelled.

They rolled out from behind the bar and scrambled towards the open door into the garden. Almost there, three hulking figures blocked their way; Romiley and two of his guards.

Max moved to the left, drawing the attention of the two men away from Sadie, who kept her eyes focused on Romiley.

His tall frame towered above her as he blocked her escape route. "You, Miss Devereaux, are an absolute pain in the arse."

She beamed at him. "Thanks. I'm going to take that as a compliment."

His mouth tightened. Quick as a flash, he pulled a pistol from a holster beneath his jacket and pointed it at Sadie.

"Oh, to hell with it," she said.

Calling on her years of Krav Maga and previous military service, she launched forward, gripping the barrel of the gun with both hands and thrusting it to the right in one sudden movement.

Romiley fired, but too late; the bullet thudded harmlessly into one of the white sofas.

At the same time, Sadie lifted her knee to his groin and twisted the gun from his hand, enjoying the sickening crack of his finger as it got caught in the trigger guard. He screamed. She stepped back and aimed the gun at his chest.

Glancing back at the raging fire spreading through the room, she gestured to the door. "Let's take this outside."

Out of the corner of her eye, she saw Max quickly dispatch the last of the guards with a nimble roundhouse kick to the head and nodded her approval.

"I'm going to marry him," she gushed to Romiley.

Romiley glowered.

Still pointing the gun at him, she watched as Max dragged the unconscious men outside to get them away from the fire. He kept going back for more bodies until all the men were safe in the garden, then closed all the doors to slow the spread of the flames.

Surveying the groaning bodies writhing on the grass, he said, "I think we need an ambulance."

"On an island?" Sadie said with a snort.

Max shrugged. "Air ambulance, then. Someone needs to call for help. These guys all need to be in a hospital."

Sadie cleared her throat and gave Romiley a pointed look.

"There's a satellite phone in the house," he said after a long pause, clutching his broken finger.

"Let's go."

Flashing her a lopsided grin, Max said, "Can you manage with Romiley if I stay to give these guys some first aid?"

"Sure. I'm not guaranteeing I'll bring him back in one piece though."

She forced Romiley to lead the way through the garden until they came to another entrance to the main house, far enough away from the fire to be safe for the moment. He took her into a large office space, with a wide mahogany desk and a bearskin rug that looked suspiciously like the real thing. The head of a young velociraptor was mounted on the back wall.

Sadie's stomach sank. "You hunt them?"

Romiley's lips curled into a smirk. "Why else would I have created them? I needed a challenge."

Before she could stop him, Romiley pulled back a curtain separating one side of the room from the other. Behind it, in a cage the size of a garden shed, three dinosaurs watched with beady eyes. They each stood on two hind legs and rose feet above the humans. A pair of thin bony crests on the head of each dinosaur caught her eye, as did the dozens of sharp, curved teeth in their mouths.

Sadie recoiled. "What type of dinosaur are they?"

"Dilophosaurus," he replied. "They're really quite remarkable. I've been studying them. Do you know, they're warm-blooded? It's fascinating."

"Studying them… You mean, taking them apart to see how they work?"

He shrugged, arms out and palms up. "Of course."

Shaking her head, she refocused the gun in his direction. "Get the phone."

Romiley narrowed his mouth into a thin line but did as he was told, pulling a black satellite phone from one of the desk drawers. A spark in his eyes was the only warning before he tossed the phone at her face and rushed at her.

Sadie fired once; the bullet grazed his arm, but flew past him and pinged off the cage holding the dinosaurs. He wrestled her for the gun, using his brute strength to pull it from her grip. Before he could turn it on her, she lashed out and sent the gun spinning across the wooden floor. Her eyes remained glued to his, watching for the slightest twitch to indicate his next move.

When he tried to attack with a brawling hay-maker punch, Sadie almost smiled. She blocked it easily, clipping his jaw with her closed fist at the same time. As he reeled from the punch, she followed up with a barrage of more, finishing with an elbow to his temple. Dazed, he fell to his knees.

Glancing around for something to tie him up with, Sadie's stomach clenched; a series of low grunts and hisses came from the area where the cage was. The scrape of clawed feet on the floor made goosebumps rise on her arms. She turned to the cage; the lock keeping it closed had been damaged by her stray bullet, and the iron-barred door now swung free. A few feet out, and moving steadily closer, the three dilophosauruses opened their mouths and watched their prey.

In a flash, Sadie calculated the distance to the door and threw herself towards it as one lunged for her. She fell just short and pulled herself through the gap. The dilophosaurus's teeth clamped down on the heel of her boot. She kicked out with the other foot, stomping on the creature's nose with all the force she could muster. It cried out and let go; she scrambled through the door.

She turned to look. "Romiley! Run!"

Bloodied and dishevelled, Romiley squared his

jaw. "They won't beat me! I just need to get to my gun!"

Instead of racing to the door, he headed in the other direction towards a gun displayed above his desk. Helpless to save him, Sadie reeled back and slammed the door shut when the dinosaur closest to her made a second attempt at her feet. Behind the door, high-pitched screams competed with the hungry growls of the dilophosauruses and the sickening sound of tearing flesh. Within seconds, the screams stopped.

Sadie turned the key in the lock and vomited all over her boots.

Walking slowly back to where she'd left Max, she forced herself to sing loud rock songs to get those nightmarish sounds out of her head.

"Sadie?" Max ran over to her.

She shook her head.

"Where's Romiley?"

Her stomach churned. "Dead. He had some dinosaurs in a cage. They got out, and he thought he was quicker than they were. He was wrong."

Max paled.

"I didn't get the phone, either."

Pulling her close, he said, "Don't worry about that. I searched the guards and found a sat phone in one of their vests. I called Shaun already; help is on the way."

"I guess we just have to wait then." She held him as tightly as she could and fought the stinging in her eyes.

Guiding her to a bench beneath a trellis of pink roses, Max gently pushed her onto the seat and pressed a kiss to her brow. "We could go and check out Romiley's museum room again?"

Her interest sparked. "Maybe."

Max put his arm around her shoulders. "Or we could do a little wedding planning while we wait? I have some good ideas now we get to plan it all over again."

Sadie sighed and rested her head on his shoulder. "Maybe later, Max. Right now, I think I might just close my eyes for a little while."

They sat in silence, enjoying the quiet peace of the distant sea, the birds in the sky, and the dwindling crackle of the fire dying inside the closed room. As the miraculous booming calls of dinosaurs drifted through the air, Sadie closed her eyes and floated in a half-dream.

Stirring slightly, she leaned closer into Max and mumbled, "Do you think we could have a triceratops at the wedding?"

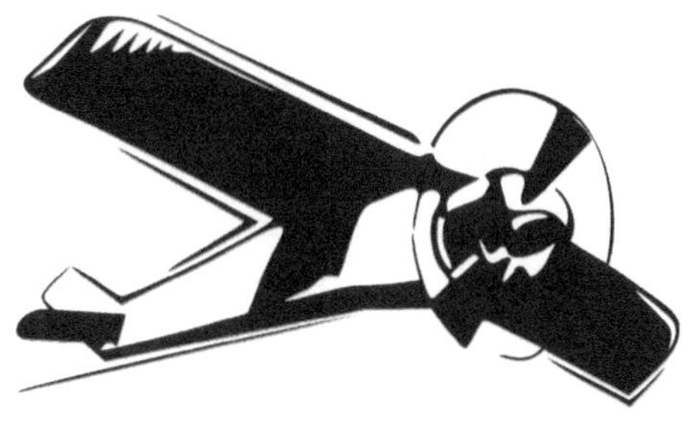

DEATH IN THE AIR

GORDON LINZNER

Even a tyrant's rule has its advantages, Jelia mused. The curfew imposed by Governor Morek on the town of Banesford since he'd taken control left her father's neighbourhood much quieter at night.

Not that Morek would have intentionally done Boruth any favours. Since her father's resignation from the City Guard, he'd grown increasingly vocal about the Governor's harsh policies. Neither his honest reputation nor his weaponry skills would protect him forever. Jelia made it her mission to keep a close watch on her last living relative.

This evening brought a more immediate concern. Boruth developed a fever that afternoon after returning from his favourite tavern. His stomach cramps were so severe even the stoic former Guard could not restrain his groans. Hours went by before Boruth's pains subsided enough that he could fall into a fitful sleep, soothed by rhythmic drumming of raindrops against terracotta roof tiles.

Jelia wrapped herself in a thin wool blanket as she settled into the chair beside her father's bed. Boruth undoubtedly would need her assistance again. Her scabbarded sword leaned against the chair, its hilt in ready reach. Since Governor Morek's usurpation of Banesford, she always kept the weapon near.

Should her father not improve by sunrise, Jelia would fetch a physician. She'd have done so tonight, save for that arbitrary curfew. Even so, she would have defied the edict had she known of any healer also willing to do so.

The woman leaned back, legs outstretched, ankles crossed. She'd shed her damp leather boots, but did not otherwise bother undressing. At least she had no memorial songs to compose. Most of Banesford's recently bereaved—and there were more than usual under Morek's rule—turned to other Composers. That was hardly surprising, given Jelia's limited availability and, more significant, her father's political views. People wisely kept their distance.

Jelia closed her eyes. The rooftop pit-a-pat started to lull her, as it had her father.

She was nearly asleep when another sound intruded, faint but clear beneath the pattering rainfall. Someone was opening Boruth's front door. Someone who botherec neither to knock nor call out.

Jelia rose, tossed the blanket aside, and drew

her sword. Her bare feet glided silently across the hardwood floor.

She stepped from the bedchamber into the entry hall just as three cloaked figures pushed their way in. The insignia on their cloaks confirmed them as Governor Morek's private guards. They were also human, rather than the expendable bestial vuks his shamans created to supplement his forces.

It could hardly be a coincidence that Morek's guards arrived now, in the dead of night, while her father lay incapacitated. The only mystery was how they knew he was ill. On reflection, that was no mystery at all. She promised to share harsh words with that innkeeper. He'd be lucky if words were all that was exchanged.

"Lost, are we?" Jelia asked, stepping forth to block the trio.

Raised eyebrows told her the intruders expected Boruth to be alone. Jelia kept her sword pointed down. She wanted it clear that she offered no immediate threat.

Yet.

The lead guard tugged officiously at his sergeant's cap. His voice made only the barest effort at sincerity.

"Our apologies. We did not intend to disrupt your household." The sergeant's fingers brushed the hilt of his own scabbarded weapon. "Governor Morek wishes to consult with Boruth about some recent statements made regarding his policies. For clarification. To reach an accord."

"At this hour?" Jelia met the man's cold grey eyes with a steady gaze.

The sergeant shrugged. "The Governor is a busy man. He often works late."

Jelia stalled, assessing the trio. "Why not send a messenger? Why his private guard? And why three of you, to conduct one man?"

"It is well past curfew. Duty requires we provide a formal escort."

"To be personally summoned by Governor Morek is an honour," added the guard, who stood behind the sergeant. His voice was little more than a growl. Perhaps he'd spent too much time among the vuks.

Jelia had no illusions about their true purpose. Many citizens of Banesford had been summoned to late night conferences with Governor Morek and never seen again. She needed to get her father out of Banesford.

"I fear your mission is in vain," Jelia replied. "My father is too ill to meet tonight. I suggest the Governor reschedule."

"Governor Morek does not..." began the growler.

"Enough, Roypo." The sergeant waved a hand for silence while continuing to focus on Boruth's daughter.

"Jelia, is it not? I am Sergeant Grolien. My associates, Guards Roypo and Marilene." He extended his left hand, palm up, and forced his lips to form an affable grin. "If Boruth is indeed ill, we can arrange for the Governor's personal healer to attend him."

She ignored his outstretched hand. "My father already receives proper care."

"Ah. Trained as a healer, are you?"

Jelia did not reply.

"Another skill to complement your renown at composing memorial songs," Grolien observed. "In addition to your reputation with that sword."

Jelia remained silent.

"Governor Morek could use someone with your abilities in his personal guard. Although he does expect a certain level of discipline." His tone hardened. "A willingness to obey orders, for instance."

"I will permit my father to be moved only if I can accompany him."

Grolien sighed. "That is not possible. Protocol." The time for talk was over. He signaled Roypo and Marilene to move in.

Never act rashly, Boruth taught her, but if you must, be swift. Jelia raised her sword as the lower-rank guards stepped forward.

Roypo came at her first, repeating his growl. One quick, deep slash across the throat took him down. His weapon clattered on the hardwood floor.

Marilene ducked low, unfurling her cloak, trying to snag Jelia's blade. Boruth's daughter half-smiled; she'd used that same trick more than once.

Jelia flattened against the wall. Damp fabric brushed her elbow. She grasped the guard's cloak with her free hand and tugged. Marilene stumbled forward. Before she could regain her balance, Jelia thrust her blade through the guard's back. The erose edge did more harm coming out than going in.

Before Marilene hit the floor, Jelia spun about to face Sergeant Grolien.

Outside, with more room to maneuver, the sergeant might have held her off. Within the confines of Boruth's home, which Jelia knew far better than Grolien, she easily deflected his attack with the edge of her blade. She added a swift kick to his crotch.

Grolien spun around, off balance. Jelia impaled him with a single thrust, then slashed his throat.

A stupid waste of lives, she reflected. Necessary, but stupid.

There was far too much stupidity in Banesford under Governor Morek.

Jelia shook off her feelings. She could wallow in regret later. Her first priority was to get her father to a sanctuary.

She looked to the bedchamber.

"No!"

Though leaking blood and intestines, Marilene managed to crawl to Boruth's bedside. She leaned over him, pressing her dagger to his throat.

Jelia leapt forward. Her right foot lashed out at the guard's head. Had she worn her thick leather boots, the blow would have snapped the woman's neck. As it was, the dagger point was deflected...

... but not enough.

Jelia shoved Marilene's dying body aside, ran the guard through again to be certain, then bent over her father. She laid her bloody sword on the bed

40

alongside Boruth, freeing both her hands to staunch the wound.

Knowing the act was futile.

Boruth stared up at his daughter. His lips moved, but he could not speak. He did not need to. Jelia knew what he wanted to say.

"I promise, father. I will keep my vow. To honour both you and my mother's memory."

Boruth acknowledged her response with a final twitch of his lips. Then his eyes glazed over, and his body slackened beneath her hands.

Jelia stood over her father's body for a long moment, unable to speak or even move. Fighting tears, she draped her blanket over his face and retrieved her sword. She gave a final kick to the female guard's corpse before stepping carefully over the other two. There would be time for proper mourning after she fulfilled her promise.

Mourning, and more.

Mid-day approached as Jelia marched steadily along the well-travelled road. She'd already covered a score of miles.

Banesford was well out of sight. The rain had lightened to a dense mist. Beneath her sodden cloak, Jelia shivered, pulling the collar tight whenever a breeze arose. She should have retained Sergeant Grolien's cloak and cap even after they'd allowed her to pass through the city gates unimpeded, but the very feel of that uniform, and the evil it represented, made her cringe.

Jelia hadn't noticed exactly when the sun rose behind thick cloud cover. Mud squished beneath her boots. The only other sounds were an occasional bird call and her own soft humming as she mentally composed her father's Song of Passage. Trees along the road seemed to reach their branches skyward, more out of habit than any hope of garnering the feeble light.

She had long ceased looking back. She'd walked for hours, with no sign of other travellers. That was the point of her departing Banesford so quickly, in the dead of night—to gain a few hours' lead.

She did regret leaving her father's body to the mercies of Governor Morek and his guards, but a corpse was only a shell. Honouring Boruth's soul, fulfilling her promise to him, meant more.

The quiet suited Jelia's mood. Her mind was a-swirl with conflicting emotions, the need to maintain a steady pace, and the creation of her father's Song. Many more miles lay between her and the Temple of Askoti, the nearest sanctuary beyond Morek's influence. She meant to reach it before dusk.

This was but the second time she had to create a Song of Passage for an immediate family member. Her efforts on the occasion of her mother's passage, ten years earlier, were tainted when she let a boy's rude taunts get to her. He survived that day, some-how, but the black mark made it all the more essential that her father's Song be performed with utmost respect.

Jelia slowed, then stopped. A chord change demanded her full attention. She repeated each variation, softly singing to herself, version after version.

So occupied, she failed to notice when the few chirping birds fell silent.

Four vuks emerged from the grove behind her.

The man-beasts' unshod feet made little sound on the muddy road, but the odour of their musk alerted Jelia to their presence. Among the strategies vuks seemed incapable of grasping was that of approaching prey from upwind—an ironic flaw, given that the creatures relied so heavily on their own sense of smell.

Vuks were trained in basic battle skills, possessed quicker reflexes than humans, could speak simple phrases, acted more or less in concert. Thick, dark grey fur provided camouflage and helped deflect sharp-edged weapons. They could also outpace the average human, being less reliant on clear roads.

Among their flaws, the creatures demonstrated obvious tells in battle. In their eagerness, they sometimes got in each other's way. Any other day, Jelia could have dispatched the quartet with ease.

This was not any other day.

Had Morek sent his second-tier guards because he knew of her vow, and how it constrained her? Or because a troop of humans could not have moved quick enough to intercept her before she reached Askoti?

Jelia promised she would find out which.

Later.

The vuks closed in, swords drawn. Dark fur bristled beneath their cloaks. Instinctively, Jelia reached for her own weapon, then stopped.

The muzzle of the nearest vuk twitched. He was the leader, then. Jelia screamed to disorient the group, then raced toward him, unfastening her cloak.

The move startled the vuk long enough for her to whirl the damp wool over his head, blinding him.

He waved his sword wildly, clawing at the garment with his free paw, stumbling into the vuk behind him. Both crashed to the ground. Jelia sped past them to engage the second pair.

These two flashed their weapons in an uncoordinated attack, as she anticipated. Jelia's right foot shot up and out, striking one vuk's wrist. His weapon flew into the grove from which they had emerged.

With a snarl, the creature scrambled after it.

Jelia whirled, digging her elbow into the fourth vuk's side. The man-beast spun sideways, avoiding the brunt of the impact, but was still thrown off balance. He tumbled howling onto the muddy road.

She heard another set of footsteps approaching; booted, from the sound of them. Morek did not trust his creatures to deal with her, then. He'd sent supervision. A single skilled human could travel almost as fast as a vuk.

Jelia did not bother looking for the newcomer. The sound indicated only one human, still some distance away. She could handle a single guard, even without her sword. First, though, she needed to attend to the pair of vuks she'd initially pushed aside, then incapacitate all four as quickly as possible.

She dropped flat to the road, dodging the blade of the vuk she'd blinded. Bracing herself on elbows, she waited for his next move.

A shriek pierced the air. The vuk froze, then turned away from her. As did the one she'd elbowed.

The human swordsman reached the battle scene faster than expected. He screamed again, rushing forward, sword raised. Jelia could not make out the man's features, but at least his plain grey cloak did not bear the insignia of the Governor's Guards.

The third vuk, meanwhile, recovered his blade and burst back out of the grove. Ears pricked forward, body tense, he leaned forward, assessing the situation. With a grunt, he then joined the pair confronting the newcomer.

Meanwhile, the vuk she'd initially knocked to the ground recovered his footing. He ignored his fellows, focusing on her.

Jelia feinted a roll to her left, then changed direction. The vuk's blade struck mud an inch from her ear.

Howls rose up behind her attacker. The vuk ignored the sounds, swung his weapon again.

"Your friends could use some help," Jelia noted, dodging his second thrust.

The man-beast shook his head, ears laid back. "Must kill," he snarled.

She narrowly avoided a third blow.

"That was pathetic," she chided. "What's wrong? Afraid to get closer?"

The taunt, though an obvious ploy, worked. The vuk leapt forward to stand over her. The tip of his sword dangled inches above her heart. The creature savoured her helplessness. Dark red lips curled upward, exposing uneven fangs in what passed for a smile among vuks.

Jelia hooked his ankle with her right leg and twisted leftward, even as she rolled in the opposite direction.

The vuk tumbled backwards but did not, as she'd expected, strike the ground.

The creature was held erect by the blade protruding from his abdomen. The man-beast's eyes widened, then turned milky white. Blood dribbled from his muzzle. The weapon's point slowly turned sideways, widening the wound before it retracted.

The vuk dropped to his knees, keening, intestines spilling onto the road. Behind him stood the man in grey, his weapon still outthrust and dripping gore.

The vuk's life-spirit dispersed in a murky swirl. Jelia scrambled to her feet as her rescuer kicked the body aside. She could see his face now but recognized neither it nor his bearing.

Three more vuk bodies lay sprawled across the road behind him. One bestial head rocked back and forth several feet from its body.

The newcomer's sword wavered, spattering the road with droplets of red.

Jelia remained in place, legs tensed, wary of the stranger's intentions.

"I appear to owe you thanks, sir," she offered at last.

He acknowledged her words with a nod, but neither lowered his weapon nor changed his stoic expression. Possibly he was a mercenary, rescuing her only to get full credit for her capture... or death. Was Morek so unsure of his own forces he would also immediately issue a bounty? Was the Governor that obsessed with making certain Jelia's father did not get a proper farewell? Was he that petty?

Of course, he was.

At last, the man broke the silence with a voice as neutral as his expression. "Just thanks? Not your life?"

"Perhaps that, as well."

"Your fighting skills are impressive."

"My father was an excellent teacher."

He glanced at the scabbard tethered to her waist. "I see you have a blade at your side."

"Where else should I carry it?"

"Yet you did not use it, though outnumbered."

"That is so."

"Had you done so, I suspect the fight would have ended long before my arrival."

"Very likely."

His blade remained outthrust. "Are you as capable with that sword as your hands?"

"That is for others to say."

"Might you show me?"

Her lips tightened. "I cannot."

He stepped closer. "Now?"

"No."

His blade made a tight circle. "I truly wish to see that skill demonstrated."

The stranger was not near enough for her to strike out, but too close for her to safely turn her back on him. Her hands flexed.

"Then you will be disappointed. I am under a sacred promise. My weapon must stay sheathed until I have properly performed the Song of Passing for my father. I swore as much to him, years ago."

The man raised an eyebrow. "A curious oath. I am sorry for your loss." The stranger sliced a swatch of cloth from a vuk's robe, then used it to clean his blade. "No exceptions for self-defence?"

Jelia allowed herself to relax slightly. "Grateful though I am for your intervention, I have neither time nor inclination to share my story."

"You said you owe me... something. I will settle for your narrative. My name is Corgan. You are...?"

Jelia frowned. Even if he was merely a random adventurer, why reveal herself? If he really did not know her...

"No one of note."

He offered a thin smile. "Very well, No-One of the Note. You can tell me your tale as we walk."

"We?"

"My company may be useful, should more beast-men come after you. Which they surely will, from what I know of Governor Morek."

She tensed again. "You know of the Governor?"

"The self-styled ruler of Banesford? All too well.

We have had... disagreements in the past, though we've yet to meet face to face. I gather you've also experienced such discord, and recently."

Without replying, Jelia retrieved her cloak. She patted off chunks of mud, draped it over her shoulders, and hastened down the road, away from the carnage.

And Corgan.

The man hurried to her side. "Your father... did Morek kill him?"

"Indirectly." As much as she resented Corgan's intrusion, Jelia had to admit the opportunity to unburden herself would be a relief–provided she did so discreetly. "We can discuss that matter later. I must finish my song before I reach the Temple of Askoti, so it may give my father's soul the rest he deserves." She glanced toward the clearing sky. "Preferably before sunset."

"You could not perform that rite at the Temple in Banesford?"

"I had to leave quickly. Even had I remained, it was obvious Governor Morek would insist my father be neither honoured nor mourned. Details of their... our... disagreement need not concern you."

Corgan's mouth twitched in a half-smile. "Then it is a fortunate coincidence that I, too, am bound toward Askoti."

"Oh?"

"On a mission of my own."

Jelia spared him a disbelieving look.

"It is true." Corgan continued cleaning blood

and viscera from his blade as they walked. "My brother was killed while in the service of Governor Morek. I had warned him against joining that man's private guard, but he was stubborn, obsessed with power. Now I must avenge him."

"My condolences. This affects me how?"

"His slayer, I recently learned, also fled in the direction of Askoti. It therefore seems we are fated to be traveling companions."

"Fated? Or cursed?"

He ignored the gibe, sheathing his weapon. "You're a Composer, then?"

"Among other things."

"How does one...?"

She sighed. "You'll not be quiet until I tell you, will you?"

Corgan shrugged.

"On one condition: no more interruptions."

"A fair trade."

Jelia took a deep breath. "My mother passed away a decade ago. Long before Morek took over Banesford. While I prepared to perform her Song, an incident occurred. I acted impulsively. There was bloodshed. It tainted the ritual. My father took me to task, and rightly so. As penance, I promised that, when he passed, I would not use my sword until I'd made proper obeisance." She grimaced. "I did not expect to have to honour that promise so soon."

Corgan turned his eyes toward the road. "I am deeply sorry, No-One. More than you can imagine."

"Now I ask that you honour your own word

and speak no more. I must finish composing before I—we—reach the temple." She softened her tone, offered a wry smile. "You may want to keep your distance once you've heard my voice."

"I'll take my chances."

The fog had fully dispersed by the time they reached the Temple of Askoti. Sunlight glinted invitingly off its polished roof tiles.

Askoti was one of several outlier Temples, unassociated with any single city or ruler, intended primarily for the use of nomadic travellers, particularly those who suffered a death in their group.

A dozen ordinary Banesford dwellings could have fit within the structure, which sat a half mile off the main road, encircled by well-tended trees. Figurines of various semi-human creatures decorated its cornices, providing an air of ornate austerity. The temple itself exuded serenity and quietude.

Too much so.

Jelia's cloak had finally dried. She paused before the main entrance to shake off the last chunks of caked mud.

"May I speak now?" Corgan asked.

She gave him a querulous look.

"Your song," he explained. "It is ready?"

"Oh. Yes. Has been for a while."

"Odd that we've encountered no more of Morek's vuks. Word of our little set-to must have gotten around."

She did not respond.

"At least one Tender should have come out to greet us by now," Corgan observed.

"Agreed." Jelia's right hand flexed. She fought the impulse to draw her sword.

Corgan scowled. "I don't like it."

"Nor do I. But I have no choice. You are under no such obligation."

In reply, Corgan drew his sword, gesturing for Jelia to precede him. She thanked him with a nod, then slid open the main door.

They barely had time to take in the magnificence of the high-ceiling main room when Governor Morek's vuks attacked. A score and more of the creatures dropped from rafters, popped up behind decorative screens, crawled out from under benches. Jelia lashed out with fists and feet but it was Corgan's sword that saved the two from immediate death.

"Sing, No-One!" he shouted above the growls and clashing blades. "Stop fighting. Sing your memorial! Fulfil your vow!"

"But..."

"I'll hold them off."

Corgan said no more, focusing on the battle.

Dodging her own attackers, deflecting them towards Corgan, Jelia took up a position in the center of the great hall, where the acoustics were strongest. She cleared her throat, then took a deep breath.

She started her father's Song softly at first, as was befitting. Slowly the tune built, echoing off the stone walls. Its growing intensity was enhanced by the Temple's interior design.

The handful of vuks following her backed off, dissuaded not by blows but by the power of her voice.

Midway through the song, she spared a glance at Corgan. He bled from a dozen cuts, none of them fatal. The same could hardly be said for the hairy bodies piling up on either side of him.

The odds were taking their toll, though.

Jelia turned away. Neither she nor Corgan could afford further distraction.

A swelling crescendo capped her paean to Boruth's life as Jelia reached the coda. Her final note bounced from ceiling to floor, and back again, slowly fading until an eerie quiet filled the main hall.

More than half of Corgan's surviving attackers then turned on her.

Jelia allowed herself a thin, grim smile. Her vow had been fulfilled.

She drew her sword.

Spin. Whirl. Thrust. Slash.

In moments, Jelia was also surrounded by vuk corpses. She leapt over them to join Corgan's side.

"Impressive," he panted as they took out the last of Morek's beast-men.

"My song?" she asked, between strokes of her blade. "Or the swordplay?"

He was too busy disarming a final vuk to answer. He kicked the creature to the floor.

"Is he the last?" Jelia queried.

"He will be." Corgan raised his weapon for the death blow.

"Wait." Jelia bent over the snarling beast-man. "Do you have a name, vuk?"

The beast-man snapped at her.

"The Governor doesn't bother to name them," Corgan explained.

"That doesn't mean they can't name themselves." Jelia returned her attention to the defiant vuk. "Never mind your name, then. Tell me what you've done with the Temple's Tenders. Do they live?"

The feral eyes shifted downward.

"Caged," he grunted.

"In the catacombs? Good."

"Of course, they're alive," Corgan added. "Even an arrogant fool like Morek dare not stir the Tenders against him."

"I don't need your explanations, Corgan." Focusing on the man-beast, Jelia continued. "You vuks are designed to fulfil your orders or die trying. You have failed in this mission. I would offer you a new one."

The vuk's eyes narrowed, but his ears pricked forward.

"Take a message from me to Governor Morek."

The vuk remained silent.

Jelia leaned closer. "Tell Morek there is a price for what he had done to my father, and more for the disrespect he showed afterwards."

Corgan cleared his throat. "For his part in my

brother's death, as well."

"He kill me." The vuk lowered his eyes.

Corgan raised his sword again. "We can take care of that now, if you prefer."

Jelia dissuaded the man with a raised hand. "I believe this vuk will accommodate us. They're made to serve the Governor, which is what I'm asking."

The beast-man acquiesced with as much of a nod as his thick neck allowed.

"Go, then."

The vuk rose to his haunches. His right paw reached for one of the discarded blades.

Jelia stamped her boot firmly on the weapon's hilt. "Leave the sword."

The creature snarled, then scurried to the temple door, vanishing into the fading daylight.

Jelia turned to Corgan. "I suppose there's a chance Morek will slay his messenger before he delivers our words."

Corgan wiped his blade on a vuk cloak. "It doesn't matter. Word of this battle, and the earlier one, will reach him soon enough."

"True." She wiped her own blade clean on another cloak. "Let's free those Tenders."

"Your song... was quite moving, No-One. I meant to say so earlier."

Corgan sat across from Jelia in the Temple dining hall. Over-generous portions of hastily prepared meats and sweets were piled on platters at the centre of the wooden table. Two of the Tenders dressed their wounds as well, ignoring the pair's apologies for desecrating the Temple of Askoti with so much bloodshed.

"Then I succeeded." Jelia shredded the last remaining bits of meat from a rib bone.

A dozen Tenders bustled about in the adjoining main room, indifferent to the sweat, mud, and blood that stained their robes. They dragged one bestial corpse after another outside, loading a cart for conveyance to a mass grave some distance from the Temple grounds. Since they were not human, or even natural, vuks neither required nor desired death rituals.

Other Tenders scoured viscera from the floor and walls, all by shadowy torchlight.

"I wish I could have heard it more clearly, without the distractions."

"You know I cannot repeat it. Each Song of Passing is unique to its subject, and the moment."

"As it should be." After a pause, Corgan asked, "Do you believe the tales?"

"Which ones?"

"About the ghosts. That those who do not receive a proper death requiem are doomed to wander forever."

Jelia snorted. "My song is a sign of respect. It is important for closure. Even those unable to compose their own songs, the grieving folk who employ me to do so on their behalf, thereby demonstrate they made the effort. Whether the Song truly eases one's passage to the next world or not, there is no harm in believing so."

"Not unlike a promise of vengeance." Corgan stared at his meal.

She nodded. "I've heard such stories since childhood but have yet to encounter a ghost. Have you?"

"Not ghosts as such. I've had sensations a few times. No doubt all in my mind." Corgan tore into his meal.

Jelia found his casual revelation intriguing and wished to hear more. Later, though. For now, exhaustion crept up on them. They exchanged no further words beyond 'good night' and then only after an elder Tender led them to a chamber prepared with the two most luxurious beddings in the Temple.

The sun was near its apex, the Temple long out of sight. Jelia continued a dozen paces further along the road when she realized Corgan had stopped. She turned to be greeted with the same lack of expression as when they'd first met.

After doing little more than grunt since they'd taken leave of the Tenders, Corgan broke his silence.

"This is far enough."

"From...?"

"The Temple. They have seen enough death for now."

"Agreed. They need not hear our plans for Governor Morek."

Corgan's lips thinned. He looked away. "There can be no 'us,' Jelia."

Jelia blinked. "I thought we.... Wait. You know my name?"

"The daughter of Boruth. Yes."

"How long have you known?"

"Since we first crossed paths. A dark-haired woman, expert fighter, Composer... who else would have been on that road, at that hour?"

Her muscles tensed. "Yet you waited until this moment to tell me."

His voice sank to a whisper. "Those vuks were not the only minions of Morek whom you slew recently. There were human vassals the night before."

"In defence of my father. Yes. I will forever bear the shame of my failure to save him."

"Sergeant Grolien..."

"Their leader?"

"... was my brother." Corgan reached beneath his cloak and tossed a bloody sergeant's cap at her feet.

Jelia's eyes widened. "Corgan, I..."

"This is why I must slay you. I am sorry, Jelia." He drew his blade but did not advance immediately.

"This tragedy is all Governor Morek's doing," she protested. "It is he you should..."

"Morek shall also know my anger. But it was your blade that took my brother's life."

Jelia stood firm. "Why did you not slay me earlier, then? Or allow the vuks to overwhelm me?"

"Two reasons. First, in honouring your father's

passing, you were denying the Governor's wishes, undermining his ego. I relished that."

"And the second?"

"The point of vengeance is to achieve justice for the dead. No honour is had in slaying someone bound by duty not to fight back. You had your vow to fulfil, and I helped you do so. Now it is my turn."

Jelia still did not draw her own blade. She hoped to talk the man down.

"You're a good person, Corgan. We fought alongside each other. You saved my life, possibly on the road, certainly in the Temple. You enabled, nay, encouraged me to pay proper respect to my father. I have no desire to fight you. Certainly not to the death."

"For you, it may be a choice. For me, it is an obligation." He took a deep breath. "No more words."

Corgan rushed forward, blade swinging, releasing the same unnerving shriek he'd used to disorient the vuks the morning before.

Jelia swerved aside, drawing her own weapon. Corgan's thrust tore her cloak, missing her by an inch. Propelled by the force of his lunge, he flew past her. His heel dug into the road, to regain his balance for the next attack.

Her sword lashed out as he flew by, then withdrew.

Corgan halted a yard beyond her. Lips twitching, he turned to once more face his brother's slayer. His widening eyes met hers.

Corgan dropped to his knees. He remained

kneeling for a long moment.

Expelling a final, shaky breath, the man crumpled face down upon the road.

The single sword thrust through his heart gave Corgan a quick and, Jelia hoped, relatively painless death. That much at least she could do.

She covered Corgan's body with a cairn of stones, to protect it from wild beasts or a rogue vuk. Eyes closed, sword held tight in both hands, the woman muttered her apologies.

That was not enough. Nothing could be.

Jelia turned, retracing her steps to the Temple of Askoti. She needed to compose a new Song of Passage.

Governor Morek's reckoning could wait.

Though not for long.

DANGER IN THE DUAT

ALANNA ROBERTSON-WEBB

The lab door creaked open, the familiar, pick-le-like odour of formaldehyde tingling Safiya's nostrils as she flicked on the fluorescent lights. Her research lab was located deep within the bowls of Al-Azhar Al-Sharif, Egypt's oldest university, and the young paleopathologist had dragged herself out of bed long before sunrise just to get a sneak-peek at her newest acquisition before her co-workers clocked on.

She had seen preserved remains before, plenty of them, but never had Safiya had a preserved human body in her workspace. It was a bit unnerving, the windowless room appearing even smaller as the bulky container towered up from the shadows where the cheap lighting didn't quite reach, but she couldn't shake the sense of excitement skittering up her spine that made the hairs on the back of her neck stand up. This person had been dead for longer than the Great Wall of China had stood, and she was about to see a precious piece of ancient history.

The sarcophagus had spent decades gathering dust in the basement of an old pawn shop before an idly browsing archaeologist had realised that there was a mummy sequestered in the coffin. A crumbling bill of sale showed that the remains had been unearthed in 1826 near the outskirts of the tiny town of Abu Minqar, and the yellowed pages detailed the arrival of the sarcophagus at the pawnshop. Now, for the first time in almost three thousand years, the ancient citizen within would be exposed to light. It, along with the coffin, would then be cleaned up, and the remains would receive a proper burial while the casket would get donated to the historical Egyptian Museum in Cairo.

Safiya halted by the exam table, hands trembling as she stretched them towards the crisp white sheet covering the coffin. She carefully peeled it back, her breathing rapid and shallow as she imagined what a diagnostics scan had the potential to reveal. What was this person's last meal? What had they looked like? Which god or gods had they followed? What was their occupation? What material was their clothing? How did they style their hair? How had they died? What age were they? Her barrage of questions floated unanswered into the void, no godly voices relieving her enthusiastic curiosity.

The lid of the sarcophagus glinted dimly, the gold paint having all but faded into a paled, flax-hued shadow of its former glory. Safiya ran a fingertip gently along one gilded hieroglyphic, hundreds of years of sand and dust rolling beneath her flesh. She was touching tiny particles of history, the very motes that their world was built upon, and even the room seemed to hold its breath in reverence as the constant buzz of the lights died to a muffled hum. The set of hieroglyphics she was caressing was where the deceased's name went, and the young paleopathologist couldn't help but wonder what the person had been called.

"Who were you, hmmmm? Let's see: Hem-net-jer-tepi…"

The ancient words meant nothing to her at first, failing to interpret themselves in her mind, until a flash of recognition from her childhood clicked into place. This wasn't a name, it was a title. Her grandfather used to be a clergyman, one of the last dozen followers of the old gods in his village, and the temple members had always referred to the old man with the title of 'hem-netjer' in place of his name. It translated to 'priest,' a moniker reserved only for those who were believed to have the strongest connections with at least one major god. Not only was this mummy special due to its archaic deathspan, it was someone who had once held an esteemed rank within society.

What did 'tepi' mean, though? Did it denote a higher ranking than a basic holy man, such as a high priest? Was it a name, or maybe a term used to show the priest was from a certain location?

"So, who were you, huh? I'd love to meet you, maybe have a nice chat over a cup of wine, eh?"

Safiya's head spun with questions, her curious appendages tracing over each letter in turn as she meditated on the mystery. She internally begged the coffin to give her answers, to reveal the mysteries of the ancient civilisation to her, not that anyone would respond.

As her index finger left the lid, the ground began to quake, each shelf and beaker quivering as they threatened to topple over. Safiya wrapped her upper body around the sarcophagus, every muscle tensed as she tried to keep it from tumbling down.

Greetings, new priestess.

The voice slithered through her mind, each syllable scratching along her ear drums. Cinnamon-hued eyes darted about the room, but there was no one else in sight. Suddenly the violent movement ceased, and the sarcophagus began to glow with a faint light. Safiya's arms tingled, and as she watched her lab coat, button-up shirt, boots and khaki pants lit up in a brilliant flash of red light. She threw her arms up to shield her eyes, and when the burst of light faded, the paleopathologist was no longer in her own clothing. A white sheath dress with broad straps now adorned her, along with woven sandals and gold bangles.

Her hair, previously in a sloppy ponytail, was now cascading down her back in luxurious waves. Small, golden beads were dangling from thin braids, their sporadic placement giving her hair a light, pretty tinkling sound when she shifted. Safiya raised a shaking hand to her face, the feel of something around her eyes bothering her. She gently touched the corner of her eye with the ridge of a nail, drawing her hand back to reveal a black line of makeup. She had kohl around her eyes, the predecessor of mascara, and she sure as the underworld hadn't been wearing anything like it earlier.

Better.

No breath had stirred, but Safiya had clearly heard that same masculine voice.

"Who are you? What do you want?"

The shrill, desperate edge to her cry echoed about the lab, but was merely met with silence.

"What's happening...?"

Her voice had shrunk, tears beginning to trail down her cheeks as she sank to her knees. She was losing her mind, right? That had to be it. She had just been so stressed at work lately, what with the government cutting their funding down, that she must have finally snapped. It was a mental breakdown, sure, but it was a fairly standard one, right? Safiya clenched her eyes shut, willing herself to see her clothing return to normal, and after thirty seconds she cracked a cautious eye open.

Damn it.

She was still in the Ancient Egyptian-style clothing, the antiquated linen softer against her skin than her typical polyester clothing. The room around her began to shimmer, the dingy, greyish walls transitioning into towering pillars of sandstone. The temperature rose drastically, beads of sweat breaking out across Safiya's flesh as scorching wind whipped sand up into her face. Everything around her was flat, sand-shrouded desert, with the structure in front of her being the only place to escape into.

Safiya pelted inside, heels kicking up puffs of dust as she ran. The entrance to the building was wide open, no door or gate barring her access to the shelter the sturdy walls offered. As soon as she set foot inside, the wind relented its attack, allowing her to breathe without sucking in lungfuls of sand. The temperature also dropped slightly, the small reprieve welcome after her horrid experience. The interior looked like something straight out of a travel magazine showcasing ancient Egypt: hieroglyphics wove in bands across the walls, and the sandstone chamber was decorated with pillars carved into the likenesses of deities. Jackal-headed Anubis, cat-head Bast and crocodile-headed Sobek were just a few of the many figures that seemed to stare down at Safiya with their chiselled eyes.

One phrase in particular appeared over and over again, the letters displayed proudly at eye level.

"Am…"

An underlying sense of panic still coated her mind, but the surrealism of the moment kept her from having a complete breakdown. She was so absorbed in her admiration of the temple that the sound of quiet footfalls was lost within the wind's whistle. At the sharp sound of a throat clearing, Safiya spun around, fists raised to guard her face.

"That would not harm me, but you are welcome to try if it will make you feel any better."

The man standing before her was elderly, his flowing white beard swooshing gently in the air currents. A thin smile decorated his face, though it didn't reach his narrowed eyes. The black pupils burned with an abhorrent mixture of rage and disgust.

"Sit and listen, girl. I do not have much time."

Something about his voice was familiar, and Safiya decided that it sounded an awful lot like the one she had heard in her head back in the lab. As though it were the most normal thing in the world, a wooden stool, the seat made of softened leather, appeared just behind her knees. Wordlessly, the young scientist sat, her eyes locked on the obsidian-hued orbs of the man before her. Quietly, as though her voice would further shatter reality, she spoke.

"Who, or *what*, are you? Where am I?"

"Very perceptive! I am relieved that I did not choose an imbecile. Humankind knows me as Am-Heh, one of the minor underworld gods, though you often underestimate my power. You have freed me, and as a reward I have granted you the title of Priestess of Am-Heh. We are in the Duat, which I suppose your kind calls the under-realm, or was it under-world? Post-life? One of those sorts of names."

"Freed? Priestess? *Underworld*? Am I dead!? What the f…"

He cut her off, his hand flippantly silencing her.

"No, no. You are very alive still, or else you would be useless to me. See, I angered the more powerful god Set a few thousand Earth rotations ago, and in one of his juvenile fits of retribution he bound me to a body, to that flesh prison, who was once my high priest."

Safiya stood, arms wrapped around herself as she swayed precariously on the balls of her feet. Her chest heaved, though she made a valiant effort to not hyperventilate.

"This can't be real…"

Inhale, followed by an exhale, was all that was keeping Safiya calm. She needed to be rational, to remain logical, and listening to this madman talk was the best way. God or no, he was the most normal-looking thing around, and she was going to fixate on that. If anything, he looked like her grandfather, and that thought made her tightening chest relax just a smidge.

"It is quite real, I am afraid. Now, the reason why I brought you here is simple: you must go where I cannot, and do what I cannot. Complete this quest, and I shall give you, my dear priestess, any mortal reward you desire."

She blinked, caterpilliar-like eyebrows arching

as she thought about that for a moment. If he was telling the truth…

"…anything?"

"Of course! Riches, love, nubile slaves, the curing of an illness or a vastly elongated lifespan are just some of your near-endless options."

A papyrus scroll appeared in front of Am-Heh, the rolled-up parchment gently unfurling itself so that Safiya could read it. The letters, or at least that's what she assumed the little groupings of squiggles were, hovered at face-height while she appraised it.

"So, this means…What, exactly?"

Am-Heh sighed, gnarled fingers yanking on his ample beard.

"Well, apparently you are not versed in the Greco-Roman hybridisation counter-cipher. I must rectify that soon, or else you shall have a challenging time reading some of the texts you will need to memorise in order to best serve me...Ah, but I digress. Oh well; for now, I shall just have to put it into layman's terms for you."

He waved his arms, a circle of light whisking into the middle of the chamber with a loud pop. Like a bubble it had a shimmering, semi-reflective surface, the rainbow of colours within swirling like a kaleidoscope.

"Go through this portal to the furthest corner of Duat. Find the cave beneath the Pyramid of Set, and make your way through it. Simply reach the other side alive by any means necessary, and your task is complete. Then my waning, godly powers shall be reinstated, and you shall be handsomely rewarded!"

"Why? What does me going through a cave have to do with anything?"

Am-Heh twirled a finger through his beard, brows creased in reminisce.

"When your world was younger, the days easier and the land more plentiful, we gods used to make wagers with humans as our pawns. I, once a fool, bet that my high priest would beat Set's high priest in a race through a simple cave. What I did not plan for was that Set would cheat, and trap my priest inside so that I would lose."

He fell silent, finger ceasing its winding movement as the corners of his mouth drooped. Safiya allowed him a few moments, then gently pulled him back to the conversation.

"If he won then why was Set still mad at you? Why punish a loser?"

Am-Heh started, wide eyes meeting her questioning gaze.

"Forgive me. I have not had someone to talk to in ages, and my social skills are in need of some polishing."

The god cleared his throat, absentmindedly shaking a small pile of sand out of one of his voluminous robe sleeves.

"Set was angry that I had enough hubris to believe that I, a lesser deity, could ever defeat him. He stipulated that my power would return when one of my followers finally got through the cave, which he thought would never happen since he had taken so much of my power. Set did not think I could ever bring someone here, but I was able to rest long enough to recover ample power to bring you, my awakener, here…"

Safiya nodded, politely encouraging him to continue.

"Get through the cave, and as soon as you do my powers will return, and I can teleport you to your home. Now you must go, before she finds us and tries to prematurely judge your soul…"

"Wait, what?"

With that Am-Heh shoved Safiya into the vortex, the mist-like gateway moulding itself around her as she stumbled. The opening instantly began to close, the myriad of colours swarming into her vision until all she could see was black. The god's voice drifted distantly from the portal, barely a whisper above the blood pounding in her ears.

"Watch out for that oversized funerary glutton!"

A moment later the paleopathologist landed with a *thunk* on a hard surface, her knees stinging painfully as the world spun. Safiya nearly vomited, the vertigo threatening to overwhelm her, but she managed to swallow the burning bile back down her throat. She forced herself to take several slow, deep breaths, and that's when she looked up. Just a moment ago she had been fighting against scorching, mid-day heat, but now the Duat was cloaked in velvet shades of purple and navy. Constellations in shapes she had never seen before danced and gleamed above her head, as if welcoming her to the new world.

"Wow…"

Safiya gazed skyward, mesmerised by the new starscape. The glowing expanse was like a river, the celestial bodies flowing gently from one side of the heavens to the other. She finally tore her gaze down, letting her eyes adjust to the darker horizon. In the distance a triangle loomed, a pulsating, ruby glow surrounding the silhouette. There was no other structure in any direction, and no obvious indication of her next step, so before she could dwell on it too much Safiya began walking.

At least in the Duat thighs didn't chafe when you walked.

As she hiked from where the portal had opened to the pyramid, she lost all sense of time. As the structure grew larger minutes could have passed, or hours, since she had no idea how fast the clock spun in this new world. Did time, or the body's ability to age, even exist in the afterlife? As Safiya traversed mile after mile of flat, sandy ground her mind tumbled through a myriad of thoughts. Sure, her situation was utterly insane, but now that she had a little time to adjust to the concept of being a hero sat well with the young paleopathologist. She was on a quest to fetch an artifact to restore the honour of a god, and would be regaled as a hero when she returned home. She could wish for fame, to be known as the greatest scientist within her field, and then glory and honour would be hers.

Safiya, thoughts wandering to what it would

feel like to accept a Nobel Prize, had failed to notice the tiny ripples spreading in the sand beneath her feet. With a mighty roar a beast barrelled out of the ground, the panther-sized monstrosity landing with a boom, massive jaws agape right in front of Safiya. Its dozens of fangs, coated in a sanguine substance that Safiya could only guess at, were easily longer than her index finger. The creature was an amalgamation of animals, pieces of lion, crocodile and hippopotamus moulded into a fearsome monstrosity.

After studying countless ancient scrolls Safiya had no doubt about who the creature was: the being looming before her was Ammit, Eater of Hearts and Devourer of the Dead. As one of the Egyptian funerary deities the demoness' sole goal was to feast upon the hearts of those unworthy to pass into the afterlife, and she likely had a nose for intruders who found their way into her domain.

"Ahhhhhhhhhhhh!"

Her scream frantically tore through the air, the demonic beast growling in response to her high-pitched wail. When Ammit had burst through the sand Safiya had been knocked backwards, landing on her side, and she flopped over as she tried to scramble backwards.

"Shitshitshitshit*shit*!"

No matter how fast she scrambled the creature kept pace, arm-length tongue lolling as it paced just a few steps behind her. Ammit stalked her movement for movement, each heartbeat bringing the goddess' gaping maw closer to the mortal's throat.

"Please, no…"

Safiya didn't realise she was crying, tears of raw fear streaming down her cheeks. She didn't want to turn her back on the deity, didn't want to give her even more of an attack opportunity, but Safiya had nothing to defend herself with. There was nothing around but sand and sky.

Sand.

Trembling fingers curled around fistfuls of grains, and before she could talk herself out of it Safiya threw two handfuls of sand directly into Ammit's eyes. The goddess roared, the sound echoing through the vast Duat, and while she pawed at her burning, grit-clouded eyes Safiya ran. The paleopathologist didn't know how close the pyramid was, or if she could easily get into the cave, but she'd be damned if she wasn't going to fight to the bitter end. Luck seemed to be on her side, for as she ran the distance between herself and the enraged goddess grew.

Safiya thought she was going to collapse. She had never been a runner, and sprinting for more than a minute wasn't exactly her forte. The pyramid was getting closer, sure, but each breath became laboured as she pushed herself to keep pumping her exhausted legs. She wanted to stop, to catch her breath, but she didn't know how close the monster was. Even a moment could mean life or death, and Safiya wasn't about to test her fate.

"Screwwwwwwwwyooooooou!"

The raw, primordial scream acted like a battle

cry, the release helping to spur the depleted warrior on. Safiya could, *had*, to make it. She would get out of this realm, get home and achieve all of her dreams. This place, and the beings within it, weren't going to stop her. The pyramid grew closer, individual blocks taking shape from within the hazy silhouette. A small opening beneath the tons of sandstone was becoming visible, and that was exactly what she needed to give her jello-like limbs fresh hope. With renewed vigour she pelted forward, but when Safiya was a dozen paces of the entrance the ground began to shake once more.

Like a crocodile Ammit surfaced from beneath the sand, snout poised towards Safiya for a killing blow. The young woman dropped to the ground, face planting firmly into the sand as a wave billowed around her. Ammit sailed overhead, her lion tail tickling the back of Safiya's neck. Safiya army-crawled forward, gasping lungs clogging as she inhaled more sand. She dragged her body to the tiny cave entrance, the sand trembling as Ammit charged towards her, but Safiya was barely faster. As she yanked her legs into the cave, curling into a ball and rolling away from the entrance, Ammit slammed into the stone.

In vain the goddess tried to dig her way in, to get at the coward who dared to escape from Osiris and the Scale of Judgement, but she couldn't. She was too big, and with no ability to shapeshift she simply couldn't follow her prey. Safiya, unaware that the funerary deity was giving up, had scooted even deeper into the darkness of the cave. The tunnel sloped sharply downwards, and the angle at which she had to crawl made her feel folded, like crumpled paper. It was uncomfortable, slow progress, the lack of light causing her to keep stiff fingers groping the ground in front of her, but at least her breathing had regulated.

She reached a dip in the cave, her aching body demanding a short rest.

"Man, what I wouldn't give for a light…"

Her wish echoed against the rough-hewed passage, the syllables bouncing around mockingly. As the last whisper died off something began glowing a few feet in front of her, the sudden light, however dim, causing Safiya to flinch. A white, smooth rock, about the circumference of an apple, appeared before her. A note came fluttering from thin air, the papyrus landing perfectly on Safiya's lap. The words, scrawled in her native Arabic, were a surprise.

شكرا لرعاية أطفالي

Thank you for taking care of my children.

Children? What children? Safiya examined the note, a small set of hieroglyphics in the bottom corner catching her attention.

They were familiar, the canopic jar and double

bread loafs tickling a memory. It was a name, a signature…

"Bast, that's it!"

She croaked out the name, throat scratching in protest. The gift was from Bast, the goddess attributed with cats, music and household protection. Safiya thought about the hours she had spent volunteering at the Little Paws animal rescue in Cairo, a soft smile upon her face. She had fostered dozens of kittens, using her own income to help provide medical care and food for them, and it looked like the Sacred Cat herself had smiled upon Safiya. Using her newfound light, she took a stock of the plastered stone, noting that she would have to duck under the dip in the rock in order to keep going.

Once her body relaxed, and it was clear Ammit was not in pursuit, Safiya realised that she would have to lay down to wriggle under the divot. She sat there a moment, hands partially under the dip with her head remaining still. She wondered if it was all worth it. Would she die in there, like the priest before her? The stone, clutched tightly in her hand, pulsed faintly, as if to reassure her. She held it out in front of her and began to squirm, feeling her back grind against the ceiling, skin being scraped even through her dress. Fortunately, the little struggle was over in seconds, and she was able to sit up on the other side.

She paused for a moment, turning to look back towards the way she had come. She could barely see the dip past the circle of light, and the darkness threatened to swallow the paleopathologist if she looked too far away. Safiya turned to the unending shadows and started her awkward crouch-crawl again, and the further she went the more the silence pressed upon her. The whistle of the wind was gone, the ambiance of the Duat failing to penetrate the tunnel. All she could hear was her laboured breathing and the shifting of sand beneath her feet; a warm, gross, thick silence that made everything feel heavy.

The cave smelled dank, like rotting leaves and rust, though Safiya had been too panicked to notice it initially. She couldn't place it, so logic dictated that she ignore it. As time dragged on her back grew sore, her spine and shoulders throbbing with tiny, sharp pains from all the scrapes and cuts. Her hands and knees were covered with dust and sand, but she didn't let it bother her. Her body, pushed to its limit, began to slip more than before. She always caught herself, but there were a few close calls where Safiya nearly smashed her face into the unforgiving rock walls.

"Yes!"

The cave was finally widening, the ceiling slanting upwards enough so she could nearly stand up. It seemed to be about as big as the entrance, though a bit thinner, and after a small turn the cave got much bigger. She was glad to stand straight, and Safiya vowed to never take her tiny lab with its seven-foot ceiling for granted again. She saw nothing of note in the chamber other than a small pool of water, which stemmed from a hairline fracture in the far wall. She didn't actually feel thirst, and decided that drinking

78

underworld water could have negative consequences. She pulled her eyes away from the clear pool, her focus shifting to find a way forward. The cave looked to be about seven or eight feet across, and as she raised her stone to get a better view a sharp sound sliced through the stale air.

Sssssssss....

It sounded like it came from right behind her. Safiya dropped into a crouch, whipping around to face the direction she had come from. Her Bast-stone slipped from her sweaty palms, and with a loud *ker-plunk* it dropped into the pool of water. She held still, glaring back at the tunnel, but nothing more happened. She glanced around after a moment, gaze flicking to the now lit-up pool, mentally praying that the stone wasn't too deep down. She dropped to her knees at the pool's edge, thrusting her hand into the water. It went almost up to her shoulder, but she couldn't feel the stone. The paleopathologist pulled back, looking closely at the water to try and see the bottom.

She couldn't see all the way down, but there, perched on the rim of a small stone shelf, was her stone. Her hand darted in, quickly snatching it before it could tip over the precipice. Her eyes met her own in the water, a triumphant grin bridging her cheeks as she hauled the stone up.

"Ha!"

Her expletive didn't echo, instead lingering by her lips, and as she was about to turn away, she saw a black shape looming across the pool. Her heart dropped and she quickly turned, scooting back on her rear. She thrust the light forward, illuminating the hulking menace.

It was just a pile of rocks.

Safiya chuckled nervously, standing up and wiping her damp hands off on her dress. She made her way forward around the pool, her feet on autopilot as she wondered if the hissing was some sort of snake. Bast-willing it wouldn't be a cobra, or something equally deadly. Past the pool was another tunnel, Safiya making her way into it easily. The walls there were smoother, and they appeared to be made out of a darker stone than the rest of the sandstone cave. She pushed onward, stepping over a few bigger, sand-covered rocks that seemed to have fallen from the ceiling some time ago. Travelling down the second tunnel was harder than the first, as the walls showed signs of damage the further Safiya progressed.

There were many more piles of rocks and dirt, and even some remnants of hieroglyphics upon the crumbling walls. Before she could reach the next bend, she swore she could hear a shuffling sound, partially muffled by her footsteps. Safiya stopped walking, but there wasn't another sound.

"Hello?"

No answer. Her stone shone, the room that she had come out of barely more than a small hole in the distance. She took a step, then stopped: the shuffling started, then stopped in tandem. Her stomach lurched as she clutched the stone to her chest, breaking into a run. She leaped over rocks, nearly dropping the Bast-stone when she stumbled. Soon she slowed to a jog, turning her head over her shoulder to see the eight-legged shadows scuttling rapidly along the walls. Her heart clenched, Safiya slamming her back against the wall as she quaked, her limbs paralysing in the tiny space. Air pumped into her lungs so quickly that her throat began to burn, her ears popping as blood rushed between her ears.

Her muscles spasmed in protest, tears pricking her eyes as the shadows swarmed around the edge of the stone's light. She was trapped, a lump rising in her throat. She let herself cry, sinking to the floor in a mix of hyperventilating and coughing. Ammit had been a threat, but that was one she could face; these eyeless, hissing beings were fear incarnate, and Safiya had an extreme case of arachnophobia. She was no Indiana Jones, no gallant knight capable of defeating any foe, and her quest was going to fail.

She was going to die alone in a cave, eaten by shadow spiders.

"No, no, no…"

She began rocking back and forth, her tear-filled whimper lost in the cacophony of dozens of spindly legs skittering across tunnel walls. As her tears dripped onto the stone a voice, as soft and gentle as a cat's fur, whispered in her mind.

Make a choice, my child: give up now, and I promise you will know peace, or fight on towards an uncertain future. If you fight, I will stay by your side.

Safiya shook her head.

"I... I'm…"

She was what, exactly? She was just going to let herself die without a fight?

"No!"

She was going to live, to go back home and change the world. She was going to get famous, open her own animal shelter, help stop ocean pollution, adopt a bunch of street children and drink a million cappuccinos, probably in that order.

This was not going to be the end.

Safiya clambered to her feet, unsteady joints cracking in protest. The light was clearly the only thing holding the shadow spiders at bay, their limbs yanking back any time one strayed into the stone's glow. She held out her hand, palm up and eyes squinched shut as she took a big step down the tunnel.

One-two step...
Three-four step...
One-two step...
Three-four step...

Each footfall brought her further down the tunnel, the spiders ever-present. She opened her eyes every few paces to make sure that she wasn't going to trip over rocks or bash her head against jutting stones, and she refused to stare at the limbs trying to shove their way into the glow. Safiya kept her breathing as regulated as possible, and counting her footsteps helped keep her mind occupied. With aching neck bent and limbs close to her side she pushed on, twisting and turning her way through miles of tunnel.

Then, finally, there was light.

Safiya had reached the end, and was alive. She had completed her quest, had eluded monsters and faced danger in the Duat. She had been on a quest that most people only read about in stories, and even if no one believed what she had gone through she now knew that amazing things existed beyond the scope of daily living. She was an unsung hero, and as that familiar, bubble-like portal appeared in front of her she knew that she was going home to make the world a better place.

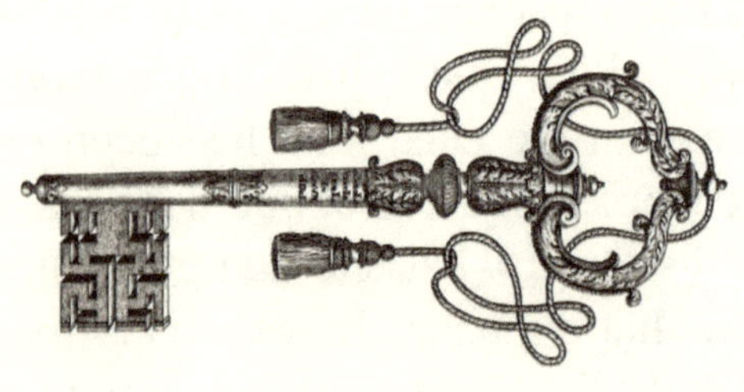

THE EBON KEY

DECLAN FLETCHER

"Halt," a voice cried as if from nowhere, "there's three bows trained on you so no sudden moves."

Henrik squinted in the early morning sun. The road they were travelling was barely worthy of the name. Overgrown in parts and little more than a trail cut by the passing of feet in the others. The trees crowded tightly around the path, making it difficult to see far into the bush. The contrast of the light with the dense foliage provided perfect camouflage. He couldn't make out any figures in the woods. Henrik looked over to his companion Manny; he didn't seem to be having any more luck penetrating the shadows. Manny was a hand taller than Henrik, but much slighter, possessing a wiry strength that complimented the agility of a natural thief.

"Alright, alright, get out here and let's get this

over with," Manny replied. His voice raspy and his hood covering his eyes.

A man emerged onto the trail, average height with the broad shoulders of a man used to physical labour. He wore a cloak that may once have been a deep green but long use had given it the hue of the forest. No wonder he was so hard to see. He had the cloak thrown over one shoulder to reveal his right hand resting on the pommel of a sword at his hip.

"We don't see many travellers in these parts." He had the air of a man leaning against the bar in a tavern, totally at ease with his surroundings. The man took in Manny's dark complexion and short cropped hair and Henrik's broad shoulders, blonde hair and heavy chain mail. "You seem to represent all the Commonwealth. The blonde barbarian of the north and the crafty Cirtan."

"We're just passing through," Henrik opened his arms wide to try to placate the man. "We'll be out of your hair soon enough."

"No need to rush. Perhaps we can assist you, for a small fee, of course?"

"Thank you, neighbour, but we don't need any help."

"I'm afraid I have to insist," the man smiled, "nobody passes through without donating to the upkeep of our road."

Manny reached into his jerkin. As he did the man's sword whistled from its scabbard.

"Easy friend." Manny pulled his hand from his jerkin, now clutching a small metal flask. He flipped the lid to one side and took a drink. "We're with Volpi."

Henrik took a medallion from inside his shirt and held it up so the men could see it. The swordsman looked from Manny to the square medallion with a stylised V on it.

"Sorry about that," he sighed and sheathed his blade. "Like I say, we don't get many travellers around these parts, getting harder to make a decent living."

Manny and Henrik dismounted their horses and slid down to the ground.

"My men will see to your horses." Daneel nodded to two men Henrik hadn't seen circle around behind them. The men stepped forward and took the reins, leading the horses out of site into the wood.

"They'll have water and a rub down while we talk," Daneel said.

"We were expecting to run into you yesterday," Manny offered the man his flask. "You're Daneel, right?"

"That's me." Daneel took a deep drink from the flask and grimaced at the taste. "Strong stuff. We move around a lot. Not many guardsmen this far out from Istrus, but we don't take risks."

Manny took another drink himself. "So Volpi says you know where we can find Bhuzon An."

"Yeah, I know it." Daneel nodded. "Old Caemaeni ruin, Hostus can show you the way. For a small fee, of course."

"Business is business," Henrik laughed.

"What do you boys want at Bhuzon An?" Daneel asked. "We've been over that ruin, no treasure there. No nothing there."

"Man came to Volpi's, asked for us by name," Henrik explained. "Paid 200 gold up front and twice as much again on delivery."

"Lot of money," Daneel whistled. "Don't see many people with that kind of money in Volpi's."

"Well, he's convinced some 'Ebon Key' is in Bhuzon An and he told me and Manny here are just the men to retrieve it."

"Bourgee fool," Manny hissed, taking another drink. "What business have I out in this wilderness?"

"The client insisted: no Manny, no Money…" Henrik grinned.

"Sounds fishy to me," Daneel said. "How does he know your names?"

"You know Volpi," Manny muttered. "For that kind of money he isn't asking questions. 100 gold more and he'd have given the fool his own daughter."

"How far is it to this ruin?" Henrik asked.

"About fifteen leagues, maybe ten of it on what you'd call roads," Daneel replied. "Five through the country."

"Great." Manny spat on the floor. "My pa always said I'd rot in a dungeon one day. Eaten by wolves, not even pa would've seen that one coming."

"Wolves don't attack people, Manny." Henrik said.

"He's right, there are wolves out there but they'll steer clear of you," Daneel said. "They understand people better than most folk and they want nothing to do with us."

It had taken three days, but they'd finally arrived. Henrik adjusted his armour, tightening it slightly around the shoulders. The weather was starting to turn, the nights no longer retained the heat of summer, but it'd still be some time before true winter. Manny finished setting up camp for the night, a deer that Hastus had brought down already roasting on the spit, filling the late evening air with popping sounds and the captivating aroma of cooking meat.

Bhuzon An sat at the top of a gentle slope. Details were hard to make out in the fading light, but the remains of a stone path ran up to a still intact arch. The rest of the structure had suffered more. There looked to be enough stone wall left to make out the shape of a square courtyard, but the only remaining tower ended abruptly in a ragged crown. No way to tell how high it had once been or if the lonely tower had once had companions.

"How long will the deer take?" Henrik sat down on a log by the fire.

"As long as it takes," Manny said over his shoulder while seeing to the horses.

Henrik picked up a piece of bread and began gnawing at it. "No obvious way into this 'treasure room,' but we'll see in the morning."

"Damn fool sent us on a wild goose chase."

"Maybe, maybe not," Henrik said between mouthfuls of bread.

"What do you know about this place?" Manny asked, taking his own seat by the fire.

"Not much," Henrik brushed crumbs from his hands. "Church doesn't much like people poking around these pre-Commonwealth ruins."

"They bother to tell you why?"

"Wasn't part of the training. Didn't tell us much, really."

"I thought paladins were the Redemptor's most trusted soldiers?" Manny said, while searching in his pack.

"Maybe they are, but I never made it past the first stage of training," Henrik said. "You think a fully trained paladin would be working as muscle for Volpi?"

Manny cut a piece of deer meat and offered it to Henrik, who put it on a piece of the bread. "Never given it much thought. Religion, not really my area."

"There's plenty of wealth in the church. You never thought about relieving them of some of it?" Henrik chuckled.

"If only! No, best to steer clear of priests altogether. You rob a merchant he might call the guard but a priest, bah! Who knows what a raging fanatic might do?"

"What did the client say about the entrance?" Henrik asked, while helping himself to some more deer meat.

"The treasure room of Bhuzon An is under-ground, the door it's said is hidden, and only men of your particular skills will be able to find it," Manny recited from memory.

"Not particularly helpful."

"Fancy words with no meaning," Manny spat. "Sounds like a priest."

They'd been over every inch of the courtyard and so far no signs of any secret door. Henrik could see no way into the tower, an opening in the one sur-viving wall section of the courtyard suggested there had once been a door into the main structure, what-ever that had been. The courtyard itself had been re-claimed by nature, grass covered it now, there was no way to tell what had once been there. The only signs of what it may once have been were two col-umns lying where they had fallen centuries ago.

"I've found something!" Manny's voice rang out from the other side of the wall. Henrik hurried round to see him examining the wall.

"I already checked there." Henrik came clos-er to get a better look at what Manny was doing. "There wasn't anything there a minute ago."

"This stone pulls out, you see?" Manny's voice more eager than Henrik had ever heard it. "Clever, very clever."

"What is that behind it?"

"My uncle was a locksmith. He was obsessed with Dwarven locks."

"Dwarves are a myth," Henrik interrupted, "like fairies or elves. They don't exist."

"The locks do. He must have had fifty of the things." Manny continued to stare at the contraption. "They were all mechanical. Designed to be unpickable as there's no key. In theory only the owner would know the secret to opening it."

"What do they have to do with Dwarves?"

"Probably nothing, just a name to add to the mystique." Manny began manipulating the lock with one of his slender knives and a lockpick.

"Can you get past it?"

"All locks have weaknesses, Henrik," Manny's brow furrowed in concentration. "Just have to find the… Ah."

Manny frowned in conversation. Henrik watched his lips move as he focussed on the task. With a loud click sound, Manny straightened up with a smile on his face. The ground shook, and a rumbling sound came from the tower. Henrik steadied himself against the wall and watched as a section of the circular tower wall sank into the ground. The whole process took a few minutes, but both Henrik and Manny took longer to recover from the shock.

"What the…"

"I have no idea," Henrik interrupted before the expletive. "How is that possible?"

"Your guess is as good as mine," Manny said. "The Caemaeni don't have the knowhow to do something like that."

"Unless the knowledge was lost somehow?"

"In the legends Dwarves were master stone-workers…"

"Dwarves are a myth," Henrik said in an exasperated tone. He liked Manny, but underneath all that practicality there was a fanciful soul.

"Whatever you say, buddy." Manny grinned. "Let's just get what we came for so I can get back to a certain barmaid who's been giving me the eye."

Henrik took a torch from his saddlebags and with a peculiar twist of his hand, muttered "Flamma." A tongue of flame sprang to life on the torch, weak at first but quickly spreading until heat and light radiated from it.

"I'll never get used to that." Manny took a drink from his flask and tucked it back inside his shirt.

"Just a simple cantrip." Henrik shrugged. "A fully trained paladin wouldn't need the torch."

"It still gives me the heebie jeebies."

"Well, so far the client has been right." Henrik paused for a minute. "Nobody else in Volpi's organisation could've found that lock, let alone opened it. So I think we can assume we'll be heading underground."

Manny took another drink. "Fine, let's go. The less I think about this the better."

Looking through the new opening in the tower wall, Henrik was not surprised to see a spiral staircase. The steps were made of stone, worn over the years, but they looked secure enough. The staircase stopped just above head height, a yard below the current top of the tower. Who knew how high it had once gone? The staircase did, however, extend downwards into the dark. Holding his torch down close to his feet, the pool of light became swallowed by the dark, unable to show how deep the staircase went. There was only one way to find out.

Henrik descended the stairs with Manny a step behind him. Manny's steps were less certain than normal, a slight hesitancy as his hand never left the wall. Henrik had no fear of the dark or heights, but the closed in staircase and stale air had him on edge as well. It was a relief when the staircase ended in front of an arch. It would've once been thought decorative, although time had robbed it of its lustre. The door within the arch would once have been robust. Time had taken its toll though, damp and rot eating the door away. A stiff breeze would blow the door open now.

Henrik kicked the door square in the middle and with a clatter, it fell from its hinges onto the floor. Henrik gasped at the room the door revealed. It was not the largest hall he'd ever seen, but still an impressive size with a vaulted ceiling. The torchlight did not reach the walls, but Henrik could see two rows of columns on either side of him. From the colour they were marble, although now covered in climbing plants, the effect of the white stone not quite what it would once have been. A square dais dominated the centre of the room, raised three steps from the surrounding room. The focus of the dais was a plinth made of the same marble as the columns, a fraction taller than a man's waist.

"Are you going to gawk all day, or can we get down to business?" Manny nudged him in the back. The echo of the room making his voice sound louder than it was.

"Sorry, got caught up," Henrik whispered, pointing to the plinth. "That must be what we're here for."

From a distance the plinth seemed empty, but as they got closer the prize resting on it became visible. A jewel black as night, around five inches tall. It had a strange cut to it, long but angular. Rounded at one end but tapering to a point at the other, it looked like a midnight black, fat pencil.

"That doesn't look like any key I ever saw," Manny muttered.

"No," Henrik replied, "but that has to be what he wants."

"Agreed, grab it and let's go."

As Henrik's hand closed around the key, light flooded the chamber, the ceiling itself glowed like the high noon sun. In each corner of the room stood a statue, creatures out of a nightmare. Each the size of a colossal bear with goat horns and cloven feet, all too human arms gripping fearsome weapons. Wicked looking hooked sword in one hand and battle-axe in the other. With the grinding sound of stone on stone, each statue turned to face them, weapons brought up into a fighting stance.

Manny reacted quickly, rolling to one knee, dagger appearing in his left hand and his own custom crossbow in the other, all in one smooth move.

He fired the crossbow without hesitation. The bolt hit the creature between the eyes and bounced to the floor as if it had hit stone.

"Henrik… I think we're in trouble." Manny's voice didn't yet have the ring of hysteria, but Henrik suspected it was only a matter of time. "The door is gone!"

Henrik's mind raced, he'd never heard of any magic capable of such a feat. The statue creatures had closed the gap and before he could reach for his own sword, an axe swung through the air. He ducked under it at the last second, only to be met with a firm hoof to the chest that sent him sprawling. He saw Manny dodging the attacks from two of the creatures. He was faster than the creatures, but they would only need one to connect once. Manny would tire, he was only human.

Rolling to one side, Henrik felt more than heard the creature's axe slam into the space on the ground where his head had occupied. Watching as the creature pulled the axe from the ground and turned to face him, the quality of the movement struck Henrik. There was something off about it. It moved like nothing he'd seen; it seemed almost staccato, as if it were an approximation of the movement of an animal it'd once seen.

Before the creature struck again Henrik made another hand gesture and focussing with everything he had said, "Denudo."

The room instantly plunged back into darkness except for the glow around the dais from his discarded torch. The creatures were gone, and a quick glance confirmed the door was where it had always been.

"Where did they go? What's happening?" Manny wheeled around, making sure there were no more of the creatures hiding.

"It was all an illusion," Henrik explained. "Somehow bound to the plinth. That level of magic is beyond my understanding, but it seems to be over now."

"So they couldn't have hurt us?"

"That was high level magic Manny, higher than anything I've ever seen." Henrik ran his hands through his hair. "I imagine they could hurt us but we'll never know for sure."

"How come we aren't dead?" Manny picked up the torch.

"Another cantrip." Henrik took a deep breath to steady himself "More advanced than anything I've ever done. Paladins use it to see through magic."

"And you've never used it before?"

"Not outside of training. It takes focus. Not all paladins can use it." Henrik's voice was hushed as he considered what had happened and what almost happened. "The threat of death has a way of focussing the mind, I suppose. I've never wanted a cantrip to work so bad in my life."

"Well, I guess I'm lucky you happen to be here then, aren't I?"

Lost in thought, Henrik didn't answer. How had the client known? The lock and the illusion. Outside of the church expeditionary force, no two other people could've done the job. The client asked for them by name…

"I'm going to have some questions for this client when we get back." Henrik picked up the Ebon Key, and they turned towards the exit.

Legionnaires blocked the path. Dressed in the traditional scale armour, they formed a barricade of square shields with spears bristling. It was Henrik and Manny's second day on the trail back to Istrus. The weather remained fine, the only danger they'd encountered so far was boredom. They reined in their horses and casually dismounted. An officer stepped forward, young as Commonwealth officers went, and like every soldier of rank Henrik had ever met clean shaven.

"Checkpoint in the arse end of nowhere," Manny smirked. "Who'd you piss off to get this crappy detail?"

"We…"

"Peace friend," Henrik interrupted. "We respect the soldiers of the Commonwealth, don't we, Manny?"

Manny grunted at the rebuke. Henrik supposed that would have to do.

"We do, however, have places to be," Henrik continued. "So what can we do for you?"

"All travellers are to have their possessions searched before being allowed to continue." The officer's stiff tone suggested a man who would not be easy to talk their way around.

Henrik and Manny exchanged a look before Manny's eyes flicked between the officer and the dozen soldiers behind him.

"There is an entire Commonwealth Cohort patrolling the area," the officer declared. "If you resist…"

"Ah, friend, you must be the youngest centurion in the army," Henrik interrupted with a disarming smile. "We want no trouble, just to be on our way. Manny, would you mind getting this fine fellow the saddlebags?"

"Thank you, citizen."

"So, what brings the legion out this far from civilisation?" Henrik asked.

"Church business."

"In the wilderness?" Manny laughed "Those churchmen like their luxury, you'd never catch one without a nice cosy bed to sleep in."

"True," the officer let out a short laugh of his own. "But it seems they're worried enough about some demonic stone. Dissidents are trying to move it from some old ruin and use it for their godless purposes."

Henrik's eyes flicked around to the horses before he could control himself. The centurion caught the glance and drew his sword.

"Hands in the air, away from your weapons!" he demanded. "You by the horses, step away."

The soldiers behind the centurion had relaxed

their formation while it looked like Manny and Henrik were no threat, but they reformed in a smooth, practiced motion. Sunlight glistening on the metal highlights of the square shields. Manny had one hand in the air and slowly removed his other from the saddlebag of his horse. In his hand he clutched a small corked flask with a round bottom, the contents impossible to determine through the opaque glass.

"Move over here," the centurion gestured towards Henrik with his blade, "next to your companion."

With a flick of his wrist, Manny tossed the flask towards the soldiers. A deafening crack split the morning air. Cursing and confused cries rose from the soldiers as smoke billowed from the flask, obscuring them from Henrik's view. Manny was already on his horse. He must have leapt onto it as soon as he released the flask. The centurion shouted to his men to reform. Henrik stepped behind him, using the distraction to draw his sword and strike with the pommel to the back of his head. The centurion crumpled to the floor. Henrik sprinted to his horse, and taking a light hold of the reins, jumped. One leg landed awkwardly across the horse's back. He had to take a second to right himself in the saddle, but at least he remained mounted.

The smoke cleared quicker than Henrik would've liked. He kicked the horse into a gallop and plunged into the treeline, Manny already off the road a few lengths ahead of. Hearing a whistle, Henrik ducked his head down as close to his horse's neck as possible. A dull thud thumped as a crossbow bolt appeared in a tree to his right. More whistling sounds, but as the distance between him and the legionnaires increased, there was only the sound of them whipping through leaves.

The horse's hooves drummed against the ground. The rhythm never quite constant as the horse picked its way between plants and jumped over logs. Henrik himself wished he had a visor as leaves and branches whipped against his face. The occasional larger branch causing him to have to duck in his saddle. Soon enough the only sounds other than his horse were the usual chattering of the forest, and he scanned in all directions there were no visible signs of pursuit.

"I think we've lost them," Henrik shouted.

Manny reined in his horse and waited for Henrik to join him.

"For now," Manny answered. "Think he was telling the truth about the Cohort?"

"Probably," Henrik sighed heavily. "Those legion types don't have the imagination to lie."

"We should be able to sneak past them," Manny said. "600 men isn't many to cover an entire forest."

"They'll have all the major roads covered, we're not going to be able to get to Istrus on foot."

"What are you suggesting?"

"I know a man with a boat…"

"Let's go."

The two wheeled their horses around and set off again, Henrik leading the way this time.

They'd been riding for about an hour when Henrik heard something. He held his clenched fist up to let Manny know to stop and stay quiet. Without the sounds of riding, Henrik could make out a sound too rhythmic and too metallic to be natural. It was a sound he'd heard often enough; the dragging sound of a sword being sharpened. The tinny sound emanated from somewhere to their left, hard to tell how far it would carry in the forest, but Henrik thought it no more than 100 metres.

Another hand gesture told Manny to dismount. Henrik crouched, moving as silently as possible.

"Soldiers, to the left." he whispered.

Manny nodded.

Both men crept through the forest, senses on high alert. The sound became clearer as they moved. It was coming from the other side of a small mound. Henrik got down on the floor, concealed by the mound. Around it, he saw a small camp. Three men in the armour of the legion around the remains of last night's fire. Tents a little further back. Henrik held up Three fingers and gestured for Manny to circle the camp. Manny nodded and slunk away. The soldier sharpening his blade had his back to Henrik. The other two on the other side of the camp were throwing dice.

A few minutes passed before one of the dice player's head snapped back. A small bolt sprouting from his eye. The dice fell from his hands and rolled into the fire pit. The two remaining soldiers cried in surprise, rising to their feet.

Henrik jumped over the mound, his blade in hand. The soldier had discarded his whetstone, but his reactions were slow. Reeling from the sudden assault, he brought his sword up but his movements were hesitant. A foot forward, but short of where it should be. His back foot not set, subtle movements betraying his nerves. Henrik struck the flat of the blade with his own. The soldier's grip broke as he stumbled off balance, and the sword clattered away. The man's dumbfounded expression never changed as he met Henrik's eyes. Henrik watched the light leave those eyes as his sword cut across his throat. As he fell backwards, blood bubbled between fingers pressed against his throat. Henrik looked away, he'd seen enough men die.

Manny had his foot on the final soldier's chest. With a grunt, he pulled his dagger from the prone figure's breast.

"Expected more," he grunted

"They were green," Henrik agreed. "New recruits, not see any action. They froze."

"Let's go."

Henrik nodded, and they returned to the horses.

They had more encounters; most they managed to avoid. Some had resulted in scuffles, but overall progress had been smooth and they hadn't seen anyone in a few hours. *Not far to the river now*, Henrik thought. They were riding at an easy trot, saving the horses where they could. The sun low in the sky now, setting fire to the tops of the trees where the leaves were turning. They would make the boat to-night at a full gallop, but if they found a secluded place to camp, that made more sense.

Henrik turned to suggest as much to Manny. Without warning, Manny rolled backwards out of his saddle. It looked like he took most of the impact out of the landing, but it was still heavy. Henrik's brow furrowed, a stinging bloomed in his cheek. Lifting his hand to his face, he saw blood on his fingertips. More arrows sped by him. Henrik looked down to check on Manny. Manny favoured his left side, the shaft of an arrow protruding from his shoulder. Manny didn't let pain show, but his grimace spoke volumes. At least he was still conscious.

Henrik jumped from his steed and hid in the bush. Seconds later, three legionnaires appeared, two with the traditional sword and shield. The third was an archer, armed with a recurve bow. A compact yet powerful bow, a soldier's weapon. Henrik watched them approach Manny as he moved through the underbrush.

"Where is your friend?" the leader demanded.

Manny gurgled in response. The soldier knelt beside him, examining his wound. Manny clutched the soldier strap of his armour as though to pull him close. The soldier shrugged his grip off, and Manny fell back to the ground with a groan.

"Find the other one," he straightened, turning to the other soldier with the sword, "he can't have got far."

Henrik focussed his attention on Manny. While the soldier was distracted, he saw Manny's dagger slip into his good hand. He didn't have much time. The gap to the archer couldn't be more than a few metres. He wouldn't have time to close it all the way.

Henrik jumped from cover, bellowing a meaningless howl of aggression. The archer fumbled the bow but managed to bring it up as Henrik closed the gap. Panicked, he loosed an arrow without being able to fully draw. The arrow wobbled in the air, glancing the off shoulder of Henrik's armour and deflecting to safety. Henrik's sword cut into the gap between the man's armour, between neck and shoulder, biting into his throat. The blade stuck for a second, dragging down on Henrik's arm as the lifeless body sunk to the ground.

Henrik looked around. Manny had taken advantage of the leader's distraction to thrust his dagger into the base of his skull. The remaining soldier hit him in the face with his shield. Manny sprawled on the floor, his dagger lying discarded to his side. Henrik grabbed the bow now lying at his feet. Dropping to one knee, he pulled arrows from the quiver beneath the dead man. With a fluid motion, he notched two arrows in succession, pulled the bow back and released. The man standing over Manny with sword raised jerked as the arrows struck his back.

Henrik threw the bow aside and dashed to Manny's side. Kneeling, he checked the wound, probing Manny's shoulder with his fingers.

"How bad?" Manny asked.

Henrik twisted the arrow slightly, causing Manny to wince in pain.

"Could be worse," Henrik said. "Tip isn't in the bone at least. We'll need to push it through."

"Ah f…" Manny rolled his head back in pain. "Pull the bastard out."

"It'll do more damage coming out than going in. Two seconds."

Manny grimaced and took a swig from his flask.

"Sit up," Henrik instructed, "and brace yourself."

With a grunt of exertion, Henrik pushed the arrow through the shoulder so the point emerged from the back. Manny screamed in pain. Taking another deep drink.

"Almost there…" Henrik snapped the arrow a thumb's length before the wound. Manny gave another twitch of pain, but no scream this time. Henrik moved round behind Manny and pulled the arrow out. There was blood, lots of blood.

"We'll need to get this cleaned up before we carry on." Henrik poured some of Manny's alcohol over the wound. Once it was cleaned, he put both hands over the word, closed his eyes and said, "Sana."

Henrik opened his eyes, but there was no visible change to the wound.

"What just happened?" Manny's eyes flicked between his shoulder and Henrik.

"Though I'd try a healing cantrip." Henrik

sighed in resignation "I've never been able to do it but I thought after the statue creatures…"

"Worth a shot," Manny reassured Henrik.

"Yeah, I suppose, we'll just have to let it heal the slow way…"

Night had fallen some time ago. Henrik checked on Manny; he looked pale but the bandage and splint seemed to be holding his shoulder. Henrik found the gurgling of the river oddly soothing. The mill and the outbuildings that supported it were the only buildings in sight. A rhythmic churning from the waterwheel the only sound in the still night. The windows of the house glowed, a stark contrast to the perfect darkness of the open countryside.

Henrik dismounted and walked up the path to the door. He knocked as hard as he dared, sounds carried in the open and who knew where the legion were.

"It's Henrik," he hissed.

The door flew open. A bear of a man filled the doorframe, once powerful but now softening. His large bald head more than compensated by a beard that bordered on aggressive.

"Henrik, my boy!" he exclaimed.

"Keep your voice down, Karl," Henrik winced. "Got the legion on our back. Manny is injured."

"Why didn't you say?" Karl rumbled. "Get him inside."

Manny slumped against the wall of the house.

Karl stood aside to let them into the room. Manny leaned heavily on Henrik as they stepped through the door, his face drawn. A fire in the middle of the room provided the light. A bookshelf on one side and chairs on the other. Food and cooking utensils were suspended from the ceiling. Henrik helped Manny into one of the chairs before turning to Karl.

"So what trouble are you in this time?" Karl asked.

"Hard to say," Henrik sighed.

"Suppose these legionnaires that have been poking around are looking for you?" Karl let the question hang. Henrik knew he was curious, but he wouldn't push too hard until Henrik was ready. "That what happened to him?"

"They ambushed us a few leagues back," Henrik replied. "We need a way to get back into Istrus."

"You're thinking of using my grain barge?"

"Looks like I need a favour again Karl…" Henrik said, with open arms and a wry smile.

"So, tell me the story…"

"Quite the tale," Karl mused.

Manny was asleep upstairs. His wound wasn't life threatening, but he'd need to see a medic to make sure he didn't lose any mobility in the shoulder. In the meantime, Henrik had been explaining the events of the last few days to Karl by the fire. Henrik took a drink from the goblet of wine his host had provided.

"Oh aye, quite the little romp we've had."

"You think this client set you up?" Karl asked. "Why would he pay you in advance?"

"I don't know," Henrik shook his head. "None of it makes sense."

"You should think about retirement yourself," Karl laughed. "None of that excitement out here working the mill."

"The quiet life wouldn't suit me, Karl."

"Maybe, maybe not…"

The two sat in silence for a minute, gazing into the fire.

"Well," Karl finally broke the quiet. "Tomorrow we'll get you boys down the river and back into Istrus. You can find your answers there. For now, I'm going to sleep."

"You're a good man, Karl."

Henrik stayed by the fire for a long time, alone with his own thoughts.

Henrik was getting a cramp from having his legs bent. He was pretty sure he'd be arriving in Istrus with at least ten splinters to boot. Without the lids, two barrels could accommodate a grown man stacked bottom to top, but that did not mean it was comfortable. He hoped Manny would be okay in his barrels. The shallow bottomed boat didn't rock too much, but in with the cargo he felt every movement. He and Manny were concealed in what he thought of as the shed, the central covered part of the barge.

In front of the shed were four ranks of oarsmen who were propelling the craft. A platform at the back of the boat allowed Karl to oversee progress with his steward, a ferret faced little man called Mickael.

Voices drifted down from the deck. Echoing footsteps caused Henrik to hold his breath. The creaking of the door and the groan of the steps.

"All these barrels contain grain?" an officious voice asked.

"Finest grain in the Commonwealth," Karl boasted. "All bound for Martin Rosten's warehouse."

"Open one of them…"

"Of course, sir, of course." Karl's voice had taken on an obsequious tone. Henrik felt his grip on the front of the barrel concealing him. Karl pulled the barrel a few inches forward.

"Not that one," the voice sounded pleased with itself, as though the officer had caught Karl in a lie. "That one on the other side."

Henrik felt Karl's grip loosen, and the footsteps faded. A grunting noise and a thud announced that Karl had taken one of the barrels from the rack. The sounds of the barrel lid hitting the floor were not far behind.

"See for yourself," Karl said, "grain fit for a king."

"The commonwealth has no truck with kings." The officer sounded disappointed. "Nevertheless, you may continue on your way."

Henrik heard the scrape of the officer turning on

his heel before the sentence was finished. His footsteps were now brisk.

"You boys okay in there?" Karl whispered.

"Oh, just dandy, thanks," came Manny's voice.

"All good," Henrik said.

"Well, the little toady is gone." The relief in Karl's voice palatable. "Looking for 'contraband.' Pah. It's a bribe he was after or I'm a gerbil."

The night air was cool and still. The sconces created small pools of light and deepened the shadows thrown by the tall houses huddling over the alley. Henrik's feet clicked on the cobblestones as he walked down the gentle slope towards his goal. The street itself unencumbered by the usual debris littering the streets of less desirable parts of the city. A barrel or two by a door, the only things visible on the pristine street. The house stood on the corner as the street bent to the left, the torch by the door lit but the windows on the second and third floors dark.

Henrik stopped in front of the solid wooden door. According to Volpi's men, this was the place. Raising his fist, he banged on the door as hard as he could.

"Leander!" Henrik shouted.

No reply after a few minutes. Henrik repeated the process. A few more minutes went by. Then the rasping sound of metal on metal as the lock was pulled back. The door opened the tiniest crack. Eyes looked out at Henrik. Before the man could talk,

Henrik kicked the door with all of his strength. The door slipped from the man's grasp as he stumbled backwards on to the floor.

Scrambling to right himself, the man looked at Henrik in shock.

"Oh God, it's you…" he babbled.

"Yes, Leander, it's me." Henrik's expression darkened. "Time for some questions."

Leander was not listening. He'd scrabbled to his feet and fled the room. He burst through the door opposite the hall into what Henrik knew to be the dining room. Henrik himself opened the door to his left, into the sitting room. The fire still burned in the hearth, a book carefully folded on the arm of one of the two wingback chairs by the fire. Henrik crossed to the decanter in one corner and poured himself a drink. Admiring the deer head mounted above the fire and the bookcase on the opposite wall as he waited.

He did not have long to wait. Leander walked into the room with Manny holding his crossbow at his back.

"Please, Leander," Henrik gestured to the chair with the book on the arm, "take a seat."

Leander's gulp was audible, his face pale. He was not a large man, a hand or so under medium height and slight. Henrik knew him to be in his mid-thirties, but he looked older. His hair was thinning and his drawn face had worry lines on the forehead and around the eyes that added years to his appearance. He had the strange combination of pallor and red in his face that spoke of a man perhaps a little too fond of the bottle. Sitting in the chair, his hands fidgeted with the arms.

"My friend here is going to ask you some questions." Manny had his face close to Leander's. Henrik tapped his dagger against Leander's cheek. "And if we don't like the answers, then I'm going to cut you."

"No, please," Leander flinched in the chair. "I'll tell you anything, I swear."

"That is a promising start," Henrik reassured him. "Now, shall we begin?"

Manny withdrew from the chair to pour himself a drink.

"You will remember that you hired us to recover an item from Bhuzon An…"

"I'm sorry, please don't hurt me!" Leander sobbed.

"Calm yourself." Without changing expression, Henrik slapped Leander, who stopped sobbing. "You asked for us by name. Why?"

"It wasn't me," Leander pleaded. "You have to believe me, I'm not the one you want."

"You'll have to do better than this performance." Manny's soft voice as cold as a winter's night. "You hired us. Tell us what we want to know."

"No, no." Leander squirmed. "I did hire you, but the job wasn't my idea. I'm not a rich man, I couldn't pay that much gold. I'm not lying!"

"A fancy part of the city for a poor man." Henrik raised his eyebrow.

"Inherited." Leander's tone now bitter. "The house, the name. That's all that's left of my family. Oh, I was rich once, but it's all gone now."

Manny and Henrik exchanged a look.

"I swear it, I lost it all in brothels and gaming houses," Leander continued.

"So how did you come to hire us?" Henrik asked. "Where did you get the gold?"

"I'm a devout son of the church. I confess my sins every week. I told my priest that I could lose the house. The last memory of my parents…" Leander said. "One day, a man came to me after confession and he told me there was a way I could keep the house and maybe I could earn some favour with important people."

"And all you had to do was hire a couple of thieves." Manny stated.

"Not just any thieves," Leander said. "They had all the details. Your names, descriptions, where to go to contact you."

"They paid you?" Henrik asked.

"Yes." Leander's shoulders slumped even further into the chair.

"Let me guess, the 200 gold we were to be paid on delivery?" Manny asked.

"They said you'd never make it back," Leander whined. "I've not seen so much gold in years. I had no choice. You understand, surely?"

Henrik turned away from the fire.

"What do you think?" he said.

"He's a spineless worm." Manny shrugged. "I

doubt he's got the stones to lie. The house looks cleaned out. Years of selling off valuables would make sense. He's probably telling the truth."

"I am, I swear it by the Redemptor!" Leander cried.

"Okay, then," Henrik sighed. "So about these people that hired you…"

The tinkling cacophony of shattering glass cut Henrik short. The shards glittered briefly in the fire as they cascaded from the broken window pane. The clay projectile hit the far wall and exploded. The liquid inside splashing over half the room. Henrik and Manny flinched back, turning their faces to avoid the splatter.

"Run!" Manny screamed at the top of his lungs. Throwing the door open, he dived into the hallway. Leander and Henrik followed suit. Henrik saw the torch from the corner of his eye. Flames ignited with a whoosh, turning the room into an inferno. Henrik felt the heat beating on his face through the doorway.

"Back door…" he suggested.

Manny led the way. Retracing his earlier steps. The three moved with caution, but with as much speed as possible. The back door hung to one side on its hinges, the doorway framing the darkness beyond. They had to go single file through the alley. The walls cramped on either side left little space. After a few hundred metres, they ducked back onto a main road and stopped at a crossroads. Henrik glanced at Manny, who nodded to confirm there was

114

nobody following them.

"Well Leander," Henrik murmured, "it seems your former employers don't want you answering any questions."

"Please, you have to help me." Leander shivered in the night air. "Keep me safe and I'll tell you everything…"

Leander lurched forward into Henrik. Confused at first, Henrik looked down to see a crossbow bolt buried in Leander's chest.

"What?" Manny looked around, trying to catch a glance of the bowman. Henrik caught Leander as he fell and supported his weight.

"The Eparch, it was the Eparch." Henrik had to strain to hear the words as blood ran from the corner of Leander's mouth. With a final shudder, Henrik felt his body go limp. Lying him on the ground, Henrik closed his eyelids with his thumb and index finger.

"Sleep in peace, my brother, may you live in eternity at the Redemptor's side."

The plush carpet deadened Henrik's footsteps, but he still moved with care. The long corridor was a monument to previous Eparchs. Portraits spaced evenly along both walls, each existing in a halo of light. Breaking into the Eparch's manse had been straightforward. The locks on the window no barrier to a professional. Just the one guard to subdue. So far. Henrik hoped Manny had the same look on the third floor. Even with an injured shoulder he was still the much better climber of the two, but Henrik was the better fighter. If all the guards were upstairs, Manny was going to run into problems.

Henrik came to a double door. Ornate and inlaid with what looked like silver, expensive but tasteful as the trappings of wealth go. Taking care to make as little noise as possible, he opened the door into a lavish office dominated by the largest mahogany desk he had ever seen. The green leather top covered in papers, a quill discarded to one side. An imposing chair sat empty behind the desk, the occupant stood by the floor to ceiling window looking out; he seemed to be lost in thought. The Eparch wore relatively simple robes for a man of his station. White, unostentatious but well-made and comfortable looking. To either side were bookcases and marble busts; Henrik recognised Placus Virius Bassus. A noted religious scholar, instrumental in the early days of the church.

"Please take a seat…" The Eparch turned and motioned to one of the utilitarian chairs in front of the desk. Henrik pursed his lips but chose not to reply. He took a seat, curious to see how this would play out.

"Ah, my son, you are a curiosity." The Eparch steepled his fingers beneath his chin. The man's face was lined with age. What little hair he had left pure white. "A thief, yes? But a man who knows the value of silence."

"A fighter learns to wait for the opening," Henrik replied. "Sometimes you have to wait for an opponent to show his hand."

"A mixed metaphor, but I assure you we are not enemies." The Eparch's smile held a note of condescension.

"It seems to me that it might be safer to be your enemy than your friend," Henrik bristled.

"You refer to poor Leander?" The Eparch made a dismissive gesture with his hand. "Unfortunate, but necessary."

"Empty words, Eparch," Henrik's voice hardened. "I'm here for answers."

"Henrik Matthiesen, former paladin in training…"

"How do you know that name?"

"You are still a part of the Redemptor's flock, Henrik." The Eparch ignored the interruption. "Abandoning your calling to the church does not mean the Redemptor has abandoned you. His plan is grand and intricate. To those who listen, he reveals those truths they need to perform his will."

Henrik should have known the church wouldn't lose sight of him. Where was Manny? He should have been here by now.

"I assume you are here to do me violence in return for these answers you seek?" The Eparch asked. "Have you considered that the Redemptor has the answers you desire?"

"My faith in him never wavered, Eparch. It's his church I have issues with."

"Henrik, my son, the church is a construct of

man. Made up of men," the Eparch replied "Like all works of men, it is an imperfect thing. That, Henrik, is why we need the Ebon Key."

"What are you talking about?" Henrik's eyes narrowed.

"It was made with a purpose." The Eparch's eyes were now filled with an almost maniacal gleam "It will open our minds, Henrik. Oh, think of it. The ability to commune with the Redmeptor himself. To fully understand his purpose. Think of the wonders the church could achieve. We could make the imperfect divine."

"You're insane," Henrik laughed. "No man can understand the will of God."

"Fool. Small minded fool," the Eparch spat before regaining his composure. "We could not allow that kind of power to rest in the hands of just anyone you understand? Leander was a simple tool, one who'd outlived his usefulness."

"Does the church not teach compassion?" Henrik demanded. "The life of one man is not expendable."

"Pah." The Eparch again dismissed the thought with a gesture. "What is one man before the glory of the Redemptor's design? But you Henrik, you have shown yourself worthy. You can retake your place in the church…"

A noise in the corridor caused Henrik to rise from his chair and reach for his sword. He turned to see two paladins in full armour, including gold highlighting, enter the room. Each holding one of Manny's arms as he hung unconscious between them. Without a word they dropped him on the carpet, his breast rising and falling slowly the only sign of life. The Paladins took up guard stations either side of the door.

"Your friend is no match for a paladin, Henrik," the Eparch declared from behind him. "Foolish of you both to think you could intrude here uninvited."

Henrik's face was grim. The Eparch was right, of course. They'd underestimated the churchman. His concern now was how to get out of here in one piece. Henrik might match a paladin for a minute, but he couldn't best one, let alone however many were in the manse.

"So, you allowed me to get this far." Henrik turned back to the Eparch, hand still resting on his sword hilt. "What is it you want from me?"

"I was hoping, Henrik, that you would join me in my grand endeavour." The Eparch's hands once again nestled under his chin. "But failing that, my offer is quite simple. The Ebon Key in exchange for yours, and your friends, safety."

"What's stopping you coming after us once I've handed it over?" Henrik asked. "Like Leander…"

"You have my word, as a servant of the Redemptor."

"What about our payment?" Henrik recognised the gleam in the Eparch's eye. Obsession. It gave Henrik a sliver of hope. If the Eparch got what he wanted, then he may be too distracted to deal with loose ends like Henrik and Manny.

"Ever the businessman," the Eparch smiled and reached into the drawer of his desk, producing a purse. "Fine. 200 gold as agreed. Now tell me where the key is."

Henrik looked at Manny's prone form and back to the Eparch. There was nothing else for it. Reaching around his back, he took the Ebon Key from its hiding place on the inside of his belt and placed it on the desk.

"You had it with you?" The Eparch's tone was incredulous.

Henrik hooked the coin purse on his belt and knelt down to put Manny's arm over his shoulder. Supporting his weight, he walked to the exit. The two paladins took a step, so they were blocking the door.

"You know, Henrik, I could simply have you cut down where you stand?"

Henrik stiffened but did not reply.

"Fortunately for you, I am a man of my word, and I have more pressing matters."

The two paladins stepped aside and Henrik left the office, half carrying Manny as he went. Leave the affairs of "great" men to them. He had to get Manny to a medic. Who knew, maybe one day down the line he'd cross paths with the Eparch again…

IMPERIAL AIRWAYS HP36

BY DAVID BOWMORE

"In 1936, Imperial Airways HP36 crashed on the lower levels of an African mountain," the well-groomed man said. His suit was of the finest Savile Row material. His white hair thick, lustrous and a little too long, giving him a slight bohemian air, strikingly at odds with the surroundings of the stiff, formal gentleman's club on Half Moon Street, W1, where he sat in a leather armchair sipping whisky and soda.

"They were always falling out the skies, weren't they?" the old buffer opposite said.

"Indeed, they were. I was a passenger on that ill-fated flight." He rubbed a finger along an old scar which ran from jaw to eye.

"Never." His moustache puffed as he exhaled. "That how you got the souvenir, eh?"

"Quite. But I have an account here that tells the

story much better than I ever could. Would you like to look it over?"

"What's the catch?" Placing a monocle over his left eye, he assessed the bohemian, knowing him to be a shrewd devil.

"No catch. But I would appreciate it if you would go about publishing it in the not-so-distant future."

"Can't make any promises. It all depends on the quality, dear boy."

"Oh, I think you'll find it's golden. Golden." When the bohemian smiled, only one side of his mouth lifted.

AUGUST 25ᵀᴴ

From the coffee table I watch the four propellers of the large silver biplane slowly spinning. Around me, standing and sitting, are my fellow travellers, who will soon board the flying marvel. I count sixteen of us, including two pilots and two stewards. Next to me sits my travelling companion, Professor Edgar Smythe, a specialist engineer and a bit of an all-round scientific genius. I have been employed to be a sort of bodyguard to the old fellow, although I have known him for several years and would have taken this trip whether he asked me or not. Gloria Young, the rather glamorous platinum blonde Hollywood actress, dressed in a long mink, chain smoking and glancing nervously toward the aeroplane paces back and forth passed our table. The scent of Vol de Nuit trails after her. Her companion is the smooth and debonair William Blake. I think he ought to shave off the dastardly looking moustache. It does nothing for his character or his cheek bones. Still, he is a movie star, so I suppose he is doing something right.

Talking to the female attendant is a fellow wearing a bowler hat, but the odd thing about him is the briefcase carried in his left hand. I can see a chain ascending the cuff of his sleeve. This immediately piques one's interest, doesn't it? What the devil is in the case? one asks oneself. The other odd thing is that he is travelling alone. With such an important case in his possession, one would think he would have a companion.

A large matronly woman sits stock still, her tea going cold. The two children, a boy and a girl, of about ten or eleven-years of age, are sitting close to her. The girl cannot take her eyes off the movie stars. The boy is busy playing with a wooden biplane that intermittently crashes on the carpet before being resurrected and continuing its imaginary journey.

A man carrying a Gladstone bag joined a woman who sat alone. He is tall and thin—well over six feet, wears spectacles and looks to my mind to be a medical sort of chap. She is dressed in tweeds, wears a little hat with a pheasant feather in it and looks the sort of woman who would be at home teaching in a girls' school. I don't think they know each other.

The steward is calling us to board now.

A little while ago, we formed a queue and ambled through the door, murmuring to each other in hushed tones. As we crossed the dusty runway, I noticed William had clasped an arm tight around Gloria's shoulder. Poor girl had, and still is having, a hell of a time. First up the steps to board was an elderly military sort. Stiff back, grey bushy moustache and the superior air of a field general.

The female attendant smiled a perfect smile as she welcomed me aboard and directed me to a seat by a small round porthole of a window.

The flight from Cairo to Nairobi is a long one, made longer by having to refuel in Khartoum.

It was a cool but clear day with only a dusting of cloud against an azure sky, as the plane began to gather speed along the runway. The noise inside one of these tin cans does little for conversation, so yet again I was forced to observe my companions and ramble away in my trusty journal. Gloria's knuckles are white from grasping the armrests. The matron type, I suspect a paid nanny, fussed the two children opposite her. The military man stretched his legs and closed his eyes. My friend, Edgar, opened a newspaper at the crossword. Others produced books. The man in the bowler hat rested his case on his knees and peered through the window.

We have refuelled. An hour of standing in the shade of a lean-too hut while fez-wearing attendants checked the plane and pumped diesel into the tank. Nothing else of note except that I found out the military man is called Powell, Colonel Powell. The children stood near their nanny. I gather their names are Tommy and Linda.

A scream woke me with a start, and a rumble of thunder resonated around the cabin.

"Everyone, fasten your seat belts," the captain called back, calmly.

Gloria grabbed William's hands.

Looking through the little window, I saw dark clouds rolling around each other. Sheet lightning surrounded us, accompanied by more thunder. Gloria screamed—a scream straight out of the talkies. The plane rocked and suddenly dropped. Thank God for the seatbelts or else we would have been thrown around the tin can.

Someone was being sick behind me. The children were crying. Their nanny did her utmost to calm them with unconvincing, soothing words.

And then a streak of lightning lit the dark sky. I saw it in slow motion. A long, crooked finger reached towards us, and touched our starboard propeller with an almighty spark that blinded me for a few seconds. And when my head cleared, and I could finally see again, not only was the propeller on fire but half the lower wing missing too.

We were spiralling out of control. I looked around for some protection, but what can one use against the forces of gravity?

The door to the cockpit swung open, and I could see the two men struggling to control our descent. We fell beneath the clouds into rain and then, miraculously, the captain managed to stop the free fall and we were at least gliding, albeit on a downward trajectory.

Gloria, it appeared, had fallen into a faint and semi-silence settled over us, for all of thirty seconds, as some sort of hope landed on our shoulders.

"Prepare for impact," the captain called.

"Put your heads between your knees," his co-pilot called.

I did as instructed.

The sound of ripping metal and cracking wood made my teeth want to fall out. Luggage was thrown all around the cabin. Someone was thrown from their seat and slid along the gangway. Hats, clothing, and paperbacks filled the air.

When I woke, I seemed to be unharmed — bit of a sore head, but essentially unscathed. But around me, my fellow travellers were groaning and whimpering.

I checked on Edgar; unconscious, but thankfully alive.

William was shaking his head groggily. I grasped his shoulder to get his attention. He looked at me, blinking blood from his eyes.

"Okay?" I asked, noticing he wore the same scent as Gloria; Vol de Nuit.

He pulled a handkerchief from his pocket and held it to the gash on his forehead. "I'll live."

"Good man."

The stewardess came to and staggered into the cockpit.

126

"Keep Gloria calm," I said. Fortunately, she seemed to be out cold.

Someone started screaming from the rear. I turned. The body I remembered being flung around as we crashed had woken. Clearly in agony, he held his arm to his chest.

I turned back to the stewards. The male was still coming around.

"You. Wake up. Wake up, would you?"

He looked at me with eyes that refused to focus. "Are you okay?" I asked.

"I think so, sir."

"Good. Tell me, do you know if a doctor is on board?"

"I'm St. John's Ambulance trained, sir."

"That'll have to do. There's a man back there with a broken arm. He needs your help. Where the hell is the captain?"

I left the steward to his ministrations, and I stumbled through to the cockpit. The stewardess stared at the men. Both looked to be quite dead. There was certainly a lot of blood.

"Miss, you need to go and help your colleague. There's a lot to do. We can't help these two now."

Once I was certain the captain was dead, I moved his body out of the way, slipped the radio earphones off his head, and searched for the radio controls. Pressing the call button, I said, "Mayday, Mayday. Anyone receiving? I repeat, Mayday." No one answered. A quick examination of the electronics and I had found the problem, a loose wire.

A scream called me back to the cabin. Linda had realised that Nanny was dead. Not to be upstaged, Gloria decided to add to the cacophony. I promised Linda that it would be okay, and that I would get them out of there, but we all needed to be calm. She blubbed some more and wiped her nose on a handkerchief her brother handed her.

"Sorry, Miss Young," I said. "The children need you, the girl especially. Her name's Linda. Will you sit with her?" I didn't wait for an answer, but turned to William Blake. "We need to deal with the dead. I've counted four so far."

"Oh, I see. Outside with the dearly departed, is it?"

"Yes. Pilots first I think."

"Right-o. Better scope the lay of the land first. See where we ought to deposit them, what." He was right, of course.

The door opened easily, and we stepped out into a sunny afternoon. You would not have thought that ten minutes earlier we had plummeted from the thundery skies, although steam rose in misty streams as water evaporated. Beneath our feet the loose clinker of a million-year-old mountain easily slipped down the incline toward what looked like a rainforest, before levelling out to a rather green expanse of veldt. A river snaked north to south in the distance. I could see no signs of life, save for the plane which had broken up; the main body and three wings which lay scattered among the sporadic heather some two hundred yards behind the wreck. One engine was

128

still on fire.

The sun beating down on us suggested we were on the leeward side of the mountain, although there was a definite chill in the air.

"Damn lucky, what?" William said.

"I'll say. The pilot pulled a miracle out of thin air."

"Definitely dead, is he?"

"No doubt about it."

The air felt thin. Whatever we did would soon drain our oxygen supplies.

Back inside, we reported our findings to the stewards. The male had a limp, but coped admirably. The female had regained her composure and was administering where she could. The lady, who had previously been in a tweed jacket and skirt combo, had ripped the sleeves off her blouse to bandage those in need. Again admirable, but not very bright. She would need her clothes for warmth. I told her so, and she told me I was speaking complete rot. She had been cross-country champion at her school and if anything gets one used to the cold, it is slogging through the English countryside on a brisk winter's morning wearing nothing but woollen underwear and a gym slip. I thought it better not to mention that those days must have been forty years earlier, but I had been right; she was a games mistress and keen to prove herself capable and equal to every task. I immediately enrolled Miss Kerr, for that was her name, into our ad hoc pallbearer team, along with Edgar who had finally come around. We deposited the two pilots, the nanny, and the briefcase man out of sight between the nose of the plane and the rise of the mountain.

When the cockpit was clear of bodies, I found young Tommy, and asked, "Do you want an important job, Tommy?" His eyes lit up. "Good, come with me."

I sat him in the pilot's chair and placed the earphones on his head.

"I need you to call for help. Do you know the word for help?"

"Mayday. I read it in a book."

"Good lad. You press this button and speak into this receiver. Like this." He repeated the instruction, and I was satisfied. Then I returned to the main cabin. The tall chap I noted in the waiting room cried out in pain as the steward set his broken arm. Beads of sweat prickled his forehead. I asked the steward if he would be okay.

"I think there's more damage internally, but I can't do anything about that. He'll be in pain," the steward said, wrapping a bandage around a makeshift split.

"No, I... won't." The patient gasped. Something was wrong with his breathing. "My Gladstone... get my... bag."

It was not hard to find. Inside, I was delighted to see it stocked with medical equipment.

"These drugs are... rough," he said, "made for animals. But... in a pinch, they'll do the... job. I'm a... vet, you... see?"

I left him to drift into oblivion as he injected himself, and went outside for a smoke. My hand shook as I lit my pipe.

Knowing she was alive and on solid ground seemed to calm Gloria. She and Linda were sitting outside on the clinker, their backs to the plane some fifteen yards down the slope. They talked about a place called Little Rock, famous actors, school and ponies.

I walked over to the bodies, lined in a row and given as much of a decent burial as we could, considering the material we had to work with. The briefcase rested on the chest of the man, and his bowler hat covered his face. The cuff still tight around the wrist prevented it from being snatched away. Having already found the plane's emergency tool kit, I returned with bolt cutters to take charge of the case.

"Grave robbin' is a capital offence," a gruff but friendly voice said behind me.

"It's not what it looks like," I said, standing up and feeling the colour rise. "I just thought that—"

"No need to explain. I recognise an officer and a gentleman when I see one." He pulled a snuff tin from his pocket and took two large snorts. Blood seeped through the silk bandage around his head.

"Are you okay?" I asked. "Should you be out—"

"Most of us are outside now, although they daren't come over here to the boneyard." He looked over at the reddening sky as the sun approached the horizon almost directly opposite the wrecked aeroplane. "It'll be dark soon. Then we'll feel the bite. You've handled yourself well so far. But do you have what it takes to keep them alive."

"I led a great troop of men—"

"I don't doubt it, but these are civilians. Different form of creature altogether. Can't see they'll listen to an old dinosaur like me. It'll be down to you."

"I won't need to lead the—"

"Of course, you will. Plan for the worst, that's what I say, and hope for the best."

The old boy was right, but it still left an unpleasant taste in my mouth. I could not possibly be expected to do this, could I?

"A search plane will be sent when they realise we're missing," I said. "They'll backtrack along our flightpa—"

"And what if we're off course? Have you asked yourself that?"

"Well, yes, I have actually. But, we can't do anything—"

"Oh, I agree. Better wait till tomorrow."

The briefcase was surprisingly light, but I kept it close to me as we went inside. I really did not know if I had what it took to lead this group, but as the old boy pointed out, I had already made a start.

"Mr Harry. Can I stop now?" Tommy leaned against the door of the cockpit. The boy looked fit to drop. "I don't think it's working, anyway."

I went back to the radio and sure enough, there was no signal, no static, nothing.

The steward sat across two seats, exhaustion

and shock finally catching up with him. I shook his foot and said, "Sorry, old man. We need to talk."

"How can I be of assistance, sir."

"I think we can dispense with the formalities now, call me Harry."

"Thank you, sir. I'm John White and this is Chloe Lawton."

The stewardess gave me another lovely smile, although it was spoiled slightly by the mascara running down her cheeks.

"How much food and water do we have?" I asked, getting straight to the point.

"One meal each. We were about to serve when the storm struck. But it's not much; soup in thermos flasks, cold chicken, some tongue slices, potatoes, and cheese. We have water, but only enough to make a few pots of tea and coffee, and most of that has been drunk already."

"I suggest you two oversee rations. Who knows how long we'll be here? Plan for two days and after that..."

As night fell, we made ourselves as comfortable as possible in the cabin, covering ourselves in extra coats and clothes from the luggage. But the cold still bit through to our bones.

AUGUST 26TH

I stood in the shadow of the mountain, looking down into the green valley below. William stood next to me, breathing heavily.

"What do you think killed him?" he asked.

"I wouldn't like to say."

"I suppose his heart could have stopped, but his breathing wasn't too good, was it?"

"No. Maybe he overdosed on the drugs? He did say they were for animals."

But my thoughts were on the undertaking ahead of us. It needed someone capable of not only navigating the jungle below, but ensuring everyone lived through the ordeal.

Edgar came to stand next to us.

"I bring breakfast in all its meagre glory. What is it they say, breakfast like a king? Pretty poor show if you ask me." He passed me a tin mug half full of lukewarm Brown Windsor soup.

"How far from civilisation are we, Edgar?" I asked as I took a sip.

"Hard to tell, two-hundred miles, perhaps only fifty. But which direction do we head in?"

"The river is the key." William nodded his head in agreement.

"You can't be thinking of striking out? We have to get through the valley first."

"What other option do we have? The radio's dead, and we haven't seen or heard a spotter plane since the crash. There's not enough food to last the day. At least down there, there might be fruit."

"But—"

"Come with me."

I brought him to the burial ground where the vet now lay. The clinker had been pulled from off the bodies that had been placed there the day before, their eternal peace disturbed by wild animals that gnawed at the dead flesh.

"Dogs of some sort, wouldn't you say?" I asked.

"I thought I heard something in the night."

"How long before they become brave enough to attack us and we're too weak to defend ourselves."

"I see your point."

"We should move while the sun is low and I need both of you to help me convince the others that we have to get to the river and follow it to civilisation."

I planned for a long journey. If we could not find water, then the very longest we could survive would be three days, but depending on heat and humidity, probably no more than two days.

My old service pistol and shoulder holster were stowed in my luggage, and I was pleased to see Colonel Powell strap his around his waist. We counted twenty-four rounds between us and we split the cache equally. His walking cane also hid a very handy short rapier. William found the emergency toolbox and took charge of a large adjustable spanner. John, the steward, disappeared into the cockpit and came back with a small flare rocket. His colleague, Chloe, tied a long-bladed knife around her waist, sheathed for safety in her neck scarf. We carried what little food there was in paper bags, and the last of the liquid in Thermos flasks. Then I cut a seatbelt from the seat and tied the briefcase to it, clipped it together and flung it over my shoulder. When questioned, I said that it was obviously important, and we should at least try to deliver it to its destination.

And thus equipped, ten rag-tag survivors set off for an unnamed river near the horizon.

Several hours later, after slipping and sliding over the loose clinker, and using the heather to help keep us upright, the vegetation began to thicken and before too long, we were deep in a valley, surrounded by tall bamboo with a thick bed of moss underfoot. And still we descended the slope.

The shade of the vegetation did little to relieve our thirst. If anything, it became hotter in the forest. The moss made walking treacherous and slow. William took the lead, hacking with his spanner, trying to carve a path through the vegetation.

The sound of jungle life was all around. Creatures scuttled away or hooted calls to each other. Birds of the brightest colours passed overhead, and small monkeys jumped from tree to tree.

The children bore it all remarkably well.

It was hard to tell but night appeared to be falling and the hope of finding a clearing to rest in was bleak, when John said, "I can hear water." This immediately caused a cacophony of delight to which he tried to quieten everybody. We all strained our ears, but Linda was the first to hear it. "This way," she said and struck a course that we all eagerly followed. Fifty yards ahead, we came upon a large pool of water with a small but radiant waterfall on the far side. We all broke into a run. Edgar warned us to be cautious.

It was clear and deep. I assumed that somewhere underground it must have drained away, perhaps providing life for the entire jungle. The children dived in. So did William, stripping off to his underwear, not caring what the women of our party might think, and everyone sipped the cool clear liquid.

With a fire drying us, we were soon huddled around it, drifting off to sleep.

AUGUST 27TH

It was still dark when I was woken by a kick to the stomach. My initial reaction to strike out was curbed by the point of a two-sided spear.

Around us stood a dozen tall men, all barely dressed and likewise armed with very sharp spears. The surprising thing about them, bearing in mind that we were somewhere in the middle of Africa, was that they were paler than one would expect. In fact, they were almost white.

The Colonel, in a rash move, drew his gun from his semi-prone position and pointed it at the nearest native. They showed no recognition and hence no fear of the weapon. Before I could warn him to put the pistol away, he had pulled the trigger and sent the nearest man tumbling with a bullet to the middle of his chest. In response the natives drew back from us and we drew closer together; Miss Kerr, the games mistress, trying to bury the children's faces in her matronly bosom. The Colonel remained seated in his attempt to keep them at bay. However, the strange natives still surrounded us. I was about to draw my own pistol from inside my safari jacket when the Colonel shot again, downing another of the white devils. This time they responded, and a spear flew with startling accuracy, impaling the Colonel to the ground. Our panic was intense. There was no way we could fight these people. I called for calm. Edgar leaned over the Colonel's body, then looked at me and shook his head. The warriors then forced us to our feet. With prods and pushes, they escorted us away from our temporary camp, leaving our gallant friend to the creatures of the forest. But I did pick up his ingenious silver tipped walking stick.

We were not bound in any way and they did not talk to us or each other, as we were brought along a winding path for perhaps a mile.

Before long, we entered a large, open clearing with many dwellings and several larger buildings. It couldn't help but be noticed that the construction was reminiscent of home, with stone and rough bricks bound together with mud. Other white natives, male and female, came to watch our procession until we were lined up in the centre of the village to be ogled at.

Edgar whispered to me, "Descendants of a lost European tribe, do you suppose?"

I shrugged my shoulders.

A portly man stepped out of a larger building, and judging by the gold torque around his neck, the crown of long feathers, and a large animal skin cloak

138

that had once belonged to a very large creature, he was their chief.

"Speak who?" he said. At least we had some sort of rough language to work with.

I suddenly found all my companions' eyes upon me. So, I cleared my throat and said, "It appears I do, your grace." When one finds oneself in these sorts of sticky situations, it is always best to employ diplomacy first.

"Kill." He had been handed the Colonel's gun by one of the warriors and was eyeing it from every angle, staring into the barrel, feeling its heft. I stepped forward partly to show him the safe way to handle it and also to gain his trust. But I was blocked by crossed spears, and then the gun went off, causing the native gathering to flee.

The chief picked the gun off the floor and pointed it at me. I honestly thought my end had come, and then he walked along our lineup. Miss Kerr hugged the two children tight, one under each arm. Gloria struck her chin forward and proceeded to lambast the chief with tales of a father who would kick his... well, let's just say I never expected such language from a lady, even an American lady. The chief sneered and moved down the line and in an instant had turned the gun on Edgar. Blood splattered those to his immediate left and right, namely myself, Miss Kerr, and the children.

Our protests and shrieks of alarm were quickly silenced as the chief continued to threaten us with the pistol. John was bringing up what little he had eaten the night before.

I sorely wished to draw my own pistol. But if I killed the chief, we would all surely die.

Nodding his head, he walked away from us and then with a maniacal grin, he turned with the gun raised in the air. Another shot. Not far from our current position was a small sty, housing three grey, brown pigs. The bullet struck one sow somewhere in the gut and she squealed like nothing I had ever heard before as she ran around her small enclosure, bleeding profusely. We were reminded of our useless predicament by the spears that threatened us.

When the hammer fell on empty chamber after empty chamber, the chief turned to me with a crinkled face and dark eyes. "More," he demanded.

I shrugged my shoulders and shook my head.

"More kill, want."

"Ended. Finished," I said.

"Finish?"

I nodded. He threw the gun at my feet. As I bent to pick it up, he pulled at the makeshift strap holding the briefcase over my shoulder. Thinking it unwise to struggle, I let him take it. But I was determined to get it back and delivered into the hands of its rightful owner. Then to my horror he pointed at Gloria, said "Her," before walking back into his larger than normal home. An immediate uproar came from our quickly diminishing group as the warriors grabbed our silver screen sister and dragged her away to her doom.

"Sacred water drink. Pay must," said the chief

from the doorway of his home. "All pay." He spat on the floor.

We were made to sit, but the warriors mostly ignored us once the chief was out of sight. I nudged Miss Kerr and handed the colonel's sword stick to her. Glancing at William, I surreptitiously loaded the pistol from the ammunition concealed about my person. I could see he was keen to save his fiancé, and he took the gun gladly. In the few minutes it took to load, I pictured all sorts of horrors happening to Gloria.

But when the chief staggered from his building, trying to stem the flow of blood running from his fat stomach, we had no other option but to take action.

"Run," I shouted to my friends, dashing for the abode and firing at a warrior who had stepped forward. The chief was on his knees as Gloria emerged from the grand dwelling, holding a dagger. "Mama always taught me to travel with a blade," she said, wiping the blade on her silk dress. Where she carried it, I know not.

I ran into the hut and grabbed the briefcase, desperate to ensure its safe return.

When I emerged a few seconds later, everyone had a head start on me, including Gloria, who ran hand in hand with William. I shot quickly and accurately, downing two spear-wielding natives. The bodies of several white warriors lay strewn as my friends slashed and shot their way to freedom. William—despite the act of being an English buffoon—proved to be more than capable with a pistol. One warrior raised a spear, and I planted a bullet between his eyes. Ahead of me, I saw another lunge at Gloria, managing to drag her to her knees, but she slid her blade between his ribs and sent him to his maker. I caught up with her and took hold of her hand. William was in a tussle with a tribesman, but Miss Kerr ran the warrior through with the thin rapier. Then John raised the flare rocket and pointed it at another pale-skinned warrior. I have never seen anything so horrendous as that man burning up from the inside but fortunately he staggered into one of the outlying buildings and the flames spouting from his mouth and eyes started a conflagration. Our departure was not so imminently important to the villagers anymore.

We staggered on, helping each other where we could, heading west. William, Gloria, Miss Kerr, Tommy, Linda, John, Chloe and I trudging through an African jungle in fear of European natives hunting us down and slaughtering us in revenge for killing their chief. The gentle slope telling us we were still travelling down towards sea level. Even when tiredness began to consume us, we did not stop. It was imperative that we be as far away from those people as possible.

If it weren't for our desperate situation the surroundings might have been considered beautiful. The sun dappled through leaves, and brightly coloured birds flew. Small creatures watched us. Tommy and Linda spotted a small friendly monkey that kept track with us, although he came no closer than a few feet.

"What time is it?" Linda asked.

"Coming up to three o'clock."

"Can we stop yet," Tommy asked.

"Soon," I said. "When we come to a clearing."

Several hours later we did indeed come to a clearing. The ground, although filthy, was at least fairly flat, and as the sun was due to set, so we decided to call it a day. We cleared a space on the ground, gathered some kindling, and within an hour had a decent fire roaring. Our bullets were fast dwindling and we counted four between our two pistols. But no one begrudged the use of one when William spotted a pig type creature. Its death was clean with the bullet aimed just behind the shoulder, midway up the body when the creature was broadside to us. We carried it back to the clearing to great applause. John set to skinning the animal and slicing strips of flesh off it that we skewed on long thin branches to cook over the flames.

We ate well and tiredness took its toll. Linda and Tommy curled up with each other next to Miss Kerr.

William came to sit next to me as I kept first watch. We had decided it was best to be cautious of the unfriendly natives who may be seeking revenge.

"Where did you learn to shoot?" I asked.

"Oh, I done a bit of this and that, here and there, when I was a younger chap, don't you know."

"You ever been in a spot like this before?"

"Not without a friendly native or two. What do

you think, old horse, will we make it?"

"We seem to be dropping like flies, but I hope so. Not making much of a success of leading us to safety, am I?"

"Oh, I wouldn't worry too much, old man. After all, we could all have died in the crash. You're doing your best. No one can ask more than that."

"How's Gloria?"

"She's more resilient than she makes out."

"Oh, I can see that. Lucky she had that dagger."

"Not so lucky for yon big chief, eh?"

We chuckled at that and then returned to whispers as someone grunted.

"Reckon your chances have gone up ten-fold, old boy," he said in a conspiratorial whisper.

"But I... well... but you're engaged."

"That's what the movie studios would have you believe, but it'll never happen. In a year or two, we will sadly part company. That way the adoring fans can fantasise about the what ifs until the cows come how. So, I won't stand in your way if you and she get a few minutes alone."

"She's not my type, Will. Can I call you Will?"

"By all means, old bean. So... what is your type?"

"A very different sort of person."

"Really? Do tell."

He smiled, and in the light of the fire, his teeth had a distinct predatory look about them.

"No, don't say anything," he said, as I was about to answer. "I do believe I can tell." He stood. "Any-
144

way, must try and get some shuteye. Let's hope we can get through this and meet up for a drink sometime."

"Nothing I'd like more."

"Abeinto."

And he went to his kip next to Gloria.

AUGUST 28TH

I woke as the sun rose to the sound of an agonising call for help. John, who had agreed to take the last watch, was kneeling on the ground near the dying fire, clutching his left wrist. The hand had turned dark purple and he swore with a level of vigour that would make a sailor blush.

I tried to assess the problem, as we gathered round.

"It's burning up," John said. "God help me, I'm on fire. This is punishment for what I did yesterday."

The veins along his arm visibly pumped.

"What is it? What's happening?" Chloe asked.

"He's been bitten, I think," I said. "By an insect or a spider, I'd guess. Everybody had better cover up your flesh and make sure no creatures are trapped in your clothing. Give everything a good shake out."

"But what about him?" Miss Kerr asked.

"The vet's bag, quick. There must be something in it that can help." But before William could return with it, the steward flung himself on his back, his legs and arms shuddering, and froth bubbling on his lips. Gloria and Chloe clung to each other while the rest of us looked on in helpless horror as John's head pounded on the soft mossy undergrowth until he stopped moving altogether.

"By God, that was quick," Miss Kerr said, slightly awestruck.

William said a prayer, which included the already fallen, then we gathered our things together and began the third day of our hike. It was a hot, sweaty and dejected group that left the clearing. Each of us no doubt pondering the ease at which we could perish.

A few hours later, I felt a distinct shift in the air; a drier, dustier quality. I was sure we would soon leave the forest behind and be on the open plans of the veldt. But what is it they say about counting your chickens too early?

A roar of tremendous volume brought us all to a stop.

"What was that?" Chloe said. The children visibly shook as Miss Kerr drew them close.

"It was big, whatever it was," Chloe said.

As if to reiterate the fact the roar sounded again. Closer. We all picked up the pace and then bursting from the undergrowth came a gigantic beast. It is the only word for it—beast. Black as night and standing on its hind legs it must have stood over twelve feet tall. It swiped at William, who at the back of the party was closest, sending him flying into the undergrowth. I immediately shot the creature, which only seemed to make it angrier.

There was no need to tell everyone to run. At

146

least my bullet had distracted the monster from his attack on William. However, I had little time to ponder his fate. I do not know where the others had run to, but I pushed ahead as fast as we could with the awesome creature not far behind. I turned and let fly with my last bullet.

Nothing seemed to slow the creature. Breathing hard and with sweat running into my eyes I was suddenly clear of the jungle. I saw my danger too late, but could not stop myself tumbling over a precipice. My arms scrabbled for a hand hold and by the merest good fortune found a tree root to grab hold of. Seconds later, the beast fell past me crying out with an almighty death roar.

Dangling several feet below the edge of the cliff, I called help.

"Is that you, old man?"

I looked up into the face of William. "That was close, what?"

"Don't be a damn fool. Help me."

"Right-o. Back in a jiffy."

I was sure the root would give way, but then I heard a commotion from above and another face looked over the edge.

"Hang on," Miss Kerr said, as if I needed reminding.

A vine slapped me on the back a few minutes later and placing my life in the hands of my friends, I transferred my weight to it. They hauled me back up, in rough jerking motions, to the surface and safety. I lay panting, thanking God for the first time since Passchendaele. Much fuss was made, which I brushed away in favour of counting our numbers.

Two children, two film stars—one trying to grip a wounded shoulder *and* a nasty flapping gash on his face—a stewardess and a burly but ageing games mistress.

William had recovered his pistol, but mine was lost. Besides which, we only had one bullet left.

"So, what do we do now?" Chloe asked.

"We can't go this way," Miss Kerr said.

"What choice do we have?" I said. "Just look around. This plateau stretches to the left and right twenty or thirty miles and if I'm right we appear to be in a slight depression. Look, it gently rises."

"But how?" Gloria said.

"Same way you got me up. We'll collect as many vines as we can and tie them together."

"There must be another way," Chloe said.

"We can debate all day, or we can walk along the edge hoping to find an easier way down. But what if we come across another one of those beasts or a whole herd of them. What if the tribe are still looking for us? We must get off this ridge as quickly as we can."

That was enough to spur them into action. Within an hour we had collected and tied together more than two hundred feet of vines. We tied one end around a sturdy tree.

"Give me that buckle and strap," William said, snatching at the briefcase.

"But I have to get it back to civilisation."

"And you will, old fruit. But we need belt and braces here."

He took the strap and threw the briefcase far over the ridge. My heart sank a little. I had taken such care of it and wanted to deliver it.

With the safety belt strapped around Tommy's chest and tied to the rope, which was also around his chest, he began his descent. Not only was the vine tied to a sturdy tree, but we had looped it around another to give us some breaking capability. Ten minutes later the makeshift rope went slack, and he called up to us. Then Linda made a safe landing.

William went over next as he was pretty much out of the hefting and pulling game because of his injured shoulder.

Gloria arrived on the ground twenty minutes later.

"I can't," Chloe said.

"You travel in aeroplanes all the time. This isn't much different."

"Oh yes, it is."

"Think of it as a bumpy landing."

"But there's only two of you." She looked at Miss Kerr.

"You hardly weigh anything, girl," Miss Kerr said. "More meat and potatoes for you when you get home. You need feeding up."

Her whole body shook as I helped buckle her up. Before going over the edge, she stepped forward and kissed me. They were very kissable lips, but right then she was a woman who needed help. Nothing more.

"Don't drop me."

And we did not.

Miss Kerr and I had a heated dispute as to who would go last. She admitted that she was the heavier of us, and insisted that it wouldn't be fair to let me shoulder the burden. My arguments fell on deaf ears as she started to hoop me into the rope and belt.

I instructed her to shorten the length of vine when her time came to descend, for she would have to climb. There was no other way. A shortened rope would mean that if she slipped, she would not crash onto the ground. Hopefully. As for my descent, it was slow going and once or twice I dropped several feet. I dared not look down. But eventually I stood on shaking legs and freed myself of the impromptu harness.

The air was cooling as the sun set, and Miss Kerr edged herself over the edge of the cliff face. I do believe none of us was breathing. Chloe had turned her back, unable to watch at all. Miss Kerr had only been going for a few minutes when she fell. Not even the shortened rope saved her. First, she jerked to a halt about twenty feet from the ground, but almost instantly she fell again. The rope tied around the tree must have come loose. Fortunately, she died quickly, and her agony was short lived.

Terrible business.

AUGUST 29TH

Despite the tragedy, we slept soundly some distance away from our fallen friend.

I was determined to get across the veldt to the river. However, I thought the brutal African sun might be too much for us and I tried convincing my friends to rest in the shade of the rock face until sunset. But Gloria was not having it.

We discovered water trickling from the rock face—probably a stray outlet from the lovely lagoon that had got us into so much trouble a few days earlier—splashed our faces, dampened our clothes. Unfortunately, we had lost the Thermos flasks before our descent of the cliff-face and we would have to endure the trek without water.

Fifty yards into our westward journey, I picked up the briefcase. All things considered, it was in remarkably good condition and still solidly locked.

Occasionally, one of us stopped to empty sand from our shoes. When we came to a lone wide-limbed tree, we gratefully took a half-hour rest in its shade. In the distance, a great herd of beast grazed. I imagined, not far away, big cats stalking them. My throat cracked as I said as much and we all wearily stood. No one spoke, least of all Linda who had been badly affected by Miss Kerr's death. She followed Gloria but the awe of being in the company of stardom had long ago left her eyes. When Tommy collapsed from heat exhaustion, I had no option but to put him over my shoulder. I had made a promise to Linda and I was determined to keep it. My legs shook with every step.

Night came and still we walked on, the boy over my shoulder like a rag doll. We held each other's hands so as not to be separated in the pitch dark, for it was the darkest night I ever remembered seeing. Gloria and Chloe broke into joyful cries as we heard running water close by. I cried as I drizzled water onto Tommy's lips, because I had known for a mile or two that I was carrying a dead body, but I couldn't just leave him. I had to do the decent thing. While the others gathered kindling, I scooped out a hollow in the soft sand and laid the child to rest, covering the mound in as many loose rocks as I could find. And when, finally, our tears had dried, we huddled around the fire, fifty yards back from the muddy bank of the river.

The bitter cold of the night only compounded the utter bleakness of our plight.

As we lay, trying to sleep, I am sure each of us wondered how exactly we would die.

AUGUST 30TH

The ladies went to wash and collect water. Although on her feet, Linda was in a dark depression. In truth, we were all feeling low. And I truly doubted my sanity at trying to get us to safety. I looked back at the sun as it rose behind the mountain we had climbed down. Had we really come so far?

It was as Gloria splashed water on her face

and neck that a huge crocodile rose from the river and grabbed the starlet's arms in its massive jaws. Her scream of terror died in seconds as the monster dragged her under the bubbling and frothing water. Silence descended as we waited, unsure of what to do. But neither Gloria or the beast resurfaced. Linda shook.

"Come on. Let's head down stream," I said.

"We can't leave her," Linda cried.

"It has been ten minutes, my girl," William said. "There's nothing we can do."

"Aren't you upset?" Tears spilled in dirty streaks down her cheeks.

"Of course, I am but..."

And right then I think he really was upset. Despite the fraud the studios made them live, he genuinely was fond of his sometimes co-star. Linda, seeing his lip tremble and his tears that threatened to overflow, stepped into his arms and held him tight. Chloe reached a hand into mine and I pulled her close. For a few minutes we took solace in each other's company. Who would have thought we still had tears left to fall?

Breaking free, I picked up the briefcase and started to head down stream, keeping well away from the reeds that could be harbouring all manner of murderous creatures.

My friends trudged along behind.

I think several hours must have passed when Chloe called to me. I turned, gun ready, only to see William had stumbled and was unable to stand. Besides the swollen and cracked lips we all sported, William's wounds were taking their toll on him. The flap on his face seeped a poisonous looking substance, and flies were particularly interested in it.

It was then that the most beautiful sound I ever heard tooted. I turned to see a small steamer chugging along at the slowest most comfortable speed imaginable. We waved and called to them with great gusto, even Linda. They came to a halt and lowered a gangplank that we all fairly danced up.

Fresh water was passed around. The crew shared their dried meat and fresh fruit with us. The captain said we were five hours from a small town with a doctor and a hotel. While we relaxed, a member of the crew chewed some dark green leaves to a pulp. He then patted this paste onto William's injured face. At least the foul smell kept the flies away. But sure enough, we docked at a smudge of a town in the early evening.

We found rooms in a shack of a hotel, but it was the warmest, driest, safest place and never did I see a finer establishment. I headed to the telegraph station and sent instruction to my bank back in London to wire money. Within twenty-four hours, I had received a message that funds were available at the Western Union branch in the very same town. Now, with cash we had the means of reaching a larger town or city.

SEPTEMBER 1ST

We have stayed in this town, called Umbrago, for two days. Mainly to rest and recover from our ordeal, but William had a fever when we arrived, and it is only now just beginning to pass. I think another day may be needed before we book passage on one of the many boats that will take us to Nairobi. We have more than a weeks' worth of travel ahead of us. But at least we will be travelling well-known waterways with people who know what they are doing.

I sometimes wonder if all the death was worth it. Shame Edgar died; he was a good friend with a brain that could win the upcoming war on its own.

Should we have waited for rescue? Perhaps, but a rescue team would have taken the diplomat's body, and with it, the briefcase. Then it would have been lost to me completely. No, my only choice was to ensure the pilot was dead, leave the radio unconnected, that we had no dead weights, convince the survivors of our hopeless cause, and take the case with me. It was after all my primary objective.

What the Fuhrer wants, the Fuhrer gets and it is an unwise man who refuses His wishes. Anyway, I have the case for the time being, and I am determined to know what is so important about it before I hand it over to my contact.

During my various escapades, I have had to find my way into all manner of locked cases, secret rooms and uncrackable safes—always for the right price of course. This should be a breeze. So, when I am ready and steadied my hand with another whisky and soda, I will find out what is in this damn case. My lock-picks are long lost, but it will be a matter of minutes to fashion two pins into L-shaped tools to spring the lock.

❧❧❧

"The blackguard." Whiskers puffed in astonishment. "And this fellow was an Englishman, you say?"

"Indeed," William Blake said, raising his glass to his lips.

"Well, I never. But how did you get hold of this journal?"

"Ah, you see, I was feeling a little better, so paid a visit to our treacherous friend and when he didn't answer my knock at his door, I entered. He was lying on the bed, half-dressed and quite dead."

"Never."

"Oh, yes. There was a faint scent of almonds in the air. It seems he'd triggered a trap when he lifted the lid of the case, which gave out a puff of cyanide gas. He would have died in seconds."

"By Jove!"

"And I've just found out who Harry really was."

"Good Lord! Do you mean he was travelling incognito."

"Oh yes, but it's top-secret stuff involving the Palace and the Foreign Office. Are you sure you want the information?"

The old buffer leaned forward conspiratorially, "Go on."

The whispered name made the old newspaper-man's eyes widen.

"Never." He sat back in his leather chair, letting all the ramifications of the revelation chug through his aging but still sharp brain.

When ready he nodded, and said, "Okay, but what the blazes was in the briefcase?"

"That's another story, old bean. Remind me to tell you about it sometime, would you?"

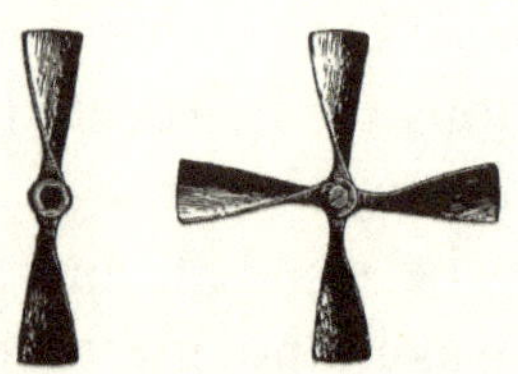

MACH 6

DONOVAN "MONSTER" SMITH

The air hissed like a demon as they soared through the sky, descending from the clouds like a wounded bird. Jack ducked behind a crate, trading lead like an outlaw in the old west. Fragments of wood splintered off and pelted him in the shoulder, a sick reminder of the miserable life he'd been dealt. He rather enjoyed his job, he really did, it's just lately he'd found himself wondering what things would have been like had he been born into another life, another existence.

Chuckling for a moment, he pondered how ridiculous the thought was of him sitting behind a desk all day, pushing papers and taking calls, like every other sad schmuck who couldn't hack it. When it came down to it, he wouldn't change a thing. Protecting the world was his purpose, and he wouldn't have it any other way. It was the only thing that kept him going, and he wouldn't stop until he secured the package.

Just last night he'd gotten so drunk he nearly puked, yearning to find happiness in the bottom of a bottle. And now here he was engaged in a gunfight with one of the most revered assassins in the world. *My, how far I'd come in such a short time*, he thought, smiling as he returned fire.

"It's mine, all mine, you bastard," yelled Bullet Lane as he ejected his empty clip and slammed in a new one with force.

"Give it up," shouted Jack. "It'll never be yours!"

"We'll see about that," screamed Bullet Lane, laying down cover fire as he sprinted toward the front of the plane.

Jack knew it was time to put a stop to the Company, once and for all. If Bullet managed to get inside the cockpit and take over the plane, then it was all over. The fate of the world was resting on his shoulders and he knew he had to move quickly, or risk the book falling into the wrong hands.

Broc Lane, better known by his constituents as Bullet, knew there was something special about him from the day he was born. He believed that he'd do amazing things one day and change the world as he knew it. However, he never pictured it involving so much bloodshed and death. But he kind of relished that part of it now. He'd become so numb to it as of late, it hardly even bothered him anymore when he offed someone.

Murder had become a big part of his everyday life, and he was very good at what he did. Just last year he'd cleared over seventeen million dollars, executing twenty-one hits across five continents. He was the highest-paid assassin in the Company, and highly sought after. Matter of fact, just two weeks ago the Director himself had personally met with Bullet and thanked him for his dedicated service and contributions.

The fact remained, though, that he was downright evil and would do absolutely anything to complete his mission. He'd been known to kill anyone who stood in his way, women and children included. Rumours surfaced years ago about a pregnant woman he killed who was giving birth, simply because she was screaming too loud while he was trying to concentrate.

Jack Finn despised people like Bullet Lane and spent every waking moment dedicated to stopping the Company. It's what he was trained to do, and it was up to him to end their treacherous reign of terror once and for all. If only he could get to the book first and switch it out for the fake;he'd be long gone, never to be seen again.

Another round zipped past him, hitting a metal bar above his head, ricocheting into one of the crates. Realising he could use the trajectory in his favour, he calculated the angle and popped off a few shots, hoping for a little luck. He decided to make a run for the captain's chair when he heard a loud groan echo out.

He'd managed to catch Bullet in his right arm, just as he was closing the cockpit door behind him. The plane was going down, and Jack knew there was absolutely no chance for a clean landing. He rushed to the lockers at the tail end of the plane and strapped on one of the parachutes. There were two extra packs hanging on hooks, and he whipped out his pocket knife and cut the cords, leaving no escape for Bullet.

Both of the pilots were dead with two gunshot wounds to the back of their skulls, execution-style, and Bullet clutched the main controls, trying to level it out. Even though he was an expert pilot, there was no way to recover in time, and the right-wing dipped, slamming Jack against some steel drums, knocking him to the floor.

Getting to his feet, Jack made his way over to the panel, bleeding from his right ear. He flipped the switch and the rear cargo doors began to open, the wind howling like a child who'd lost its mother. It whistled and hummed as little red lights flashed silent alarms, warning them to stay back or unless they wanted to be chewed up and spit out like all the rest.

Jack thought about how he'd ended up here at this moment, and not in some cosy old cabin sipping hot cocoa, wrapped in a warm thick blanket, his feet kicked up by the fireside. He grew up an orphan, never knowing his parents or where he came from, and his birth was a mystery with no legal documents to prove he was even born. He was the perfect candidate for the position; no ties to anyone, alone, vulnerable, invisible.

From a very young age, he was plucked from obscurity and taught the ways of the Ohgen Tribe. They trained him how to hunt and kill, and he'd become fully self-sufficient by the age of nine. The Elders were amazed at how quickly he picked things up and how easily he retained information. There was talk amongst some of the Elders who claimed that he was the one their ancestors had spoken of; an ancient spirit forged in fire and sent to protect the earth from all who seek to destroy it.

The tale had been handed down for centuries, each believer hoping they'd be one of the lucky ones to observe his true divinity. His birth had been foretold for by some of the greatest minds in history, and they rejoiced in anticipation of his arrival. After searching for what felt like forever, he'd finally surfaced when a story was printed about a young boy who possessed no identity; no birth certificate, no proof of existence. He was the one they'd been searching for all along. heir last hope.

Stories spoke of the magical son who couldn't be hurt and who was incapable of dying. He was the protector of all things holy and righteous, and he would bring peace to a restless wasteland. He would restore life and combat evil at all costs, with honour and dignity.

Suddenly there was a loud boom, and an engine exploded, shooting fiery chunks of debris throughout the air like miniature missiles. Chaos infected the bright blue sky, and the plane continued to plummet, leaving trails of choking black smoke as it made its death descent. He knew it was now or never and he checked his pack once more just to make sure he'd be making it home safely, even if they were hovering over the ocean in the middle of nowhere.

Jack was just about to jump when something tickled his ear and he spun around to find himself bombarded by a barrage of gun blasts. Bullet was out for blood and he was going to beat his opponent, no matter the cost. He always succeeded and believed himself superior in all facets of the profession. There wasn't a soul alive that could beat him, not one.

Another bullet whizzed past him, and Jack knew that his time was up. He needed to go now, or risk being pumped full of lead. Taking a couple of steps backward, he got a running head start and pushed off right as engine number two erupted somewhere above him.

Jagged pieces of shrapnel rained down on him as he graced the big blue devil with his presence, praying he wouldn't be swallowed whole. He zigged and zagged as best he could, but he couldn't avoid everything, and something tagged him in his ribs, slicing open his suit. It began to fill up with air and inflate, and soon his body went numb from the intense pressure.

He pulled the ripcord on his rig and his chute deployed. The ocean was speeding up toward his feet, and he did his best to lessen the impact as he made contact with the surface. However, he hit it at a pretty decent speed and it plunged him deep underwater, vomiting him up a few minutes later as he gasped for air. He felt like he'd been body-slammed by Hulk Hogan, and his ribs were badly bruised and battered.

As he looked up, he saw the plane explode and split into two separate sections. He hoped his enemy was dead, but he'd be a sore loser if he was a betting man. The chips were stacked against him. However, he'd gotten a really nice head start.

Bullet watched as Jack made his exit like a coward, running away from a good old-fashioned gunfight. He'd sabotaged Bullet's only chance of survival, leaving him trapped and spiralling out of control in the burning tail section. Little did Jack know, there was still one chute left inside, next to the dead pilot in the cockpit.

Flaming crates, barrels, tools, and anything else that wasn't tied down, shot through the sky like rogue meteorites. Luckily, Bullet had managed to grab the last pack before the plane split in half, and he strapped it on, preparing to jump. Suddenly a strong gust of wind caught him and sent him flying into a hunk of the wing that had been dislodged and discarded, knocking him unconscious.

A minute later he came too, just in time to pull the cord and make a safe splashdown without any risk of serious injury. His arm stung like hell and it hurt when he lifted it above his head for more than a few seconds, but despite all of that, he wouldn't quit until the job was done. Bullet always got what he came for, even if he had to kill to get it.

He landed about a mile offshore from a secluded fishing village, and swam toward it, hoping to get his feet on solid ground and find something he could patch his arm up with. Jack had a substantial lead on him, and time was of the essence. His competition was fierce, but he was a master at the game and was always thinking six steps ahead.

There were a half dozen boats along the dock, and he'd simply commandeer one and beat Jack to the punch. He was patting himself on the back for his quick thinking when out of nowhere something came speeding right at him. He dove and pulled at the water, trying to get out the way as fast as possible, as the boat came barrelling toward him.

Jack went speeding past, watching as Bullet disappeared in the wake from his craft. He hadn't expected to see him, thinking he'd met his demise when the plane crashed and sank to the bottom of the ocean. But there he was, alive and well, and Jack wasn't too happy about it.

He knew it was only a matter of time before

Bullet confiscated a vessel and came after him, and he needed to be ready. The next time they'd meet face to face, it wouldn't end so well for one of them, and Jack was going to do everything in his power to make sure that wasn't him. His only concern was keeping the book from falling into the wrong hands.

The books were reported to be the oldest known relics in human history, although they'd been lost for over a century. Their whereabouts remained unknown, except to a handful of the most powerful syndicates in the world who were vying to get their grubby little meat hooks on them. Controlling the books meant ultimate power, and the Company wouldn't stop until they had them in their "possession."

They were referred to as the Codex of Knowledge, which consisted of three sacred volumes; the Book of Life, the Book of the Dead, and the Book of Magic. The Company had already successfully recovered two of them, and now only one remained. If they were to gain ownership of the last book, there was no telling what they might do, and Jack wasn't about to let that happen.

All that was left was The Book of Life. It was written that the last book contained the secrets of creation and the essence of existence. Supposedly, whoever wielded its power could bring about an end to the darkness, banishing it once and for all. They could breathe new life back into the world and stop all the suffering, if used correctly.

It was written that only someone with a pure

heart could brandish it and utilise all of the knowledge concealed within its tattered, withered old pages. Man was a cowardly beast and the direct cause of all the death and destruction since its conception. However, Jack was different; special in a way, unlike those who came before him. He was exceptionally determined and strong willed, and that's what made him the best at what he did.

There was a downside to it all though, as far as the book was involved. If the Company managed to acquire it, they could potentially destroy it and dispose of the information inside, which could, in turn, cause catastrophic damage to life as we knew it. Cities would collapse and crumble and eventually humanity would die off, the species would cease to exist. And that would be the end of it all, humans just a speck in the dust.

But Jack wasn't going to let them win. Not as long as he was still alive and breathing. He had no idea when that time would come, but he knew it wasn't going to be today. He shoved the throttle up as far as it would go, and he held on as the waves whacked away at the bow of the boat like Paul Bunyan.

Soon enough he'd find Mount Thorn and brave the labyrinth of tunnels underneath, each one laced with its own individually crafted defence mechanism. He took his gun out of its holster and dropped the magazine, removing each bullet to make sure they weren't waterlogged. One by one he dried them and inserted them back into the cartridge, loading them up for action.

It was only a few more miles until x marked the spot, and he checked the boat for any remnants of food or water. All that fighting and adrenaline had made him thirsty, not to mention exhausted. There was nothing on board except for half a bottle of water, which he happily gulped down with haste. It had never tasted sweeter, and he thanked his lucky stars for the heavenly respite.

He took hold of the wheel and directed it around the horn of a floating island, relaxing for a moment as the water splashed up and hit him in the face. He smiled and wiped himself clean, enjoying the beautiful scenery while he had the opportunity. It was times like these that stuck in his memory, the other stuff easily forgotten and ignored.

The warm ocean air blasted him in the chest, and he embraced it with open arms. He began to think back to when he was a child, when suddenly a choir of loud bangs descended upon him like a swarm of locusts. Glass shattered to his left, and he ducked, drawing his weapon in retaliation.

Bullet had almost drowned and was furious as hell as he climbed out of the water and onto the dock. His arm was killing him, and he was in no mood to negotiate. There were a variety of fishing boats and trawlers to choose from, and a speedboat that guaranteed he'd catch his enemy in time and beat him to the destination.

As he boarded the boat, two barrel-chested men stepped toward him, asking him what he thought he was doing. Instead of going into his usual pitch of why it's beneficial not to mess with someone like himself, he kicked the man closest to him in the groin and tossed him overboard, leaving him for the sharks to feed on. The second guy laughed, then turned back to Bullet.

Without hesitation, Bullet picked up an empty bottle that was lying next to him, and he broke it over the second man's head, sending him to his knees, clutching his bleeding skull. He then proceeded to choke the man until his legs stopped twitching and he was no longer breathing. Once he made sure the man wasn't moving, he grabbed him by the collar and belt and sent him flying overboard, right alongside his partner.

Bullet fired up the engine and jetted off at warp speed, hoping to catch up to Jack before he made it to Mount Thorn. If Jack got to the book before him, there'd be no telling what the Company might do. He'd never failed a mission in the past, and he wasn't about to start now.

He'd lost his sidearm when the plane exploded, and he fumbled around, searching for something to use to combat his opponent. As luck would have it, he lifted the cover of a cooler to reveal a small cache of weapons hidden in the stern of the boat. Apparently, the owners were gun runners, and he'd hit the jackpot. There was a bundle of assault rifles, and he snatched one up, checking to see if it was loaded.

Jack knew Bullet was gaining on him, he could feel it. But there was something deep inside him that said he'd win, no matter what. He was a lone wolf and used to fighting for what he wanted. Sometimes he wondered why he chased the thrill, the wind in his hair, the sun on his back.

Multiple gunshots rang out, and immediately he knew who it was. He hit the deck and wiggled between the seats, trying to get a decent shot off as the boat rocked with the waves. Panelling splintered, and the glass cracked, littering the floor with torture devices as he crawled around on his hands and knees.

Any moment they'd be rounding the curve, and he knew exactly what to do. It was his chance to catch Bullet off guard, and he prepared for his opportunity. There would be a little less than a minute where he'd be out of view of the other vessel, and that was when he'd make his move.

He tucked himself between the seats, and at the last second, he reached up and guided the boat around the bend. As soon as he was in the clear, he jumped up and throttled down, making a swift one-eighty before accelerating back up to full speed. He headed directly at Bullet as he rounded the corner, causing him to lose control of his boat.

It flipped about six times before finally coming to a stop, settling in the water. Jack couldn't see the assassin anywhere, and it worried him. Normally you'd see the body somewhere, but as always, until you actually laid eyes on them, anything was possible and you never underestimate your enemy. That was the number one rule, Jack recalled, and it was there for a reason.

There was a secret opening just a little further down, unfortunately, it was a bitch to get to. It was rumoured that adventurers had to swim a significant distance under the island, where they'd eventually come to a hole in the ground that led to the maze of underground tunnels. If they managed to make it through those alive, they'd be deposited into a room where the Book of Life was said to be encased in stone.

From there, all Jack had to do was open the door and free the book from its enclosure. Once it was in his possession, he'd take it back to the Elders and let them bury it, along with all the other ancient artifacts that had been recovered over the years. Saving the world was a full-time job, and somebody had to do it.

The boat slowed and headed for the beach as Jack jumped into shallow water. He sprinted up the sand and into the brush, trying to locate the secret entrance. Supposedly there were three large trees that crisscrossed and pointed to a slim crevice in the rock face, and he quickly spotted it without too much trouble.

He squeezed through the narrow space and popped out on the other side, rubbing his eyes to make sure he wasn't dreaming. He'd never seen anything so clear, and he cautiously dipped his feet in as he waded into the spring. The excitement was spilling over, and he took a long, deep breath before diving in.

It was colder than he was used to, and he fought against the shock, his chest tightening with each breath. Somehow he was able to continue swimming, and he kicked and paddled until he thought his lugs were about to burst. He started to gulp for air and he panicked, frantically checking every direction for somewhere to go. Just as he swallowed his last few breaths, he began to question life and why he was even here.

Everything went black, like someone had thrown the switch, and he knew he was dead. Except he really wasn't dead, not one bit. Somehow, his lips had found a sizable pocket of air and before he knew it, he was breathing again. It must have been the way they discovered the underground maze of tunnels in the first place—pure dumb luck. There was no way of knowing the pocket was there, unless someone had accidentally stumbled across it like he just did.

Once he gained enough strength, he took a deep breath and continued his journey. It was almost the same distance he'd gone already, and right as he started to gasp again, he eyed what looked like a hole in the surface and headed for it. He didn't know if he was going to make it or not, but he prayed for forgiveness anyhow.

Thankfully, after a few more seconds, his head pierced the skin on top of the water and he was able to breathe again. He took in as much air as he could, hoping he wouldn't pass out, which he almost did. However, he managed to hold on and stay alert without losing consciousness, and a moment later he found some giant rocks and pulled himself up into them.

Lying on his back with his eyes closed, he was listening to the sound of his own breath when suddenly he realized where he was and he sat straight up. He began looking around, and his jaw nearly hit the floor as he caught sight of it. The entrance to the tunnels stood between two enormous columns that were topped with weird, gargoyle-like statues.

Before he entered the maze, he grabbed one of the old torches off the wall and pulled out some flint and used his knife to create sparks, lighting it up. There were six different tunnels that led to the book, and without thinking, he chose one and started his trek. Down here he needed to keep a mindful eye and watch his step. One false move and it could mean his life.

As he walked along the passageway, he thought about the time when one of his Elders had taught him to hunt. He'd shown him the ways of moving amongst the shadows and how to stay hidden while stalking his prey. Silence was key and the quieter you were, the easier it was to sneak up on an unsuspecting foe.

The tribe showed him how to be patient and disciplined and how to stay focused on the task at hand. He learned to become a master manipulator and an expert craftsman. He was well aware of his surroundings at all times and had a strict eye for details. He'd earned a degree in four separate styles of martial arts, and he'd won multiple shooting competitions by the time he was a teenager.

When it came down to it, he was ready for anything. He'd trained his entire life for times like this, and he watched every step he took. He could see something up ahead and he paused, bending over to pick up a rock. Making sure he was far enough away, he chucked the stone in the direction of the rubble, and it came as no surprise when two gigantic cinder blocks came out of the walls and smashed together, causing the ground to shake beneath him.

Picking up another stone to toss, he did his best to gauge the timing of the trap and he knew he'd be cutting it close. He wound back and let it go, his heart pounding anxiously as the blocks clashed and retracted. He saw his chance, and he raced past as fast as he could, trying not to get pulverized.

Just when he thought he was in the clear, the wind from the impact sent him flying face first into a veil of spiderwebs, which triggered something in the ceiling, and dozens of snakes fell from above. Jack was terrified and for a moment he just stood there, not knowing what to do. If there was one thing he disliked, it was slick, slithery serpents.

He jumped up and hurdled the barricade, letting out a huge sigh of relief as he landed on the other side. He wiped the sweat from his forehead and checked his torch to make sure it was still useful. Wanting nothing else to do with the reptiles, he

174

bolted down the tunnel until he came to a dead end.

There was a small hole at the bottom of the wall, and he got on all fours and crawled through it. When he was able to stand up again, he found himself in an underground cave that was split right down the middle by a stream of rushing water that ran deep under the mountain. The only way around it was to climb the surrounding rocky terrain and try not to fall in.

After climbing for what felt like ages, he reached the other side without being swept away, and he rested for a minute before going further. He was dead tired and beginning to believe he might never find the book. The thought had crossed his mind, and he was haunted by it.

He was at the end of his rope and he didn't know how much longer he could keep up the pace. It was the first time in his life that he felt vulnerable, and he was scared out of his mind that he might actually fail. It wasn't something he was used to, and doubt began to creep into his mind like a cold heartless mistress. But he had to keep pressing forward, regardless of the challenge in front of him.

There was nothing he couldn't do when he put his mind to it, and he buckled up for the ride ahead. Things were about to get hectic, and he knew he was going to have to get down and dirty if he planned on making it out of this in one piece. He was going to give it his best shot, and whatever happened, happened.

It was time to find out what he was really made of, and he stopped at what appeared to be another dead end. However, after checking around, he touched something and a section of the wall ascended, revealing a hidden room. Inside were three separate entrances, each with a series of hieroglyphics carved into the door, and he had no idea what to make of them. They looked like spells of some kind, and instantly he knew the book was behind one of them.

Three podiums stood in the centre of the room, and as stupid as it seemed, he decided to try the middle one. Each one had a place to stick his hand, and he figured he'd give it a go and see what happened. He reached out and jammed his palm in the moss covered print, hoping he'd chosen the right one.

And just as he had thought, the big door in the centre popped and moaned as it separated from the ground, the dust clouding the room all around him. It was so thick and heavy that he couldn't keep from coughing, and he covered his face while he watched in awe. A bright light engulfed him from head to toe and he threw his arm up in protest, shading his eyes, saving himself from going blind.

He'd never seen anything so beautiful in his entire life, and he brushed away a tear as it streamed down his cheek. It was like he'd stepped into heaven itself and a warm, fuzzy sensation washed over him, sending goose pimples up his spine. It was the Book of Life, and it seemed to be emanating light. Glowing unlike anything he'd ever seen before.

Right then he knew everything was going to be alright and all his fears melted away. No matter what happened, he knew he was going to be okay, and he had nothing to worry about any longer. He'd been beckoned and answered the call, and for that he'd be rewarded.

Snapping himself out of it, he headed over to where it sat, standing mere inches away from it, his palms sweating as he reached out to clutch it. He couldn't take it anymore, and the moment his fingers kissed the cover everything went blank and he couldn't remember a thing. He removed it from its stand and held it up, yelling out in glee.

Tears continued to roll down his cheeks and before he knew it, he'd turned around and walked right out of the room, completely unaware of what he was doing. He was stunned when he finally stopped to look up, finding himself face to face with the notorious Bullet Lane. They stared at each other for a moment, the two giant doors with hieroglyphics all over them breaking their seals as they started to rise.

Bullet looked at Jack. "Give it to me, now," he said, his face shredded from the crash.

Jack couldn't believe his eyes. Bullet was still alive and had gotten the drop on him after everything he'd been through. How was it possible the assassin was still here and not fish food? It made no sense, but then again it was his fault for not confirming the kill like the Elders had taught him. He knew better than that.

"You can't have it," said Jack. "You'll have to kill me first."

"That can be arranged," said Bullet, grinning as

he crouched into a fighting stance, preparing to do battle with the legendary knight.

"Do what you must," said Jack, winking at him.

"Ask and you shall receive," said Bullet, as he lunged at Jack.

Jack sidestepped and Bullet tumbled forward, tripping over a sliver of stone that was higher than the rest. Right as the giant doors opened, the ground shook violently, knocking them both to the dirt. All of a sudden they heard growling from somewhere behind them and they both glanced back to see two abnormally sized wolves exiting the doorways, drooling and snapping their razor-sharp teeth as they readied to attack.

They were giant and hairy, and Jack guessed that they were a fail-safe of some sort in case someone tried to remove the book from its safe keeping. He started to run, and one of the wolves chased after him, ignoring Bullet as he laid on the ground unflinching. This couldn't be happening, but it was.

The ground continued to shake and shift, and the mountain started to crumble from the force of it all. Chunks the size of small vehicles began falling from overhead, and the walls cracked on all sides while the place collapsed around them. There was no escaping it. They were doomed.

Bullet hopped to his feet and ran, yelling, "Use the book! Do something," as the wolf closest to him bent down and snatched him up in its teeth.

Unfortunately, Jack was already headed back out the way he came, the first wolf nipping at his heels. As the place continued to cave in, it provided the beast with an array of obstacles that kept Jack from being eaten alive and somehow he found himself back at the underground river again, being swept away by the rapids as the place came crashing down around him.

Caught in the beast's mouth while it chewed him like dog food, Bullet pulled his knife out of his boot and began stabbing it in the eye over and over until an enormous stone fell on it, trapping him inside its mouth. He could feel its skull compress under the weight of the object, and he didn't know if he was going to make it out or not. Could it be the end of Bullet Lane?

TWO MONTHS LATER...

Having no idea where he was, he gently pried his eyelids apart, peeking out through thin slits while someone tended to him, dabbing his forehead with a cool, damp cloth. His body was sore all over and he hesitated to check and see if all his limbs were still attached. Right now he felt like sleeping, and before he knew it he'd dozed off again.

It had been close to nine weeks since they'd found him, and he needed all the rest he could. He could move his feet and hands, but not much else besides that. Luckily, he'd survived, but he couldn't remember what had happened or why he was here.

An old man approached and kneeled next to him, grabbing his hand as he spoke. It was a language he wasn't familiar with, and he shuddered as the man squeezed his palm. Tilting his head back, the man held a cup to his mouth, forcing him to take a drink of its contents. He coughed and spit some of it back up, accidentally spraying his helper in the chest.

The old man laughed as he opened his mouth to speak again, concerned for his patient's well being. It was then that and finally he understood what the man with the face paint and feather headdress said.

"Jack, I'm glad you're back," he said, titling the cup to his mouth for another sip. "We have work to do."

ПOT CAMPING

BY NEEN COHEN

Stale beer, sweat winning the fight over cologne, and that pull of scotch wrapped around her, familiar and cloying. Haley Robins leaned closer as Sasha tried again, raising her voice and squinting her dark brown eyes.

"You're not going to go camping for your thirtieth. I thought I had nudged that country bumpkin out of you."

"I'm going camping, Sash. Whether it makes me boring or not." The mediocre skills of tonight's live band covered the feint huff in Haley's words.

"I give it until 2am before you call me and beg me to come back and get you."

"I'm going for a week, and I won't call you."

"But it's your birthday," Sasha whined, already on her third drink, the sun only now sinking over the horizon.

Thursday nights were the new Fridays.

"Yes, my birthday. Mine. And I've taken a week off from the hell hole and I'm spending it the way I want to."

"2am." Sasha smirked, tossed the last of her drink into her mouth. Standing, she wiggled the empty glass at Haley.

"Nope, gotta be sober to head off early in the morning." Haley finished her first and last drink as Sasha rolled her eyes and headed to the bar.

Haley checked her watch every few minutes. Twenty minutes had passed, and she stood with a little too much enthusiasm.

"You aren't walking, are you?" Sasha narrowed her eyes at Haley over the tan shoulder of the girl with the pixie cut. A work colleague from level two, whose pout slurred with her fourth or fifth drink as she swivelled in her chair to face Haley.

"What, too adventurous for you?"

"No, too bloody stupid. The sun is down," Sasha shot back.

"Well, the vampires and me are homies, I'll be right." Haley winked.

"Message when you get in."

"Yes, mum."

Haley kissed Sasha's cheek, waved goodbye to the pixie*what the hell was her name?*—and headed home to officially begin her annual leave. Working in a call centre was mind numbing, but she had met Sasha. When Sasha wasn't ribbing her for living in the past or having her nose stuck in a book, they had

182

fun.

But in three days, she would turn thirty.

Although her thesis had been written, she hadn't finished her degree—Bachelor of Arts majoring in Ancient History, she didn't have a career—call centre forever, no thank you, no partner. She hadn't even gotten laid in months, and no kids—Yeesh! What an idea.

Sasha frowned at the thought.

The light showers created a rhythmic background to her excitement, as the drive continued on well past the announced forty-five minutes on her maps app; the rain creating morons out of the already inept drivers in the city.

But the rain had its advantages. Once they pushed through to the suburbs, there were fewer cars on the road, and Hailey smiled. Buildings gave way to homes, and then farms. The view outside glistened, evidence of the rainy weather in the bright green landscape and the rushing waters of creeks and rivers they passcd.

She cracked her window so she could hear the gurgling rush, and to stop the driver whose questions had started intrusive and turned to bizarre.

Who asks how long someone has been on the planet? And didn't he know it was rude to ask a stranger's age?

Soon Haley fought against the claustrophobia of the rock face to her right as it smashed her against the fearful openness of the sheer drop to her left. They sped up a narrow dirt road that climbed too quickly. She flinched at every bump, and quickly wound the window back up as the sound of tires slipping sent begging help of a deity she didn't believe in.

Don't let there be any cars, don't let there be any cars.

The mantra flowed as her fingers pulled at the hem of her shirt.

The false air in the cab suffocated, creating gooseflesh on her bare legs, making her wish she'd worn pants not shorts. She jiggled her legs, fearing if she asked for the air-conditioning to be turned down, the taxi driver would begin his questions and narrowing looks through the rear-view mirror again.

"You are here."

"Holy Hannah!" Haley blinked through the rain-streaked windows to the front of the cabin she had booked. "This is cabin one?"

"Yes." The questions were replaced with one-word answers and a clipped tone. She paid and got out, tightening her pack onto her back and hauling the suitcase from the boot without assistance. Slamming the boot closed, she stumbled back as the taxi sped off in a slosh and spray of gravel.

Well, that's reassuring.

But she was here, she had done it.

"Cabin one. Wow."

Haley stood in front of a two-story building surrounded by trees and bushes. A small carport sat to the right of the brushed off path leading to the veranda and front door.

Okay, so she hadn't exactly told Sasha the whole truth. Camping for a week with actual tents and no hot water or flushing toilets? No thanks. Plus, she wasn't stupid. Nothing like camping alone in a forest up a steep mountain to become the first victim of a B grade horror movie.

The clouds hung low, but the dull grey dissipated. Snatches of blue sky and white fluffy clouds peaked through.

The cabin door opened soundlessly.

You expected it to creak?

A small, self-deprecating laugh bounced around the dining room she had stepped into. Taking a deep breath, her limbs relaxed in anticipation as subtle hints of ground coffee danced among floral scents she couldn't name.

"Wishful thinking, Robins."

Flinching at the echo in her voice, Haley forced a smile to stretch her lips. This was good. This was what she needed. Down time and self-ruminations. A return to the 'boring geek' she had been before she met Sasha. Biting her bottom lip, she put the twist in her stomach down to hunger.

The suitcase was filled with more junk food than clothes. She'd been told it was only a twenty-minute drive to restaurants and a small grocery store, but the whole point of this trip was some much-needed isolation.

She nodded to herself.

"Alone time is good." Her teeth grazing her bottom lip and tasting the remnant of her peanut butter toast wasn't convincing.

Upstairs she opened the suitcase on a double bed and took the shopping bag of treats back down to the kitchen, which sat between the dining room with the front door and a cosy living room. The living room was set up with two-seater couches adjacent to each other, both half-facing an old box television in the opposite corner with a large glass rectangular coffee table that filled over half the space. It was cosy, despite the hideous yellow wallpaper.

After rifling through her bag of goodies, she groaned, an image of her jar of coffee sitting on the kitchen bench at home.

"At least there isn't anyone here I can murder," she muttered, as she hauled open cupboards to find the usual mismatched crockery and the occasional dead cockroach. As though teasing, another waft of the smell tantalised her nose.

Despite the frustration she smiled, images of herself in cartoon form flashed through her mind—legs lifted off the ground, carrying her toward the colourful lines of tempting scents.

"Screw this."

She slammed the small cedar wood door, having only checked half of the cupboards, and grabbed her backpack from the pink floral printed couch.

"Yeesh." She snapped a photo with the intention of showing Sasha. If and when she eventually dobbed herself in about her camping trip.

Her shoulders rose and fell as she stepped out

on to the balcony at the back of the cabin and looked down at the sloping hill of trees and scrub.

"Nature, it's nice to see you again."

She bit back thoughts of bugs and deadly creatures. Fear and distaste of the country was a recent addition. It hadn't raised its head until her mother called and asked about her next visit to the farm. She winced remembering the cow shit she had slipped in last time, grateful it hadn't been a video call.

It had been the beginning of this adventure.

She had changed, but how and when she didn't know. And who that made her now, she was even more clueless about.

The straps on her backpack slid through her fingers as she tightened them, heading down the slope, stepping into the bush via a small gap in the trees.

A walk surrounded by nature. That's all she needed. She would recentre and remind herself what she was doing with this life of hers.

She rolled her eyes.

When did I start thinking like a self-help book?

Oh, about the time I realised I was old and had nothing to show for it.

"Shut up!" She muttered to the voices warring in her head.

Take a deep breath.

Finally, a calm and sensible voice.

The walk helped. A sweaty sheen of sweat stuck her tank top to her back and clung to her bare arms. Better still, she no longer flinched every time a rustle or snap of twig came from a nearby hiding spot. The darkness above the canopy of the trees was encroaching and the canteen from her backpack gave its last drop of water ten minutes ago. She rifled through hoping there was something to eat. Her stomach growled.

"Bandaids, wallet, reusable shopping bag, pencil case." She threw the case back into the pack, "helpful, Robins. Real helpful. Bloody city slicker."

Standing up again she pulled her phone from her back pocket. Her stomach growled, again.

"Oomph."

Air rushed out of her lungs as one moment she was heading up the hill toward the cabin, fingers tapping out a text to Sasha, and the next she was on her back, looking up into the clearing sky framed with tree tops and a blurring pulse at the corner of her vision.

"What the hell are you doing here?" A face, while presumably female had features obscured by the waning light and blocked the view. The voice grabbed her attention and punched her ovaries a little in the process. *WAY too long since getting laid.* It was a mix of an accented European but the articulation of the British.

"Huh?"

Brilliant!

"Get out of here while you can." The face disappeared and Haley was certain her mind had imagined the stranger muttering something about humans as she vanished.

By the time Haley got back to her feet, she caught only the last snatches of wavy shoulder length red hair disappearing into the trees further down the slope. Flinching, she touched the back of her head.

Haley pressed her lips together tightly.

Alone time, she needed alone time.

"Fuck that." A smile, the first natural one since she slipped into the taxi that morning, spread like molasses across her face.

She made her way, slower than her hit and run, following the path of snapped twigs and eerie silence. An hour earlier she had flinched at the constant noise of nature. What she wouldn't give for that unintrusive lull now.

Her head pounded and excitement slipped into impatience. She cursed the twigs that grabbed at her shorts and shirt, scratching the bare skin of her lower legs.

"Great," she muttered, hearing the tear of cloth as she untangled the hem of her shirt once again.

"Where is the weapon, Olin?" The voice was velvet, sending shivers up her spine. Arousal or fear?

Both?

""I. Don't. Know!" A deep rumbling voice rolled toward Haley, like thunder coming across the sea.

"The humans will not be so easily quelled into submission. They will only manage to bring more chaos on to all of us."

Humans? Haley covered her mouth with a

laugh.

Oh god, she had stumbled upon a movie set. She had heard these mountains were used for some of those teen god movies.

"I didn't give 'em the weapon."

"But you know where it has gone!" It wasn't a question and the laugh that came from the man was the creak Haley's cabin door didn't have. This was incredible.

How were they doing that with his voice before post production?

Haley couldn't stop smiling. She slipped closer toward the voices as they continued speaking words she couldn't quite catch. Sasha loved those movies, she could see her best friend's green-eyed monster raising its shackles now.

Don't go camping, huh?

The trees in front of her swayed slightly and she shuffled, slow and quiet up to them. Peeking through, shoving aside branches and ignoring barbs that dug into her palm she finally got a view of a small clearing, the red head standing over a man on his knees in front of her.

Haley's limbs pulled toward the earth as she took in the details at once.

It looked like a set, but something was off.

There was a large rectangular hole in the ground, a slab of dirt encrusted grey stone pulled away and to the side. The end of it balanced precariously over the end of the pit. She could see what she assumed was a step before it fading down into the darkness.

A tomb. She smiled.

It was always a tomb in the movies, right?

As she noticed what was there—layers of golden fiery leaves shiny with the recent rain—her breath caught.

She knew what she didn't see.

Not a single cord or camera. Not a hint of a hidden person behind a tree, or the poor unfortunate sod holding up the boom mic to catch the rumbling words. No too bright lights or the snap of a clapper board.

Her eyes searched the clearing and fell again on the man at the red head's feet. A band of watery blue light wrapped around his arms, pinning them to his body. She could almost hear the sizzle as it wavered around him, reacting to the man's every breath and movement.

Warmth burnt in Haley's chest. Her mouth flapped around indecision. Did she scream, laugh, sob uncontrollably as she collapsed to the ground in a foetal position?

Why the fuck was she smiling?

Her heart raced, breath panting too loudly over dry lips as her eyes remained fixed, and her flight instinct refused to kick in.

"I told you to get out of here." The red head looked up and locked eyes on Haley with her last word.

"What are you?"

Stop smiling.

"What?" A V formed in the centre of Red's eyebrows.

"Well, you aren't an actor, that's for sure. Right?"

"An actor?" The V grew deeper.

"I thought this was a movie set. But it's not a movie set and I'm either completely delusional—it's a valid option but I don't think so—or some of the shit about history is actually literal."

Red's mouth opened and snapped closed again as a sound like splitting tree trunks rendered the air. Both Haley and Red turned their eyes back to the man.

He was no longer bound in blue light.

"Thanks." He winked at Haley before he disappeared.

He didn't fade into oblivion, there was no smoke or puff of where he had once been. He was simply one moment there and the next the space was empty, no ripples in the air to indicate a shift of atoms.

"Son of a demon whore." Red stomped her right foot.

"Damn did the movies get it wrong." Haley laughed as she pushed herself into the clearing, hissing a little as rain water from the tree's leaves hit the cuts on her hands.

"Who the Hades are you?" Red regained her voice and Haley felt her bravado slip.

"Sorry. I—" Haley stepped back and yelped as her shoe lost footing on the slippery leaves beneath her.

Cold hard hands wrapped around her waist before she could fall. The hysteria bubbled up around her chest and slipped out as she closed her eyes.

"Oh god, if you tell me you are a shiny vampire, I'm going to go back to believing it's all just movie bullshit."

"What are you?" Red threw Haley's question back at her.

Haley laughed again and shook her head.

This was one hell of a dream.

Haley woke with her face, sticky from drool, pressed against an ugly pink floral pattern.

"What…" the words trailed off as she shuffled up. Red sat across from her, long legs clad in black crossed at the knee. Her ankle slowly bouncing up and down.

"Finally. I thought you were never going to wake up."

"What happened?"

"That depends." Red raised an eyebrow. Why were the stunning ones always able to do the eyebrow?

"On?"

"Whether you are going to be hysterical or helpful?"

"Not sure I really have a say in that." Haley sat up properly, wiping the drool from the corner of her mouth before reaching for a bottle of water sitting on the coffee table in front of her. The snap of the safety seal was too loud in the small room.

"Oh, I assure you, you all have a lot more control than you think. You're all just too cowardly to admit it."

"Great, thanks." Haley gulped down half the bottle of water, muscles tensing at the familiar barb. "Yes, cowardly and boring. Why the hell are you still here?"

"You made me lose my Underdemon. I need your help to find him again." Words were spat out, like someone expecting the sweet taste of strawberry on their tongue but getting the bitterness of lemon instead.

"And who are you?"

For a moment silence lingered as Red tilted her head like a question mark.

"You aren't scared of me."

"Oh, I'm scared."

"But not enough."

"Meaning?"

"Meaning, you can help me without becoming a burden."

"I'm not exactly the helpful type. Didn't you hear the whole cowardly and boring part of my speech."

"Urgh." She stood and brushed down the tops of her thighs with long pale fingers. "You humans and your self-deprecating bullshit."

"Excuse me?" There was being impatient, and then there was being downright rude. "I just found out that some otherworldly shit is actually real and all you can do is attack my race?"

194

My race?

Jesus, wake up Hals.

Haley got the impression from Red's opening and closing mouth that she wasn't used to being snapped at.

Well get used to it Hotty Mchot a lot.

"If you really need my help, I need food and a damn explanation first."

Haley held her breath. Waiting to be struck down or something. Instead, Red burst into laughter and shook her head.

"Very well, that sounds reasonable."

"Reasonable." Haley tasted the word like a foreign meal on her tongue.

"Yes, fuel is necessary for you to think."

"Coffee is necessary for me to think, but I forgot it."

"Ah," Red's smile sent a pulse through Haley, echoing down her body until it reached the tops of her thighs.

Seriously? What the fuck is wrong with you girl?

Haley gulped, keeping her thoughts to herself.

"Come." Red didn't check to see Haley following after her. "You find food, I have the coffee sorted."

Haley was still blinking trying to process as she watched Red reach into cupboards she hadn't gotten to and make fresh ground coffee.

I knew I smelled coffee!

Haley opened the bag of goodies she had left in the kitchen, grabbed a packet of chips and followed

Red back into the dining room. They sat across the table from each other.

"So." After the first handful of chips Haley asked, "who the hell are you?"

"It doesn't matter. Why would a human take something from a tomb, and where would they take it?"

"To the museum to study it." Haley looked around, a chuckle shaking her shoulders.

"Okay, how do I get to this museum?"

"Okay, so not a movie, a prank. How didn't Sasha get you in on it?"

"Oh, for demons' sake. This isn't a movie, and it isn't some prank. Believe what you will, but you need to take me to the museum."

"Why? I haven't had an explanation yet. Tell me who you are and what's going on and I might believe you enough to help."

"Fine." Red pursed her lips, Haley's muscles pulsed. "I'm the demon of Doorways. The Underdemon you helped escape plans to steal Silas' weapon to tear open the doorway. Bad for everyone on all levels and realms."

Silas' weapon. The words rang a bell inside Haley's mind. Her memory ticking over the files from her studies, a school excursion, lessons about Silas and his ruthless nature. But she hadn't called him Silas, she had called the Underdemon, Olin. Another name she remembered, but this one didn't bring up the memories too easily.

"I didn't help him escape."

"You distracted me; it was all he needed."

"Oh." Haley pulled the mug of coffee to her lips and took a sip. "Oh my god." She stared at the black brew.

"What?" Red looked at Haley over the rim of her own cup.

"This is orgasmic."

"Really?" Red smirked and raised that single damn eyebrow again.

Good one brain, let's try the other foot.

"I, I, I just mean... It's really good."

"It bloody better be, I've been making it long enough."

"You." Haley closed her eyes and shook her head.

One thing at a time, Robins.

"Okay, so." She took a deep breath and opened her eyes on the exhale. "You're a demon, he's a demon and you're both looking for the barbarian's weapon which I assume will be a whole wipe out the world ploy."

"I am a demon, he's an Underdemon. Opening any doorways between realms won't wipe out the world, just the inhabitants. The doorway he is trying to open will steal the oxygen and kill all sentient beings. But, you know the museum and Silas, you called him the barbarian?"

Score one for the mere mortal.

"Yep. And I know exactly what to do to get his weapon."

"Then enough fucking around. Let's go."

"Ha." Haley laughed and shook her head as Red glared. "Sorry, just. You swear. That's so cool."

"You are a very strange human."

"I know." Haley's head dropped and silence rested over the room. "How do we get there? Can you teleport us and shit?"

"Well, seeing as I'm in this realm and stuck in this." She ran her hands up and down indicating her body, Haley's eyes followed and felt the warmth from her chest creep up her neck and pool in her cheeks. "I'm stuck to the limits of human transport."

"Really?' Haley laughed before quickly covering her mouth with a hand. "But you did the whole light band thing. And where did the Olin go when he snapped away? Surely a demon has other powers."

"Demons do, and as the Demon of Doorways I have quite a few. But we are moving away from any doorways and," her head tilted left and then right as though weighing her thoughts, "things become tricky."

"Tricky?"

"To use that kind of energy you have to sacrifice equal energy."

"Sacrifice? As in kill?"

"Yes, now please. I will answer what I can later, but he will find the museum soon enough and I don't plan to have the human race wiped out in the next four days."

"Four days?"

"Silas' weapon becomes inactive for another hundred years. Please?" Her eyes, cracked emeralds, stared with a pull that caught Haley's breath.

"Fine." Haley looked around her.

"Are you looking for that thing over there?"

"My phone." Haley jumped up and followed Red's pointed finger to the bottom step leading up to the bedrooms.

"What's it doing here?"

"It kept chirping at me. I thought it was you for a moment until I found it in your pocket."

Haley shook her head forcing away the image of Red's hands on her, digging into her back pockets.

"Okay." Haley picked up the phone and the display showed thirty-two messages.

She unlocked the now cracked screen and pressed the number of the only saved contact.

"Ha! Not even 2am." Sasha's amusement made Haley close her eyes and breathe deeply.

"Yeah okay, you win. But I need your help."

"You wonewy?"

"Shut up Sasha, shit just got real. Or unreal. Anyway, listen to this..."

Sasha showed up in her rusted Kermit green Mazda 323. It had seen better days ten years ago.

"I told you it was important Sash, what took you so long?"

"What took me so long?" Sasha jumped out and slammed her driver's door closed. It was the only way to engage the lock but the ferocity of the swing to Sasha's arm made Haley take a half step back.

"You said cabin one."

"Yeah."

"This," Sasha pointed to the two-story cabin they stood in front of, "is Cabin three, moron."

"What?"

"Ah, yes." Red stepped out of the cabin's front door.

"Ah, yes?" Haley prodded.

"Tyler got a little too enthusiastic. Thought your weirdness was my kind of weirdness."

"What? Who's Tyler?"

"Never mind." Red smiled and nodded toward the car. "Is this how we are getting to the museum?"

"The museum?" Sasha was not impressed. Her hands jammed on to her hips and her shoulders moved up and down with her rapid breathing. "What the fuck? And who the shit is this?"

"Stay here and I'll bring the car back afterward. I'll explain then."

"Ah, no." Sasha pulled back her hand clutching her keys, "not happening, bitch. Kermit's my frog."

"Kermit?" Red asked, her eyes darting back and forth between Haley and Sasha.

"She named the car." Haley shrugged.

"Humans are so weird."

"Speak for yourself, Dracula's bitch."

Haley burst out laughing as the two glared at each other.

"Alright, either fuck or let's move on." Haley's cheeks burned as the words came out before she could stop them.

"Fuck?" Red raised an eyebrow, her top lip quivering with a scowl.

"I've seen her bed people with less sexual tension." Haley lifted her hands as if to say, *sorry but it's true*. Haley enjoyed the look that passed between the two again, until the sound of distant rumble skittered shivers down her spine as memories of the Underdemons growling voice returned.

"Okay, let's go then." Haley stepped toward Kermit.

"Where?" Sasha hadn't moved.

"We really are going to the museum, Sasha."

"Fine," Sasha called out before she slammed herself into Kermit, "but you better explain this bullshit and Drac's bitch before the night is out."

"Do you want me to drive?" Haley asked as Kermit swerved for the third time, Sasha's laughter bouncing around the metal frame. A low hum of what Haley interpreted as impatience came from the backseat where Red sat.

"No," Sasha waved her hand at Haley, gulping in air trying to catch her breath and wipe laughter tears from her cheek at the same time. "Damn you're awesome, Robins."

"Not so boring now, huh?" Haley muttered.

"Oh, shut up." Sasha laughed, softening the blow with a smile at Haley before looking up into the rear-view mirror. "And what a story, you could have just said you were sick of camping. Which, by the way, cabins aren't camping."

"It's not a story, shit, I thought it was a prank you had pulled on me to begin with."

"Me, I'm not the history geek. But you really expect me to buy that a Demon of the Doorways has to hitch a ride in Kermit to get to the museum because humans have thwarted her plans by grave robbing?"

"Yes." Sasha shivered as the growl rumbled from the back seat.

"What is your name?" Haley felt her eyes bulge as she realised the question slipped from her mouth.

"Miera."

"Miera." Haley whispered.

Sasha's laughter stopped as the word crackled from Haley, singeing her lips as though she'd just taken a bite from food too hot from the oven.

"As in the Goddess of Light you did your damned thesis on?"

"Believe me now do you, Sasha?" Haley felt her cheeks warm as eyes bore into the back of her skull.

"Fuck!" Sasha breathed out the word.

"That's a yes in Sasha speak." Haley looked back over her shoulder, a shiver straightening her spine as she met Miera's green eyes.

Haley's smirk dropped as she looked back at Sasha. Her friend's face faced forward as though turned to stone, her lips pressed white.

"It's okay. She's not going to hurt us." Haley's voice was hot chocolate smooth, memories of talking

202

to her niece after a nightmare flashing through her mind.

Sasha flicked a look at Haley, eyes wide and filled with an unfamiliar shimmer. Her fun loving, adventurous friend looked scared. Haley shook her head.

Of course, she's scared, she just needs time to adjust.

You weren't scared.

Haley couldn't refute the internal dialogue.

The car stopped and Sasha kept her bloodless fingers on the driver's wheel.

"Are you coming with us?"

Sasha shook her head at the question as Miera opened the back door and slipped her long legs out of Kermit.

"You going to be okay?" Sasha's voice squeaked and she looked at Haley.

"Yeah. Are you?" Haley squeezed Sasha's hand.

Sasha's eyebrows furrowed and a moment ticked by before she nodded.

"Let me know when you get home, okay?"

"You aren't boring."

Haley laughed.

"You were never boring you idiot." There was no fire in Sasha's words. "Why do you think I always wanted you to come out with me. You make things interesting and fun."

"What?" Haley laughed again. "You always called me boring."

"Yeah well, jealousy is a weird thing."

"So why tell me now?"

"Because I can't be as brave as you." Sasha leaned over and waited until the door closed behind Miera. "She scares the shit out of me."

"Oh."

"Be safe. Call me if you need me to come back."

"I'll be okay."

Sasha knew she would be. She was always okay.

Hailey waited until Kermit drove into the mass of Friday night commuters before asking the first question that fell out when she opened her mouth.

"What did you do to her?"

"Me? I didn't do anything."

"She's scared of you." Miera tilted her head in that same question mark and Haley felt as though those emerald eyes might bore through her skin. "What did you do?"

"You aren't scared of me."

Haley shrugged and began walking toward the museum. "It's this way."

"Why aren't you scared of me?"

"I don't know." Haley refused to look at Miera as she shrugged again. "You don't seem to have any desire to hurt me, unless I should be scared of you?"

"Most people are."

"You already said I was weird."

"And you assumed it was a bad thing."

Sasha didn't hear Miera's words as she faltered in her steps. A group of women laughing and talking loudly stood between them and the front doors to the museum. She recognised the pixie haircut of Sasha's previous night flirtations.

"We need to go around the back."

That perfectly raised eyebrow rose, almost meeting Miera's hairline.

"Just trust me."

To Haley's surprise Miera did, following her as she walked around the side of the building.

"Want to explain?"

"Not really keen to be recognised breaking into the museum. The people in front of the doors know me. It might not bother you, but I still have to live here after we get the chakra."

"Wait, break in?"

"The museum is only open during the day."

"And you're okay to break in?"

"Well, I figure it's more important to stop the demon ripping open doorways but," she smiled at Miera as she dropped onto a park bench near the staff exit of the building and patted the seat beside her, "that doesn't mean having a criminal record is what I want."

"Why didn't you tell me it would be closed?"

"Would it have stopped you?"

"No."

"Would you still have needed a ride to get here?"

"Yes." Miera sat down next to Haley. The warmth of Miera's thigh sent a rush through Haley. "But what now?"

"Joel finishes in about twenty minutes."

"Joel?"

"A mate of mine who works here."

"Continue."

"I will say hi to him, while you make sure the door he comes out of doesn't close behind him."

"You've done this before."

Haley felt the warmth in her cheeks.

"Only once."

"Why?"

"There was an exhibit I wanted to see but couldn't get in during open hours because of my work schedule."

"You really are a surprising creature."

"If only I used these superpowers for more interesting endeavours though, right?"

"Why would you say that?"

Haley shrugged and for a moment the sounds of the Friday night revellers echoed filled up the silence that lingered between them.

"What's a chakra?"

"Oh, you caught that, huh?" Haley laughed. "It's a disc-like kind of weapon a character on my favourite TV show uses."

"Like Silas' weapon."

"Yeah, I didn't know it was a weapon, the museum has labelled it a disc, but it always reminded me of that."

"It is a weapon."

"It kills people?"

"Indirectly, yes."

"But it's not razor edged or anything?"

"No." Miera's laugh was light and made Haley smile as she leaned back on the park bench.

"Who is Tyler?" Haley asked, remembering the name the demon mentioned back at the cabin.

"Oh, you caught that did you?" Miera spoke Haley's words back at her. Their eyes locked and Haley took a deep breath in, starving for oxygen.

"He's a mortal familiar. He brought you to the cabins, thinking you were a wayward demon."

"Me?" Haley spluttered as she stiffened. "I'm just boring old me."

"I don't think you are boring."

"Really?"

"Not at all. All these people," Miera spread her arm to take in the nightlife of people clumping into groups, playing chicken with cars, and trying to out-do each other in clothing and laughter, "they are all scared to just be. They need to be seen and acknowledged without being different. You are braver than all of them combined."

An undignified sound akin to a goose honking escaped Haley's mouth.

"It's true, even your friend Sasha tried to tell you how special you are." Miera placed a gentle hand on Haley's arm.

"Sasha thinks I'm boring."

"She explained that."

"You heard her?"

Miera smiled. "Yes, but now I think our time is up."

"Time is up?"

Miera nodded toward the staff door that was opening.

"Oh." Haley jumped up and raced toward the door.

"Haley." Joel jumped as Haley helped open the door.

"Hey, Joel."

"Hey." Joel's shoulders slumped forward.

"Sorry, you look exhausted. I just wanted to say hi."

"Oh," Joel looked up, "it's your birthday, isn't it?"

"In a few days."

"Are you having a party?"

"Nah, but if I did, you'd be invited."

"Oh." Pink flushed his cheeks. "Have a good birthday."

"Thanks." Haley smiled and waved him off, hoping his exhaustion was enough to stop him looking back. Joel slipped around the corner toward the bus stop and Haley turned a wide smile to Miera. She held the door open in one long fingered hand.

"Easy, peasy."

"After you." Miera pulled the door all the way open, Haley ducking under her arm and stepped inside the low-lit bare brick corridor.

She led the way without hesitation, having been here more times than she cared to admit. She hadn't lied, she had only snuck in there once. The other times she had been escorted by various workers who had gotten to know her during her many lingering

208

visits.

"You spend a lot of time here then?"

"I like it. It's filled with history."

"Ahh, the history geek."

"Yeah." Haley sighed.

"History is important. More humans need to pay attention."

Haley pushed her shoulders back and stepped into the large atrium of the museum.

"Where is the weapon?"

"Just take a moment and look around." Haley admonished the impatient Demon of Doorways. "Isn't it beautiful?"

Several displays dotted the area. Thick red ropes cordoned off some, while others were scenes displayed on raised dais. There were large sculptures hung from the roof with clear wires and the silence made Haley nostalgic for the slapping waves soundtrack that played during opening hours.

"There are a lot of things here that are dangerous."

"Really?" Haley couldn't stop smiling.

"I tell you it's dangerous and you smile?"

"I'm weird. We have already established this."

"Ah, but at least this time it's making you smile."

"Shut up." Haley still smiled as she muttered the words.

Chewing on her bottom lip she warred between prolonging the adventure and showing off her knowledge. A splinter of broken glass echoed from the other end of the museum, taking away her thoughts and indecision.

"Stay behind me."

"Is it the Underdemon?"

"No, the coward will use a human to find the weapon and take it back to him."

"Use a human?" A lump formed in Haley's throat.

"All demons, and Underdemons have the power to influence human decisions."

The blue light, like that which had wrapped around the Underdemons body when Haley had first seen him, flowed from Miera's fingertips. Haley couldn't have pulled away from the flickering flash of light as it sailed toward the man even if she had wanted to. It was more hypnotic than a lava lamp. The man's body jerked upright, away from the cabinet, surrounded by the broken shards no longer protecting the items that lay among them. The shiver rippled over Haley's skin, pulled a bubble of sound from her lips as the man turned around, stiff and reminiscent of a puppet. Their eyes locked for a moment before he crumpled to the ground.

"Have you influenced me?" Haley asked as she let out a heavy breath.

Miera cocked her head and blinked several times as she looked at Haley.

"I did try. It didn't work."

"Something's wrong with me?"

"Hardly."

"But you have influenced others?"

"When I've needed."

"Well, he was in the wrong place anyway." Haley shook her head, her muscles bunching and her skin breaking out in gooseflesh as she moved back toward one of the other displays, pointing toward the weapon, fingers trembling.

Will I finally get to touch it?

"You really do spend a lot of time here."

"Yes, fine." Haley watched as Miera wrapped her fingers over the disc and pulled it from its display. "I'm a huge geek. I don't do anything fun or anything adventurous without Sasha dragging me behind. And I usually kick and scream."

"I can imagine the kicking and screaming."

Haley laughed and shrugged, turning away to hide the heat in her cheeks. She could imagine the neon red beacons she had seen too many times in mirrors.

"But you are definitely not boring or lacking in the adventurous spirit."

"Why, because I brought you to the museum?" Haley rolled her eyes.

"You found out about Demons, about the other realms of existence. You brought the Demon of Doorways to find a weapon that could open a hell on your realm. You didn't balk once about any of it. You barely even asked."

"Well, I did think you were making a movie."

"Yes," Miera smiled and nodded, "but you didn't flinch when you realised you were wrong."

Haley took a deep breath. It puffed out her chest

and pushed back her shoulders.

"I didn't, did I?"

"You, Haley Robins, are an adventure all on your own."

"Cool." Haley was smiling so wide her cheeks ached a little as she followed Miera back toward the exit they had broken into.

"So, what does it actually do?"

"And now you ask," Miera laughed but there was no meanness in it. "As I explained earlier, the doorways stop the realities from bleeding into each other. If that shithead gets the weapon and breaks open the door, the atmosphere you all need to breathe will be taken over by the poison of their realm."

"And you have to stop Underdemons from doing this." A nod was Miera's reply. "Well, that's a shitty job."

"Only four more days, and the weapon is useless to him."

"What do you need to do with the weapon until then?"

"I take it back to the tomb, replace the wards on it."

"Can it be brought back after it's inactive?"

"I suppose so." Miera narrowed her eyes at Haley.

"Okay, but then what do you need to do?"

"Spank some Underdemons' arses."

Haley laughed. "Hang on a tick." She raced back to the display and began to tidy up the remaining items, ensuring they were in the right place.

212

"What are you doing?"

"It's going to be bad enough when they find this guy here, at least the display won't be wrecked as well."

"Fine." Miera rolled her eyes and the corners of her lips quirked up.

Haley watched as Miera walked over to the man. She wouldn't kill him now, surely. Haley shook her head and focused.

After making sure Miera's distraction with the man kept her eyes averted, Haley grabbed a piece of paper and a pencil from the nearby suggestions table, and scrawled a quick note:

This object has been removed for the benefit of humanity, to stop an ancient demonic force from partying with our air supply. Also, to be cleaned. Will be back Wednesday.

Three months passed since Haley's 30th birthday. She had quit her job in the call centre, found a part time job in the university bookshop and returned to finish her study. She would one day curate the museums, and she would find all the weapons hidden around the world. She might even find her way to bumping into Miera again.

She scoffed at the thought.

Her legs dangled over the edge of the large sandstone border of the garden that tried to make the large old building of the university that held the administration and bookshop more inviting.

"So, taken out any more demons recently?"

"Hey, bitch, it's the Underdemons I want to take out." Haley shielded her eyes with her hand as she looked up to Sasha who stood on the stone next to her, arms out either side as though the stones were narrow and not three feet wide.

"Hey, yourself." Sasha dropped down and nudged her shoulder into Haley's. "Not the way I saw you looking at her."

"What?" The blush crept up Haley's neck and called her out on the unspoken denial.

"Look, she was an intimidating bitch from hell, literally." Haley didn't bother to explain, though the desire itched every time Sasha got the details wrong. "But she wasn't all bad. She got that human puppet out and no one ever found footage of what happened at the museum. I guess that was pretty decent."

"Decent," Haley snorted, "and her job saving our ozone layer is demonic?"

"Maybe, but I don't think it's the last we're going to see of her."

"Really?" Haley couldn't hide the hope in her eyes.

"Behind you, moron." Sasha shook her head, a half-smile pulling up the side of her mouth.

Haley turned around, warmth turning to a raging fire along her neck and up to her cheeks.

Miera jerked her head toward the open back door of the taxi she learned against. Haley nodded, kissed Sasha on the cheek and jumped up.

"2 am." Sasha called after her with a laugh.

Haley ran toward the taxi.

THIS GARDEN

C. MARRY HULTMAN

People called it the Path of the Gods. For centuries, it had been a whispered legend in small hillside communities and the dive bars of Peru. Adventurers seeking their fortunes had ventured up the Andes to locate the entrance but had all failed. Returned, mad from starvation, egos and bodies bruised or shivering with fear at what they had encountered on their journeys. It seemed destined to remain part of South American lore.

Then one fateful evening, as the thunder rolled across the mountaintops and lightning threatened to strike the party, Dr Juan Cruz located the door. Unexpectedly, it materialised atop one of the great Inca structures, an old sacrificial pyramid where bodies had lazily rolled down the steps, gutted and drained of blood. They had sent word to the research facility in the capital before the group of ten explorers had ventured inside. It was the last anyone ever heard of them.

The door stood before them, odd, otherworldly, in fact. Just a frame holding a stone slab carved with intricate patterns of figures. Standing on what looked like a suspension bridge flanked by great winged gods. The door had not been there when the party arrived the day before. Dr Bendtsen had been quite disappointed and in a rage proclaimed that someone had led them astray, but the guide Lupe assured the expedition that it was the correct location and to everyone's surprise, the portal was there as day broke over the isolated ruins of the ancient civilisation.

The door opened with ease to reveal a moss-covered staircase going up. It was impossible to see the top of it, for white billowing clouds obstructed their view the farther the steps climbed.

Bendtsen ordered Lupe and the other guide, Jesus, to take the lead with their rifles at the ready. He was not a superstitious man, the good doctor, but they had heard enough stories of travelers seeking their fortune and never returning to use caution.

It took almost half a day to climb the steep incline of crumbling stone steps. Higher and higher, they ventured until they must surely have been thousands of feet above the ground. There were six men in the party; Dr Bendtsen of the archaeological department, Dr Birch the biologist, Dr Ehlert of the historical society, the two guides and the young journalist Jason Olsen. They rested at regular intervals and then carefully moved on, amazed that they did not need to use the oxygen tanks on their backs. The staircase was wide enough to accommodate two people side by side, but there was no railing and as they climbed ever higher, they saw the ruins become smaller and smaller below and they were aware that a single misstep would send them tumbling to certain death. This became even more poignant as they traversed the thick mist of the clouds.

The fog was so dense that one could barely see one's own hand, let alone where the steps ended. Jesus passed down a thick rope for them all to hold grab, so not even one was lost.

The bright evening sun welcomed them as they were free of the clouds and that was when they could see the plateau clearly for the first time. Like the image on the door, it resembled a large suspension bridge, but to their amazement, it was hanging freely.

Once they reached the top and passed through the stone arch, the true scale of the construction was evident.

"What the bloody hell?" Dr Ehlert said, as he gazed out over the structure.

It appeared to be a floating platform made up of cobbled stones. Like a broad street stretching out as far as the eye could see. Side paths branched off in various directions like some great labyrinth. Trees and various vegetation either grew from the stones themselves or from cyclopean structures built along the edges of the paths. They marveled at the wonders presented before them as they investigated the place. Jason Olsen took photos with his camera, while Dr Ehlert examined the stones; Dr Birch vigorously took samples from the plant life and stored them in his pack.

"This is amazing," he said as he plucked a bright purple flower. "I have never in my entire life seen such flowers or plants. This will put the entire biological community on end."

"How did they even construct this?" Dr Bendtsen asked in general.

"There are no signs of suspension or supportive elements," Dr Ehlert replied. "The only object visible so far would be the stairs we just climbed."

"And if there were suspension, what would they be attached to?" Dr Bendtsen pondered. "And if there were supports, we would have seen them below."

"There are more questions here than answers, that's for sure." Jason was feverishly taking notes on his tablet. "Like how come airplanes haven't registered this at all?"

Dr Bendtsen tried to lean over the edge to investigate what supported the platform. "As far as I can tell," he reached down into nothingness, "this structure that we are standing on is about ten inches thick. It is not resting on anything at all, just floating on air."

"That's physically impossible," Dr Birch exclaimed.

"And you feel that a door suddenly appearing on top of an old Inca pyramid was plausible?" Dr

Ehlert remarked sarcastically.

"No, of course not. That could have been a trick of the light. Because it was not visible when we arrived. None of us actually climbed the pyramid to check. This though. We are in fact standing on a manufactured construction, a complex network of streets and various edifices hanging miles above the Andes. Is it proof of alien technology?"

"Surely you can't be serious?" Dr Ehlert replied and scoffed. "Do you mean to say that this was made by distant travelers from the stars?"

"Only that it might be a possible explanation. Several ancient texts detail how gods, as they call them, came down and helped various civilisations with feats of engineering, only to return to the sky. What if they never left us? What if this is where they lived and how they remained out of sight for centuries?"

"Now I know you're joking. I hadn't realised Mr. von Däniken had joined the expedition," Dr Ehlert threw up his hands and walked to his pack.

"What if there are doors like the one we just passed all over the world, at every ancient site? What if there is one by the great pyramids and we just don't know it yet?"

"It is too early to speculate on such things," Dr Bendtsen interjected. "We are first and foremost here to do research and document our findings, and maybe discover what happened to the three expeditions that came before us. I am convinced that we will find a logical explanation to everything in the course of our journey."

Since light was fading and the hour was late, Lupe and Jesus set up camp for the team. A small two-man tent for the guides and a larger military grade one for the rest of the expedition. The plateau bathed in red light as the sun descended and caused the flowers to glow with an incandescent neon light.

Jason was leaning against the arch, looking out over the clouds below, smoking a cigarette as Dr Ehlert walked up to him. They were waiting as the guides set up a fire pit for cooking. They had found remnants of an earlier pit and had assumed it was from the last expedition, ten years ago.

"What do you make of all this?" Dr Ehlert asked the journalist.

"Not sure," Jason replied absentmindedly. "I have no expertise in any field, really. Dr Birch's wild explanation, though irrational, seems as fitting as not. How does anyone construct something like this?"

"In my experience we still have a lot to learn about ancient engineering. The more we discover, the less we know."

"I am also wondering about this whole expedition." Jason lit another cigarette on the butt of his old one. "We are the fourth one in a span of thirty years to attempt this venture. None have returned, yet the University of Wisconsin decides to fund it anyway, without proper precautions?"

"Well, I would speak softly about the funding part." Dr Ehlert glanced over his shoulder. "It is true that UW Madison is footing the bill here, but they believe it is for a different expedition."

"You mean to say?"

"Mums the word, my friend," the doctor placed a gloved finger to his lips and nodded. He wandered over to the top of the staircase and gazed down at the heights they had climbed. "To answer your other question, Jason, there have been numerous expeditions and government involvement, but they have either not found the door or they have not returned. The three teams before us were merely the scientific ones. How many groups have vanished in the sky, no one knows, because no one will say."

As the moon rose on the darkening backdrop, a flock of birds alighted in the distance. Jason raised his camera to catch them mid-flight. They seemed far away, leaping off some edifice ahead of them on the stone structure. The light played tricks on his eyes, for their wings looked pointy and sharp, not made up of feathers at all.

"The first sign of life," Dr Ehlert sighed. "We shall see what tomorrow brings, my good man."

He retired to the tent and Jason remained a while. Finishing his cigarette and following the route of the birds as they circled each other, silhouetted against the moon.

That night, as his companions lay snoring in their sleeping bags next to him, Jason woke with a start. There had been a sound, soft but still audible through the thin fabric of the tent. He was still, staring up at the canvas ceiling, waiting to hear more and it came. The deft footfalls of padded feet moving across the cobbled stone. It reminded him of the way his cat moved across his tiled floor at home. Determined yet elegant. Jason slowly turned on his belly to see if he could catch shadows against the dim glow of the smoldering fire, but there was nothing. Just the sound of footsteps, several pairs of them moving about, maybe the clicking of claws, he was unsure. He waited, holding his breath until the sound faded, as if whatever it was had decided to leave the same way it came. He did not sleep the rest of the night; the event had rattled him too much.

The following morning there was a large tear in the guides' tent. It had only ripped the outer layer, but it was enough to rattle the two men who were in such a state that they were having a difficult time not spilling their morning coffee.

"No debris flying through the air," Dr Birch put up a wet finger. "In fact, there is no breeze at all for us being this high up. Very odd."

"It was clearly some form of animal, scrounging for food." Dr Bendtsen pulled at the slit. "Once it identified that there was nothing here it moved on. Simple as that."

They confirmed the doctor's suspicions once the party discovered that the supply packs overturned, but not opened. This caused Dr Birch to assume that whatever had invaded the camp had not been carnivorous at least. Jason kept his nightly experience to himself.

After packing up their belongings and leaving the oxygen tanks, they moved on. Since the expedition did not have any other mission than exploration, and to locate older parties, Dr Bendtsen decided that they venture straight ahead. The vegetation was thicker that way, and there appeared to be some larger structure in the distance, visible in the bright morning sun.

"I believe there is a tower off in that direction," Dr Ehlert claimed as he peered through his spyglass. "It looks like an ancient minaret, rounded from what I can tell."

"We press on," Dr Bendtsen said as he let the guides, both still armed, lead the way.

The trek continued across an ever-widening path. Lush bushes brimming with berries of varying colours sprouted from the rock itself. Roots snaked along the edge of the path with trees shooting straight up against the heavens and at various parts. The branches with their vibrant green leaves hung over them like a vaulted ceiling, shading them from the sun beating down from a clear sky.

About midday, for their watches had stopped and the screens of their cell phones had gone blank, they reached a fork in the road caused by a tall cyclopean wall approximately ten feet in height, from which a fall of clear water fell. It collected in a pool before them. A variety of colourful fish swam around

224

in the pool and they paused to gaze at the wonder of activity played out before them.

Dr Birch leaned over the clear water and touched it.

"It's so cold," he exclaimed. "Of course it would be, but where does it spring from?"

"Maybe it is collected rainwater." Jason attempted an explanation as he photographed the collage of fish."From what rains?" Dr Ehlert snapped. "There isn't a cloud in the sky and no wind. Where would this magical rainfall come from?"

"Something hydrates the plant life around her and this is obviously a stream. So it comes from somewhere." Dr Birch absentmindedly let his hand glide atop the surface, mesmerised by the bright creatures below. "If I could only bring a sample. They don't look like anything I've seen before."

A small frog jumped up from the depths. It was crimson in colour with large yellow eyes. It licked its eyeballs and considered the group.

"That thing looks normal to me," Jason exclaimed.

Dr Birch was about to answer when he cried out in anguish and pulled his arm from the pool. The others hopped to as he fell to the ground, writhing in pain. Attached to his hand was a dark blue fish, roughly two feet in length, with bulbous yellow eyes and scales reminiscent of metal rivulets. The guides came over and tried to pry the thing off the flailing biologist who called out not to damage the specimen. Blood was pouring from where the animal had latched on to his hand, between thumb and index finger and its mouth extended far across the back of the extremity.

Dr Ehlert came up and smacked the fish at its center with a shovel he had brought from his pack. There was a horrible wet snap as he cleft the fish in two. The bottom half, flying over the edge and fell towards earth. The head of the thing remained attached to Dr Birch howling in equal amounts of pain as in dismay over his lost prize.

The head kept moving, gnawing at the doctor's limb as they tried to beat at it with various tools. Finally, they had beaten the remains to such a bloody pulp only a row of sharp teeth persisted to sit in the flesh, like rows of jagged splinters.

Dr Birch lay on the ground as Dr Bendtsen attempted to remove the teeth one by one. It was not until they had cleaned the wound that they could assess the injury. The creature had ripped and torn at Dr Birch so violently that it had reached bare bone. Completely shredding through tissue and muscle until it resembled the bloody remains of the fish that had caused it.

"We need to get him back down," Jason remarked. "That injury is pretty bad."

"Well, we could send one of the guides with him to base camp and then they would drive him into town." Dr Bendtsen scratched his white beard and cleaned wiped fish remains from his spectacles.

"No, we press on," said Dr Birch said through gritted teeth. "I did not come here and make this discovery to be hindered by some outlandish fish."

"That thing needs to be looked at by a physician," Dr Ehlert said. "If not, it is going to get infected and gangrenous."

"Just douse it in alcohol and wrap it up. I'll be fine."

So they did. Dr Birch, being of Finnish stock, had brought several bottles of Koskenkorva vodka and had no qualms about pouring the contents over his tattered hand.

"Where to next?" the guide Jesus asked.

"I would assume that either one of these paths snakes around and leads us to the tower," Dr Ehlert claimed as he looked at his compass. The needle was spinning erratically, making it impossible to tell which direction they were facing.

They decided to take the path to the right. Not due to any superstition, but because they had all been taught to do so when faced with the choice.

The path brought them round the great wall of stone, keeping it on the left side while a jungle of vegetation kept the open drop on their right side hidden. Occasionally they thought they could hear rustling among the thick branches and would stop to listen, but the sound vanished just as quickly as it came. It was eerily still. Unnaturally so, without a sign of a living thing around them.

Dr Birch soon became more and more lethargic and the guides were forced to grab his backpack as his legs buckled under the weight of it.

"He's burning up with fever," Dr Ehlert remarked as they paused for a moment to eat and drink.

"What do you want us to do?" Dr Bendtsen answered back. "He was the one who refused to head back."

"At this rate he is going to succumb to infection before we have a chance to go home."

"Neither one of us here is a physician. We don't know. He might still make it. We have some antibiotics in one of the packs. Just give them to him and he'll be fine."

There came another rustling from the brush again, and they rose to their feet. Dr Ehlert sent the guides over to examine the wall of vines and branches that were now shaking more vigorously.

Clutching their rifles, the Peruvians reluctantly moved in and tried to pry the thicket apart to see what was happening.

"What is it?" Dr Bendtsen inquired.

"I can't quite see," Lupe said. "It looks like something climbing on the other side."

"On the outside?" Jason raised his camera and followed the investigation through the lens.

Lupe attempted to move a big vine obstructing his view. The movement ceased for a moment and the party collectively held their breaths.

Then there was a high-pitched scream, a flash of reddish fur, the glint of teeth, and a long arm shot out and grabbed at the guide. Lupe screamed and moved back. Jesus attacked the flailing and bloody arm sticking through the mass of tangled vegetation and it vanished. The brush shook violently, as if the

228

greenery itself was agitated. He fired a couple of shots at it, and there were more cries. Jason knelt by Jesus, who was completely still, his hands covering his face.

Dr Ehlert tried to speak to the man in a soothing voice, but there was no reply. He slowly pulled the hands from Jesus' face. There was nothing there. The hands came away, palms covered in blood and gore only to reveal a white grinning skull, eyeballs still in their sockets, staring up at them. Lidless and lifeless.

They wrapped the body in a sleeping bag and left it as close to the stone wall as possible.

"We'll pick him up on our way back," Dr Bendtsen explained.

"If we can find our way back," Dr Ehlert said under his breath.

"What's that?"

"That is, if we can find our way back," he replied in a louder voice. "None of our instruments work and we have no clue where we are or where we are going. What of Birch? Once he perishes, do we wrap him up in his sleeping bag and leave him like so much dead waste?"

"We press on and make camp before nightfall." Dr Bendtsen was adamant. "This is obviously not a safe place to stay. We are duty bound to our investors."

Dr Ehlert let out a sigh and walked away.

They picked up the pace and were soon free of the claustrophobic alley made of stone and foliage. Visibly shaken by the two vicious attacks upon the party, they threw tentative glances over their shoulders and recoiled at the slightest shift among the branches.

The path led them to twin carved columns standing eight feet with a wrought iron gate between them. Someone had carved the columns to resemble men standing with arms folded over their chests and bearing lion heads instead of human ones.

"So now we have crafted metal as well?" Dr Ehlert exclaimed. "And carved deities."

"They have the same symbolism as ancient Egypt." Dr Bendtsen went over the carved stone. "Note the crossed arms, like the pharaohs of old. It means that they are dead."

"Dead lion headed people?" Dr Ehlert scoffed at the claim.

"There is old writing at the base as well," Dr Bendtsen continued.

"What does it say?" Jason asked, frustrated by the constant conflict between the two men.

"The characters predate ancient Inca writing, but I can read some of it." He wiped the column free of debris. "It appears to be a standard warning. Beware treading beyond this point sort of thing, but this word I don't recognise. Kar-ki-on, maybe." He shrugged his shoulders and jotted down the find in his notebook.

The gate was ajar and Jason ventured to stick

his head inside. On the other side, the path opened up to a lavish garden. It was like a rainforest. Dense hanging branches, thick leaves touching the stony ground and moss-covered rocks everywhere. He thought he could see a brook lazily move through the trees.

"You guys should see this, it's like another world in here," he said in amazement.

As soon as they had made Dr Birch comfortable against one of the columns, they each took their turn to peek inside and marvel at what lay beyond as the sun once again began to set. Jesus, calling for their attention, suddenly interrupted them.

There, in a corner close to the left column, lay a mass of faded fabric. Jason carefully moved the heap with his foot and they heard the familiar sound of aluminum tent poles rolling inside. He leaned down and picked up part of the scraps.

"From an earlier expedition?" he wondered.

"Most likely," Dr Ehlert answered the rhetorical question. "It has been faded by the sun, so it's been here a while. Oddly enough, there is nothing else here."

"This might explain why," Jason opened up a large tear in the cloth. Something had ripped through both the outer and inner layer. He partially turned it inside out to reveal brown stains of dried blood.

"Animal attack?" he pondered.

"Or accident," Dr Bendtsen suggested. "If there was an attack, there would be evidence of something else left behind. Not only a damaged tent. Since they didn't go back down, they probably just left the tent after it ripped and headed beyond the gate."

They settled down for their second night in the strange, elevated world. They tended to Dr Birch, who was shivering with fever. The antibiotics were having little effect on the remains of his hand. It was turning green and beginning to smell. The heat from the sun was baking it, making the infection spread faster. They fed him broth and then put him to bed. They watched the large birds fly overhead as they had the previous night. They seemed bigger now, gliding on invisible slipstreams on giant wings. They seemed impossibly high up above them and headed in the direction of the tower, like them.

Dr Ehlert came over to Jason, who was leaning against the wall, staring out over the opposite side where the brush had given way to open air again.

"Regretting your decision?" he asked the journalist and smiled, removing his glasses.

"Not sure." Jason scratched his stubbly chin. "On the one hand, I have quite the story once we return. On the other, at the rate we are experiencing accidents, we might not return at all."

There was a moment's silence as they both considered the possibilities. They both knew that even if this was the most modern expedition to venture up in the atmosphere, they were ill prepared for what they might encounter. This was already evident.

"Have you heard of the Joyce-Armstrong Fragment?" Dr Ehlert said to break the silence. "No. What is that?"

"It is a notebook with the first two and last pages missing. It was found near a farm in England, stained with blood."

"And?"

"Joyce-Armstrong was a pilot who was convinced there were, what he calls, air-jungles at great heights. He based this on the fact that several of his friends had disappeared in their airplanes. On one occasion, they had found one of them decapitated. The notebook details how he climbed up to 40,000 feet only to encounter such jungles and strange gelatinous creatures, like jellyfish, floating around. It seems as if he found something even more dangerous, for the notebook ends with hints of something ghastly and more solid approaching him."

"And you believe this?"

"I didn't. Until we ascended those stairs and arrived here." Dr Ehlert sighed and tossed a small fragment of stone at the torn tent. "They found his plane crashed outside Kent, but not his body."

Silence again. The snoring from Dr Bendtsen inside the tent, the sound of tobacco burning at the end of Jason' cigarette and the gentle crackling of the fire, the only audible sounds.

The following morning, they all awoke to the smell of cooking food. As they carefully exited the tent, they found Dr Birch sitting by the little portable stove, cooking breakfast for them. His face was still a sickly pale pallor and his eyes bore the sheen of a man ravaged by fever, but he was otherwise in fine spirits.

"Good morning, gents," he said in a chipper tone. "I have already taken a little stroll on the other side of the gate and even prepared breakfast for you."

Dr Ehlert walked up to him and placed a hand on the man's clammy forehead. He then grabbed his afflicted hand, only to find a stump wrapped in stained gauss.

"What the hell, Lars?" he cried. "What have you done?"

"It was dead," Dr Birch replied nonplussed. "It needed to come off. It was going to kill me."

"Where is it?" Jason asked, eying the frying pan with suspicion.

"I gave it to one of the flying beasts last night."

"What flying beasts?" Dr Ehlert backed away from him.

"The ones who have been following us since we started. They come on large leathery wings, they look like feline angels."

"He's gone mad from the infection," Dr Bendtsen exclaimed and began rifling through their medical kit.

"Not at all, John," Dr Birch grinned. "They have spoken to me and have invited us to their tower."

"You hold him down and I will sedate him." Dr Bendtsen had a syringe in his hand and started to approach the rambling man. Jason and Dr Ehlert nodded in reply and moved in on him as well.

Dr Birch, noticing what they were up to, rose to his full seven feet, five-inch height and prepared to take them on. Jason tried to wrap his arms around the man's waist, but Dr Birch clobbered him in the back of the head, sending the journalist to the ground. Dr Ehlert went in high, but his colleague punched him in the face, breaking his nose and sending him on top of the tent. Dr Bendtsen attempted to catch him with the needle, but Dr Birch kicked the frying pan into the air, sending hot grease into his attacker's face.

Dr Bendtsen dropped the syringe and covered himself, crying out in pain. Dr Birch looked around and then ran past the gate into the world beyond.

"Let him go," Dr Ehlert called to Jesus who was about to pounce on the large biologist as he bowled past. "We need to take care of Bendtsen here."

Jesus took a water bottle and dowsed the archeologist's blistering face. Fortunately, hot grease had only splashed Dr Bendtsen's left side and missed his eyes, but red irritated soars covered it all the same.

"Now can we return?" Dr Ehlert said after gingerly wiping his colleague's face.

"No. We press on," Dr Bendtsen replied as he assessed the damage in a shaving mirror. "We can't go back with nothing to show for it and poor Lars lost up here, delusional and imagining things. What would I tell his wife? That we left him?"

"So we are going to risk our lives to find that crazy son-of-a-bitch?"

"Yes. He is a friend of ours, so we don't leave

him behind. We find him, pump him full of drugs and bring him back home. All the while prepping for a return in a few months."

"So, we're still exploring?"

"We can easily do both," Dr Bendtsen smiled a pained smile through his damaged skin.

"This is insane," Dr Ehlert kept repeating as they passed the columns and ventured further into the unknown.

They had decided to keep the tent and most of the equipment on the other side and spend the day searching for Dr Birch. They only carried energy bars and water. Jesus was clutching his rifle, visibly shaken by the goings on of late, and he kept reciting the Lord's Prayer under his breath as his eyes shifted left and right. Dr Ehlert carried a machete that he used to remove large vines cutting off their path. As far as Jason knew, Dr Bendtsen was unarmed, while he himself carried a Colt .45 stuffed in the front of his pants.

The stone path was narrower now and most of the area covered in a variety of exotic plant life. To Jason it resembled one of the wild English gardens he had seen on television. It all had some kind of mad logic behind it. As if someone had meticulously placed each shrub, weed or seedling there. Dr Bendtsen speculated that this was in fact the fabled Hanging Gardens of Babylon, for some of the plants were tiered, resembling pyramids. As opposed to the path they had walked before, they no longer followed a straight line. Instead there were various paths intersecting each other in an elaborately engineered system and more than once the party had to decide which way to attempt. They tried to keep the little stream to their right at all times and follow the tower in the distance.

There was a lot more noise there as well. Invisible birds chirped high up in the foliage, and every now and then there was a rustling beside them. Jason tried to take pictures as best he could every time, they chose a particular direction, identifying what he thought were important markings that they might find their way back.

They walked in silence as the sun began to set.

"We need to decide if we are continuing or heading back for the night." Dr Ehlert halted. "It will be impossible to find our way back in this labyrinth in the dark."

"The tower is just around the bend here," Jesus pointed out, having scouted ahead.

"We find the tower, take a breather and then head back," Dr Bendtsen decided. "We have flashlights and Jason here knows the way back."

"Oh, I wouldn't make that claim," Jason just finished saying as something came out of the bushes behind them.

Lars Birch barreled out of the thicket and into Jesus. The rifle went off. Firing straight into the air. The guide cried out as the large man carried him off into the brush on the other side of the trail. It all went so fast that the others could scarcely react. At the same time, the garden came alive. The sky darkened by large birds bursting into the air from all around them. Jason had enough wits to snap pictures at the objects swirling above them.

Dr Ehlert had grabbed the rifle dropped by Jesus and fired after Dr Birch, but it was impossible to tell if he managed to hit anything.

As the cloud of winged animals threatened to block out the setting sun, they blindly ran in the direction of the tower.

They reached a raised dais built from the same cobblestone as the rest of the structure. Panting, they paused and looked behind them to see if the flock of birds had followed, but the sky was clear.

"This was such a bad idea," Dr Ehlert said while checking the ammunition in the rifle.

"Why?" Dr Bendtsen was already looking around. "The only threat is one of our own. Those big birds weren't looking to harm us. We find Lars and get out of here."

The platform was about an inch or so higher than the path, but the tower in the centre of it stretched fifty feet in the air. The structure seemed to be made of limestone and was octagonal instead of round with lion headed figures similar to those guarding the gate lining the base. There were windows at the very top under a red spire. Sticking straight out from under one of the windows was something resembling a flagpole.

Carefully, they walked around the tower in order to avoid ambushes by something hiding behind it. Instead, they found the remains of a camp.

This flattened tent was older than the one at the gates. The heavy fabric revealed that it must have been from the turn of the century. The tent poles constructed from sturdy metal yet had buckled under the weight of something heavy crushing it. There were faded backpacks strewn about and evidence of a fire. A single tree stood a couple of feet from the deserted camp. It resembled an ash or olive tree with light objects hanging in haphazard fashion. Slender, with elongated branches reaching towards the tower, like hands stretched in the worship of a higher power. Dr Ehlert walked over to have a closer look at the long objects hanging from the lowest branches. Long snake like white things, stained with flecks of brown. He touched them and then recoiled in disgust.

"They're spines," he exclaimed and unexpectedly retched on the ground, turning away from his horrific find.

"What are you talking about?" Dr Bendtsen came over to examine the discovery.

"Human spines." Dr Ehlert was on all fours, dry heaving between words as Jason tried to comfort him.

"It's true." For the first time Dr Bendtsen agreed. "They are attached to the branches by tendons or some such. Lars would know, but these are definitely human, you can tell by the curve of them. Clear signs of walking upright."

"So, what does this mean?" Jason was at his breaking point. Tears filled his eyes as he slowly came to the realisation that these human remains were what was left of earlier expeditions.

"We have to return." Dr Ehlert was sitting with his head in his hands, rocking back and forth, trying desperately to make sense of the situation. "Whatever hung those spines does not want us here."

Night had fallen and the moon looked down at them, nearly full.

"There is no way we are going to make it back through that labyrinth tonight," Jason said in a resigned tone. "We wait through the night and try to find our way in the morning."

They leaned against the tower, eyes on the path they had come from. It was the only way in or out. The rest of the area was a dead end. Only open air surrounded them, a fatal drop back to earth. Dr Ehlert held the rifle in his hands as he stared out into the night while Dr Bendtsen had borrowed Jason' .45. The journalist was busy cycling through the pictures on his camera, trying to get a feel for the way back. Sleep would not find them, and if it had, they were not about to welcome her.

Jason stopped at the myriad of pictures he had snapped of the cloud of birds swirling in the sky. He zoomed in on a group that appeared closer. They were so unlike other birds he had seen. Their bodies longer and there was a suggestion of arms and legs almost human in shape instead of that of a fowl. The wings were bat-like in form instead of feathery and the head was close to feline with pointed ears. He shuddered and chalked it up to a trick of the light.

Suddenly the night erupted in brightness. A multitude of lights were floating all around the platform. The three men rose in unison and walked around in awe of the incandescent soft bluish glow, briefly forgetting their situation. Dr Ehlert and Dr Bendtsen walked over to the edge of the platform to get a closer glimpse.

"They look like jellyfish," Dr Bendtsen whispered at the floating mushroom caps with their long tendrils hanging below them.

"Gelatinous creatures in the air..." Dr Ehlert whispered as the things swirled together in a magnificent translucent orb and then rose towards the spire above them.

They followed the mass as it circled the top of the tower and in the light from the floating jellyfish, they noticed a body now hanging from the pole. A body. That had not been there before.

Jason grabbed the binoculars from his pack to get a clear look.

"It's Jesus," he said as he dropped the binoculars to the ground and let them shatter at his feet.

"Are you certain?" Dr Ehlert suppressed another bout of nausea.

"Someone's gutted him and then hung the body by its intestines. Those jelly things are feeding on his carcass now."

"Lars."

Dr Bendtsen interrupted them. He was aiming his rifle at the figure of the biologist standing several feet away from them, barring the exit. "It's time to go home, Lars" Dr Bendtsen continued, his voice less than confident.

Dr Birch, his skin still so pale that it reflected the light from the moon and the glowing jellyfish, smiled and shook his head slowly. His eyes looked upwards and as they did, several shapes dropped from the heavens.

With an almost inaudible sound, several figures surrounded the trio. Dr Ehlert kept aiming at his colleague, and Dr Bendtsen held the .45 steady as the beasts encircling them. The creatures must have been eight feet tall, with naked, muscular human-oid bodies covered in reddish fur. They had black bat-like wings that easily spanned twice their height from side to side. The most terrifying things about these monstrous fiends were their heads. Where one would have expected a human face was instead a feline one. A large head reminiscent of a lion with glowing yellow eyes. Some of them snapped their giant maws, revealing rows of sharp teeth capable of rending flesh to shreds.

The trio moved back towards the tower to keep their backs free from attacks. Jason turned a dial on his camera and without thinking snapped a picture at the beasts as they closed in. The flash lit up the partial darkness, causing the creatures to halt and shade their eyes, he was sure he heard some of them

242

whimper. As if on instinct, Dr Bendtsen fired at Dr Birch, but the shot went wide and the biologist vanished into the night. Dr Ehlert tried to fire at one of the winged cats and his shot went through its wing, leaving a gaping hole. The beast did not react and pounced on the doctor, who desperately tried to fight back. Dr Bendtsen turned his rifle at his friend's attacker, but another beast mauled him for his trouble. The clawed paw ripped his face from his skull, leaving a tattered mess of bone and muscle. Dr Bendtsen froze in shock as another claw tore his jaw clean off, sending it clattering off the edge. As the body collapsed on the ground, blood pouring from the wounds, a group of the creatures piled on top of it, tearing at it with teeth and claws.

The one Dr Ehlert had winged grabbed his throat with a powerful hand, causing him to gasp for air. The beast shoved its free arm into the mouth of Dr Ehlert and dug deep. Dr Ehlert tried to cry but was hindered by an arm of fur and muscle. There was a soft crack and the thing pulled out the man's spine through his mouth.

Jason had managed to move away from the melee of bodies, attempting to find an escape. He moved towards the exit when he heard the soft bounce of padded paws land behind him. He tried to pick up speed when a powerful hand grabbed his shoulder, claws digging deep under the soft tissue of his collarbone. He gritted his teeth, desperately trying to fight the pain and avoid passing out. The beast spun him around and he could smell the stench of blood upon its breath as it roared. Staring at certain doom nearly paralysed Jason, but as the maw closed in on him, he remembered the flash and how it had affected the monsters. Without even thinking he raised the camera and took a picture. There was a high-pitched sound and then the feline face with its soft yet vicious features was bathed in white light. Jones felt the grip relax, and he did not wait. He turned and bolted for freedom, not looking back as he clearly heard wings extend and bodies taking off into the air.

He followed the narrow path to the best of his ability, first keeping the stream to his left, all the while clutching his camera. Once he was back down on familiar ground, he needed proof so that he might warn other expeditions. A million thoughts rushed through his mind, firing off quicker than he could sort through. What if those things were waiting up there? Biding their time until it was time to descend to earth. Were there in fact several of these elevated air jungles hiding above them, and if so, what did it mean? How was he going to find his way? There was no time to stop and check his pictures, and it all looked so different in the dark. He did not recognise a single thing, and it felt as if the gardens were shifting right before his eyes. He continued to run, panting heavily, the sweat stinging his eyes and the taste of blood in his mouth. He thought he heard the rustling of leaves close by him and the flapping of large, leathery wings above. He ran left and right and sometimes straight through the thorny vines before him to find his goal. It tore at him, cutting his face and ripping his clothes to shreds.

Then all of a sudden, he burst through the thicket with the roar of beasts ringing in his ears. He crashed on the cobblestones and rolled crashing to a halt against one of the columns.

He took a moment to catch his breath and wipe the blood from his mouth. His lungs were on fire, and every muscle in his body ached. He looked back at the gardens from whence he had come. Truly, it was as if it was alive. The vegetation moved before him, and in golden rays of a rising sun, it looked like it was settling back to its original position.

Jason crawled through the gates and towards the camp that they had set the previous morning. He assumed that he was far from safe, but he needed to rest before he headed towards the steps and then made his descent.

He found water and the few remaining energy bars and began replenishing his system. Shadows darkened the ground in front of him as the massive bodies of flying beasts flew overhead. He ducked, but they seemed to ignore him. He relaxed and then felt a sharp pain through his back. It burned, as there was a sensation of something pushing through his torso. He coughed and spat up blood. Slowly he looked down to see a tent pole protrude from his abdomen. In disbelief, he turned around to find Lars Birch smiling at him.

Jason Olsen fell to his knees, and the world was spinning as he tried to keep his focus. His body gave out, and he landed hard on his side. He could feel the beat of his heart in his ears and he tried to catch his breath, but he could not. Instead, he kept spitting up dark liquid, and he covered his mouth in a vain attempt to keep the blood inside. As his vision started to fail him he saw the dirt covered boots of the biologist return to the hanging gardens, vanishing into the depths of the air jungle. Walking the Path of the Gods.

VOLCANO OF THE WOLVES

CHISTO HEALY

APRIL 3ᴿᴰ. 1970.

Wolf Island was a small island in thc Galapagos. It was mainly a volcano surrounded by marsh. It was closed off to the public to protect the many birds that called it home. Professor Gary Smith wasn't interested in the birds. Sure, they were interesting, especially the vampire finch that fed off of other birds and stole their eggs, but his interest in the island was far more personal.

"This is it," Professor Smith said to his friend and the owner of the boat that took them there, Carlos.

"It is," Carlos agreed. "So that means now is probably the last chance to turn back."

"If I get caught, I won't let anything fall back on you," Professor Smith said.

"That's not what I'm afraid of." Carlos looked ahead at the island and the volcano that took up most of its mass. "I'm afraid your grandfather was right."

It had been said that the island was named after geologist Theodore Wolf, but Gary's grandfather had a different idea. He believed in a race of wolves; wolves that lived as men. He had been determined to prove it when he went to the island and never returned. That was before the island was closed to the public. Gary had been itching to go to the island for most of his life, as he had just been a child at the time. The fate of his grandfather dug deep into his subconscious and it wouldn't let him go for his entire life, taking him to this moment. He ached to find out what happened to his grandfather, to know what became of him, and to know if he had been right. If he had been, were the wolves dangerous? The world deserved to know, didn't they?

In his 20s, Gary became a wildlife conservationist and a geologist. He even met with the Galapagos national park looking for a job and got rejected. They were very particular about who they took. It was about more than credentials. Almost seemed like they were working to keep a secret. *Could it be so?* he'd wondered.

People with live aboard boats were allowed to scuba dive in the area. It was the best chance the professor, now in his forties, would have to get close to that volcano and whatever was inside of it. He didn't have a boat of his own and a professor's salary didn't allow him to afford one, so he contacted Carlos. His childhood friend was reluctant to help, but in the end he agreed. During their travel to the island, he never ceased to show his reluctance, even down to this very moment.

"My whole life," Professor Smith said to his friend. "Forty-seven years to make it to this moment. There's no way I'm turning back, but I understand if you don't want to wait out here for me. You've done more than anyone else would have, Carlos. You can go."

"No, I can't," Carlos told him. "If I leave and you disappear and there is no news as to what happened to you, I will end up just like you, needing answers and unable to let it go. I want a better life than that."

Professor Gary Smith laughed and shook his head, although he wasn't laughing because his friend was joking. He was laughing at the truth of the statement. "So, you gonna don scuba gear and come in after me if I don't come out?"

"Just come out," Carlos said. His eyes were on the island. His gaze was pulled away when Gary patted his shoulder and said, "I will."

Wolf Island. This was it. Almost half a century dreaming and striving for this moment. Gary couldn't help but fear being let down. There was too much hype, too much build up. What if there was nothing inside that volcano? Nothing on that island? Then he had to know. If nothing else, it would be closure, something he desperately needed. He was already in his wetsuit, prepared for his dive. He would scuba in like everyone else, but Professor Smith was bringing gear with him on this dive, gear that would allow him to break the law and scale the mountain of molten rock. He was going to go up, over, and into the heart of the volcano. That's where the answers lay. The fate of his grandfather, good or bad, was somewhere inside that dormant behemoth. He took a deep breath. His heart was racing just taking in the sight of this. Tears warmed his eyes.

The volcano was only ten feet above sea level. Professor Smith felt he could do it quickly enough to not be seen by the authorities and stopped. At least that was his hope. He prepared for the moment, for the fact that people would be watching, guarding the enormous structure. Gary had trained a long time for this. Some people didn't understand what it was like to go your whole life needing closure, needing answers. You couldn't live the rest of your life without them. All that existed was the question. It lived with you, showered with you, ate with you, came to you in your dreams. It didn't allow you to have healthy relationships. It enslaved you. There was no freedom from the question without the answer. Carlos was the only real friend he had, and he hadn't seen him in almost twenty years before he showed up looking for help. Thankfully, Carlos was a good person and understood the complexity of his situation. He saw the question as an addiction, like a drug. His sister, Maria, had an addiction of her own

250

and it ate away at his heart, watching her succumb to it. When Gary came to Carlos, he saw his friend felt this was an addiction he could actually put an end to. It felt like a chance at redemption after not being able to help the girl he grew up with.

Gary's grandfather had his own addiction, his own dreams and theories and needs, and it had taken him out here to this god forsaken island where he was never seen again. The authorities that worked so hard to keep this place private and keep everyone out didn't seem to have any knowledge or information about what happened to the older Smith. Their lack of information helped to construct the mystery that drove the younger Smith and led to this very moment. He needed to know. It was more important than the rules and laws that were in place; more important than the consequences of breaking them. If he got the answers he was looking for, then Professor Gary Smith was prepared to go to prison. He would be freer in prison with the answer he spent his life seeking than he would be out in the world without them. It had come that far.

The island was originally called Werman Island, which was consistent with his grandfather's theory. Gary had read all his papers and journals a thousand times over, combing them for clues. The old man had said that the name of the island changed when the wolves had been discovered. If the island had been named after the geologist that discovered it, as the local authorities and Wikipedia claimed, then why did it have a different name at first? Why wouldn't it be dubbed that from the beginning? There was definitely something about the island that didn't add up.

Grandpa Smith declared that the local authorities wanted to cover up the existence of the ancient species in order to keep people away, maybe even to preserve them and keep them from going extinct. Perhaps it had been out of fear and legend. They could have believed the wolves to be gods or feared a curse would come from exposing them. With no one willing to tell the truth, there was no way to know. Shortly after the elder Smith went to explore the volcano, he disappeared, and the island was closed to the public almost immediately after. How was that not supposed to be a red flag to his family? Somehow Gary's parents found a way to accept it and let it go, but he couldn't do it. He couldn't understand how they could do it.

Gary hadn't ruled out the possibility that his grandfather had actually been insane, as many people, including his own father, had claimed, but it didn't stop him from having to know for sure. It didn't change the fact that he never came back from his trip and the fact that they closed the island afterwards yet had no information on his whereabouts.

"Last chance," Carlos said. "We can turn around now and move on with life and live happily ever after."

"I can't. How can I?" He had dedicated so much of his life to this that it was literally impossible for him to abandon it now.

In the years that Gary and Carlos hadn't been

talking, Gary had met a woman at college, an amazing, intelligent, beautiful woman, named Clarissa, but she discouraged this trip. She pushed him towards therapy and begged him to let go and move on. Gary had loved Clarissa more than anyone he had met in his life, but he knew that he couldn't marry her like she wanted him to. After seven years of him refusing to take that step, she left him. He regretted losing her, but he didn't regret his commitment to his grandfather, to this trip.

He also knew that she had a valid point when she had said, "If you insist upon doing this and something happens, something like whatever happened to your grandfather, then I would be left alone as a widow, and don't you dare say that's why you haven't married me, Gary, like having a ring or not having a ring would change my heart."

Gary had known that she was right. He had known that she was right about him, and she was right to leave him. He didn't blame her, but he did miss her and think of her often. It was this that drove him to go ask Carlos for help, despite the fact they had grown apart and not spoken in so long. He had to do this first, to find out first; then he could live. Once he came out of that volcano with the information he needed, he could finally be who his parents wanted him to be, who Clarissa wanted him to be, who he wanted to be. He took another deep breath and rolled his shoulders. Carlos massaged them to help calm his nerves.

"What if it's active, full of lava?" he asked as he

rubbed his friend's tight anxious shoulders.

"The volcano was ruled extinct," Gary told him. "It hasn't erupted in almost a million years. Of course, it had to be dormant if Grandpa's man-wolves called it home, right? If the volcano erupted that would have kind of solved that mystery for us and burnt up Grandpa's bones in the process."

Carlos sighed. "Point taken."

Professor Smith broke away from his friend and nodded to him. Then he took the dive, going backwards over the side of the boat before he lost his nerve. It was now or never and never wasn't an option.

He was immediately amazed by how clear the water was. The fish swam around him fearlessly as if he was one of them. He followed the designated visitor's route to the island and made land, but he didn't follow the path back to the ship as intended. Instead, he climbed over the roped banisters, the chains, and avoided the security cameras. He used a harness, carabiners, and climbing rope to scale the side of the volcano. After all the time he spent on simulation walls doing the same, he made quick work of it. The only ones that saw him were the birds, and they didn't seem to mind his company.

Well, the birds and Carlos who stood on the deck of his houseboat. Gary glanced back to see his friend's black hair blowing in the gentle breeze, a pair of binoculars pressed to his eyes. Gary saw him breath a sigh of relief when he spotted the professor climbing into view, and he gave a wave.

Now Professor Gary Smith stood at the top of the Wolf Island volcano, gazing down into its shadowy depths. His entire life had led up to this moment. It was a strange feeling for everything to be about one moment and then for it to actually be happening. It was surreal, strange, hard to grasp as reality.

"Alright, Grandpa," he said. "Let's go meet your wolves."

With that, he went over the edge and started to descend. It didn't take him long to see that the rock itself carried design. It had been carved, and not just for practicality. It was art. It had been carved stylistically. The patterns were intricate and complicated, beautiful, and mesmerizing. He had barely ventured a few feet into this thing, and already his sense of wonder had been invoked. The Professor could only imagine what the rest of this place held.

He knew that the ornate carvings in the wall of the volcano were definitive evidence of life within. The proof was already in front of him that someone resided within this behemoth, or at least they did at one time.

Planes couldn't land there, and men were not allowed on this island, yet within the confines of this volcano was an artistic masterpiece that no one would ever bear witness to. Gary used the waterproof camera he had brought with him to take pictures, to do what his grandfather was never able to do; have proof. If nothing else, the world deserved to see the marvel that he witnessed in person. It was a sight to behold.

Even with the ledges and carvings, the paintings and etchings interwoven with gold, the way down was steep. A less experienced climber would probably have fallen to their death. He was glad that he spent his life working up to this moment and he didn't rush here prematurely. He was glad that he had done this right. He felt confident now, motivated, excited even.

"Soon enough, they'll all see, Grandpa. They'll know you weren't crazy."

There was what looked like a cave entrance off to the right and down a ways. Professor Smith repelled and swung over to it until his feet touched down firmly on the ledge. When he stood firmly planted on solid ground, he disconnected himself and ventured into the cave.

It was surprisingly well lit.

As he continued on, Gary realized why. There were lights of sorts. They were fishbowls full of water that contained some kind of glowing fish swimming around within. They were set in designed window-like ledges carved into the walls. Whether or not they were put there by wolves was yet to be seen, but it was clear to him that some level of sentient beings had been down here. On the off chance they were dangerous, he had his revolver in a waterproof sealed pouch on his back and his knife strapped to his leg. He had trained long hours with those tools as well. He wanted to be prepared for anything.

As he moved further into the cave it branched

off different directions, including down. The need for spelunking was over. He had found the entrance to an entire tunnel system that he was willing to bet went the entire circumference of the volcano. If it went down into the depths, who knew how far down that was. It could go for literal miles. Maybe his grandfather had found this place and just never found his way out. Maybe he never did find his wolves but he had been living here, surviving all this time. Maybe the fish lamps had been put there by him.

It was a wild thought and he put it out of his mind fairly quickly because of the architecture he saw above. His grandfather was an explorer and a survivor but one thing he was not was an artist. What few diagrams existed in his journal were childlike and simple. Gary noticed then that there were strange markings on the edge of every turn of the tunnel. Could they be like street signs? Was it a way to keep track? It was possible that it was just more art but his gut told him otherwise. Since he was choosing directions at random, he was taking pictures of the symbols to help him find his way back when the time came. Whether they were intended to be a directional resource or not, they were going to be exactly that for him.

As he went along, he headed further and further down and further in. It was exhilarating and terrifying all the same. His heart pounded with adrenaline. Then the lights went out. It was sudden, like they had been shut off. Were they covered? The fish removed? It didn't seem like they were the type of lights you could flip an off switch for.

If that was the case, then he wasn't alone and there was someone ahead and behind him. Someone that saw him go in and came in after him? Or someone that was already down here when he arrived? That was the real question, but either way, the danger of the situation was evident.

Professor Smith cracked a glow stick and put it around his neck, then he got another for his wrist. He held a thicker one in his hand. He himself was aglow and the area around him was lit up enough for him to see a good three feet in any direction. Everything beyond that was complete and utter darkness. It felt darker than any other darkness he had known. Maybe he wasn't as prepared as he allowed himself to believe. It was so pitch black that it actually felt blank, empty. He knew it wasn't, though. It wasn't empty at all. Someone was there, maybe multiple someone's. He could feel them watching him despite not being able to discern their location. Could it actually be his grandpa? He couldn't assume it was anyone friendly, but he had to make sure they knew that he wasn't there on a mission of ill intent. If they saw him as a threat, things could get ugly quick, no matter who they were.

"I mean no harm," Gary said into the darkness. "I come here in peace."

"Then what need do you have for the gun in your pouch," a voice said from the dark.

His pouch was black and he wasn't sure how

they could even tell what he had in it. He didn't feel like that was the right question for the moment though. The small details could come later.

Professor Smith swallowed the rising lump in his throat and said, "Coming in peace didn't guarantee being received in peace. I brought it to protect myself. I'm sure you can understand that."

Whoever was there was someone well spoken. They had an accent that made him believe they were probably multi-lingual as well. He didn't imagine his grandpa's Wolfmen to be highly educated civilised people so that was steering him towards believing that it was someone else that had caught him. Then again, he thought, what was he expecting exactly? Lon Cheney? He really had no idea what to expect.

"I appreciate your honesty," said the person unseen. "Now remove it and place it on the ground outside of your light."

Gary nodded. He slowly reached behind him and took the gun out of his pouch. "I appreciate your English," he said as he knelt down, and gently tossed the gun into the darkness as a show of good faith that he hoped didn't wind up getting him killed.

"I speak many languages."

I knew it! Gary thought excitedly. The stranger proved his point by issuing a command in a tongue that was definitely not English. It was not a language that the Professor had ever heard before, in his time at university or during his years of training. In fact, he was willing to bet that it was a language no one had ever heard before, outside of this volcano.

His chain of thought and fascination with the moment was shattered by the disturbing sound of scurrying feet and the sound of someone grabbing the gun from the ground followed by more scurrying feet. He could almost smell whoever retrieved the gun. It was a primal smell, wet, earthy. Gary wished more than anything that he could see who was there, who now had his weapon.

"Men are not allowed here," the voice spoke from the darkness once more. Now it sounded like it was behind him. Professor Smith turned around despite the fact that he couldn't see a damned thing. "Why have you come here?"

Professor Gary Smith took a deep breath. He exhaled it slowly. This was it. This was the moment he had been daydreaming of since childhood.

"Forty years ago, when I was just a child, my grandfather came here. He never came back. All I had of him were his journals. I have been waiting all my life to come here, to find out what happened. Maybe to find him or whatever was left behind by him. I'm not really sure what I expected to find, to be honest."

"You are related to Smith?" the voice asked from the dark, the tone changing to one of interest and curiosity.

Gary smiled at this. *Did they know him?* It doesn't sound like they hated him or killed him if they did. Gary felt renewed, invigorated. What would Carlos say when he showed up back on the boat with the pictures he took? He couldn't wait to see the man's face.

"Yes, yes. I am also Smith. Professor Gary Smith. That is me. Arnold Smith was my grandfather. Smith are we."

Suddenly the dark was gone and the lights returned. Gary breathed a sigh of relief until he turned around and found himself standing face to face with the largest wolf he had ever seen. It was on its hind legs and towered over him by a good foot and a half. Gary wasn't a small man. He stood six foot tall which meant this wolf had to be close to eight feet in height with a build to match as it was almost entirely muscle from what he could tell. As friendly and sophisticated as the creature had been up to this point, it was impossible not to be intimidated by the sheer sight of him.

"Come with me, Smith," the wolf said to him, in the same smooth baritone English he had heard in the dark. "I will show you the way."

Even as afraid as he was, Gary couldn't help but smile. It was true. *It was all true!* He couldn't have imagined a better outcome. This was everything he had dreamed of. He was so simultaneously terrified and filled with excitement and awe that he could barely contain it. He thought the moment might actually stop his heart and bring forth his end.

Professor Smith allowed the wolf to lead him through the tunnels then. Interestingly, the creature continued to walk on its hind legs as it led him. It didn't drop to the wolf's more natural fours as he had expected it to. Gary couldn't help but wonder how many more were out there. At least one, he knew for certain. He decided to voice the question.

"How many of you are there?" he asked as he walked.

"Many," the wolf said.

He led the professor down a maze of winding tunnels and corridors. The deeper they got, the less the surroundings seemed like primitive caves and more they looked like lavish palace halls. The wall art, carvings lined with sparkling gold had returned. There was a blanket of hardened molten lava down the centre like a red carpet. But where did it lead? Where was this wolf taking him? Did it have something of his grandfathers? Was it possible that his grandpa was still alive after all these years? He felt the magic of it all filling his heart and it made him feel like a child again.

"This place is beautiful," Gary said with a sense of childlike wonder. "Has it always been like this? How long have you been here?"

"We have been here as long as here has been," the wolf told him.

Then he walked over a sparkling threshold and led Gary into what appeared to be an actual city. There were buildings all carved out of volcanic rock and designed with the same stylish architecture he had previously seen. There were light posts topped with the familiar fish bowls. There were paved streets with wolf cubs playing in them. Everything sparkled and shined.

"My God, it's gorgeous!" Gary exclaimed. "It's

absolutely gorgeous."

"Come, Smith," the wolf said nonchalantly, unimpressed by his enthusiasm.

He led the Professor down a cobbled molten street, between buildings Gary couldn't help but touch as he passed, feeling the smooth surface and the surprisingly cool temperature. They continued on to a residential area full of single-family homes, all built out of volcanic rock and hand painted in various colours, reminiscent of a suburban neighbourhood like any he had seen above. How could this even be? How could no one know about it? Or did they?

"I'll be honest," Gary said. "I never imagined this level of civilisation could exist down here. It's hard to believe even while I'm looking at it, feeling it."

"As is our hope," the wolf answered. Then he gestured towards the front door to a house with one giant paw. Gary couldn't help but take notice of how intimidatingly long and sharp his nails looked to be. "Go. Enter."

Professor Smith looked at him curiously for a minute. *Why? What's inside?* The creature had a strange disinterest in him but he didn't seem particularly threatening. Of course, that could change if he didn't comply. He took solace in the fact that they didn't take the knife strapped to his thigh. Then, with a shrug, Gary pushed the door open. Inside, another wolf was sitting in a large chair, reading a book beside a fish lamp. He looked up when Gary entered. "Who are you?"

Gary felt nervous and intrigued. He smiled and waved and did his best not to show fear. "My tour guide brought me to you. I am Professor Gary Smith."

The wolf looked him up and down for a moment. Then he set his book on a nearby table and stood. "Little Gary Smith, a professor? My grandson. How on Earth did you find your way here?"

Gary stared at the wolf with wide eyes. He was awe-stricken. Not only did he find his grandfather, but he was alive, and he was a wolf. "I have your journals. I have spent my life trying to find this place, to find you. How?"

"These people are peaceful, majestic and wonderful Gary," his grandfather said. "Once I found them, I couldn't leave and now neither can you."

Gary felt suddenly nervous. He looked around at everything. "What do you mean? How did you become a wolf? What is happening here?"

"If I had left, people would have hounded me wanting to know what I found down here. They would be curious to see for themselves. They would come. They would take these magnificent people and use them, test them, do horrible things to them. A civilisation that has existed long before ours would be rendered extinct in no time flat. I needed my answer and I got it, just as you needed yours and got it, but it is not an answer that can be shared. These people must be protected."

"So, you stayed. You felt obligated. It makes

264

sense. What about the wolf part?"

"The wolves are immortal, grandson. I protected their life, so they protected mine. They can change you too, make you one of us, but they won't demand it. The choice is yours."

Gary thought for a moment. He looked out the window at the city beyond. He looked around this exquisitely designed house, at the handmade furnishings and decor. Then he looked back at the wolf standing before him, and he nodded. The gesture was returned. Then his grandfather, the wolf, led him out into the open area where the children played. The wolf howled and its call was answered by other howls in different pitches and octaves.

Gary looked around, wondering what was to happen, how he would achieve his immortality. He felt anxious but excited, until he saw all the wolves closing in from every side. Suddenly, he was nervous, sweating, afraid and confused. One of the children bit into his leg and he cried out in pain. A female sank her teeth into his shoulder. When he cried out, he looked to his grandfather. "What is this? Why? You said I could join you!"

The wolf that was once his grandfather nodded its thick head. "This is the way. You must be consumed. Then when a female has her next litter, your soul will belong to one of the newly born. When you're born as a wolf and you're part of the tribe, our safety is secured."

Gary's eyes widened with terror as a wolf bit through the meat of his side. Something bit into his back and he screamed. "I changed my mind. I don't want it anymore!" he cried out.

"We cannot let you leave here," his grandfather said, his voice laced with sadness. "For the safety of our culture and community, this is the only way. I'm sorry. You should not have come here."

Gary grimaced in pain and reached for the knife strapped to his thigh. Then all the wolves moved at once. Professor Smith was buried beneath the furry bodies. Teeth sank into every inch of his flesh, tearing and ripping at him, chewing and swallowing him, bit by bit as he screamed and cried, and begged for mercy that wouldn't come. Their numbers were so many that they made quick work of him, and soon there was nothing left but bones, bones that the wolves chewed on and sucked the marrow from, bones that would be gone soon as well.

Outside, Carlos waited and waited, his heart sinking as the hours passed and turned into days. The local authorities came to his boat to ask him to leave and questioned why he had been docked there so long. He lied of course, which he wondered if that was the right decision. Gary could have been trapped down there, pinned with his leg broken, in need of help. Eventually, Carlos was forced to leave. He knew that his friend wouldn't be angry with him, but he was angry with himself. He had wanted to help the Professor get past his addiction and only succeeded in helping him get consumed by it, and he had no idea just how literally. He couldn't let it become his own addiction though, to take him over and become his own holy grail. He had to allow himself to live. He apologised to Gary as he closed the book on that chapter of his life.

6 MONTHS LATER

As Gary suckled milk from his new mother's teat, he couldn't believe he was alive, again; that it had actually worked. The other wolves in his litter were arranged on either side of him, fighting for a drink as well. He couldn't let them though. He needed his strength. Gary was immortal so time no longer mattered, and he already knew how to take things slow. He had already proven himself adept at remaining dedicated to cause, a mission, a purpose. They should have spoken to him about the terms, given him time to mull it over. He didn't really believe there had ever been a choice, not really. The wolves had no intention of allowing him to continue on as a human, as a threat to their very existence, but even now, that's exactly what he was.

When the time was right, even if it was many years from now, he would leave this place. He would escape, and he would document it all. Then he would spend his eternity finding out what other magic the world had hidden away in its shadows. This one small brown wolf had a single answer, but he had a mind full of questions and the heart of an adventurer. Human or not, Professor Smith was far from down.

Belly full, he trotted away from the wolf that birthed him and padded his way into the centre of town where he could still remember his death, see flashes of it in his mind; the fear, the pain, every bit of it, or bite of it. Gary lay down there, craned his head back and howled.

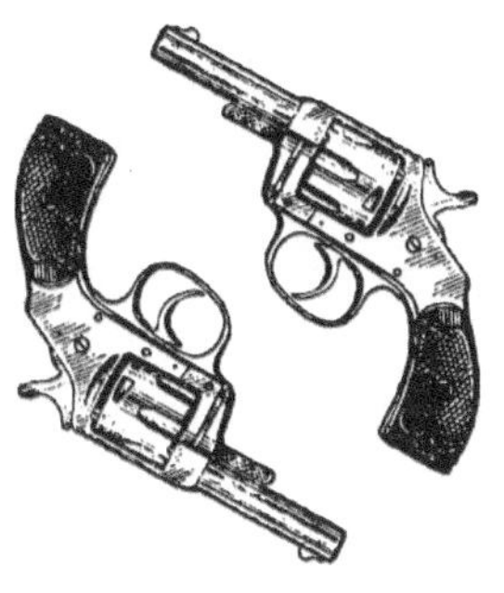

EUGENE ANGOVE AND THE QUEST FOR THE BLACK STONE

TIM MENDEES

MARCH 25TH, 1938. THE PERUVIAN RAINFOREST.

"Cripes, sir! That was deuce close." Hampton panted. "That fellow nearly took your head off with that shot?"

Eugene Angove took a nip of brandy from his dented hip-flask. "Funnily enough, Hampton... I believe that was the intention. I'm just glad that fellow is a worse shot than you are."

Hampton rolled his eyes. "This is no time for levity, sir. Those scoundrels will be here any minute."

Eugene carefully started to reload his revolver. "On the contrary, dear boy. If I'm going to be shot down like a blasted animal, I'm going out with brandy in my belly, a smile on my lips and my buttocks bared at the bounders!" With a *click,* he closed the barrel and peeked out from behind the pile of rubble they were using as cover. Through the temple door, he could see furtive figures with rifles moving into an attack formation.

"Do you think Sarah, Hank, and the Professor have found somewhere to hide, sir?"

"I bally well hope so, Hampton. They ran off down that passageway over there." Eugene raised a finger and pointed over to the right of the perfectly square chamber. "If they have any sense in those academic noggins of theirs, they will have found a decent hiding place by now." He weighed his revolver in his hand and pursed his lips in thought. "Here..." After an agonising minute of silence, he passed the Webley revolver to Hampton.

"What? ... I can't..." The terrified valet babbled.

"Take it, Hampton. I have a plan. You need to cover me." Eugene started rummaging in his pockets.

"But, sir... I can't shoot. You said it yourself, I couldn't hit a barn door."

"Doesn't matter," Eugene grumbled as he continued to search for his recently acquired cigarette lighter.

"What? ... Sir, what the Dickens do you mean, it doesn't matter?"

"Just fire in the direction of the door, man. If they have any sense of self-preservation, it'll keep them away long enough to plant this..." With a flourish, he produced a stick of dynamite from his leather satchel.

Poor Hampton nearly had a coronary. "Where the hell did you get that?"

Eugene grinned. "Remember that construction site we found those bearer chaps at?"

The butler was aghast. "You... you mean, you pinched it?"

"I prefer the term, *requisitioned*, but you could say that I pinched it, yes... Now stop gawping like a beached haddock and get ready to shoot... here they come!"

Scrambling over onto his knees, Hampton slowly raised his head to peek over the rubble...

Pew!

A bullet ricocheted off the stone debris, kicking up a plume of dust and narrowly missing Hampton's cranium.

"Keep your head down, man." Eugene scowled. "Just poke the gun over the top and fire blind. You don't have to hit them, just don't let them into the temple... Here, take this ammunition." Passing him a crumpled box of .455 cartridges, Eugene noted the blank expression on Hampton's face. "Pointy end to the front, old chap... pointy end to the front."

As the first shadowy figure appeared in the doorway, Eugene bellowed: "Now!" Hampton poked the barrel over the top of the debris and fired. The bullet *pinged* off the corner of the doorway. The cultist yelped and jumped out of the way. Eugene took advantage of the distraction and raced over to one of the large stone pillars in the centre of the room.

As soon as he was safely hidden, two of the attackers poked their guns around the entrance and started firing. The bullets from their Mauser rifles slammed into the stone floor, off the pillars, and into the walls. Everywhere except their bodies. As their clips emptied, Eugene gave Hampton the nod, and the butler poked his gun over and fired two shots. By sheer luck, one of the bullets caught one of the men in the shoulder. The man bellowed obscenities in a deep voice that sounded like custard being sucked down a plughole and dived away from the aperture.

"Good shot, Hampton!" Eugene chortled, as he raced over to the next pillar and took cover. As they waited for a return salvo, a voice cut through the dust and drifting gun-smoke...

"Hold fire!" The voice was deep and gravelly, with a distinctive American accent.

Eugene peeked around the pillar. The sun was shining directly behind a heavy-set man in a trilby hat and a rumpled pin-stripe suit casting his face in shadow. "Keep down," He hissed at Hampton. "Let's see what this ruffian has to say for himself."

"Hand over the book and the Professor and the rest of you can go free."

"That's a good one, sir. Tell us another one, my sides are splitting." Eugene snorted. He'd been in enough scrapes since leaving the army after the First World War to know grade-A manure when he heard it.

"You have my word, Mr Angove. All the Order wants is the book and that thieving academic... The rest of you are insignificant... Now, hand over the damn book!"

"What's so special about the book?" Eugene asked, playing for time as he prepared the fuse on the dynamite. He already knew what they wanted, but he was looking forward to seeing what nonsense the man fed him.

"It is a holy text, Mr Angove. My people want it returned. Wouldn't your Archbishop want his bible back if some bastard had stolen it?"

Eugene sniggered under his breath. "So... it has nothing to do with the parchment of human skin the Professor found in the binding then?" Wrapping his finger around the fuse and pulling sharply, he cut the fuse to a bare minimum. "You see, I thought you were after the black stone."

"Don't play games with me, you asshole!" The man raged. "Hand over the book or I'll tear you apart with my bare hands."

Saying nothing, Eugene caught Hampton's eye and mouthed the word, "now."

Hampton raised the gun and opened fire. Eugene danced around to the final support pillar. He was now less than a metre from the door.

The man in the suit sighed. "Very well. I gave you the choice... Take them, boys!"

As the bullets started flying, Eugene flicked the lighter into life and touched it to the fuse. With panic surging through his veins, he twisted and dropped the stick of explosive on the other side of the pillar. Counting down the seconds, he waited until the last possible moment before diving out of the way and rolling for his life into the far corner of the room.

Boom!

The sound of the dynamite exploding was swiftly dwarfed by the tremendous *crash* of falling masonry. The pillar was decimated, bringing the roof crashing down in front of the doorway. The sunlight was completely cut off as the entrance crumbled and piles of ancient stone filled the aperture.

Coughing and spluttering through the dust and smoke, Hampton took his flashlight from his pocket and switched it on. After scanning the room, he left cover and raced over to his dishevelled employer. "Sir? Are you alright, sir?" He panted as he wafted the dust away from Eugene's face with his bowler hat.

Eugene chuckled. "I'm quite alright, Hampton. A bit banged up but I've had worse hangovers if I'm honest... Help me up, won't you?"

Hampton took Eugene's hand and hauled with all of his might. Straightening up, he took one of the torches off the wall and lit it. Looking at the mess he had made, he grinned. "Well, that should keep them out for a while."

"Indeed, sir," Hampton replied drily. "But... how in all that is holy are we going to get out?"

Eugene patted Hampton on the back and held out his hand for his revolver. "Let's cross that bridge when we come to it, old chap. Revolver, if you would be so kind?"

Hampton hadn't realised that he still had it in a death-grip. His knuckles were white. "What? Oh, yes, here... take the frightful thing. Take the bullets, too."

"Thank you, Hampton. You didn't do too badly there. You hit one of the blighters."

"Did I?" Hampton beamed. "Jolly good."

"Right, let's go and find the Professor and Miss Sarah before they can get us into any more damned mess." Eugene then took the only remaining doorway and started walking slowly down a narrow tunnel. "I'm sure it will be plain sailing from now on."

After a moment, Hampton shook his head in resignation. "Very good, sir." He sighed. Hoping that his employer hadn't just jinxed them both...

MARCH 15TH, 1938. CHYCOOSE, CORNWALL.

The events that led to that festering temple in Peru were set in motion just over a week earlier. Eugene Angove, former Captain of the British Army, was enjoying several gin and tonics in the sunshine as he watched his beloved cricket team, Truro, thrash fellow CCL side, Newquay, in a charity match at Chycoose Manor. The crowd was rapt with attention as six after six was bowled. The Truro side was in rare form, much to the delight of the cu-

cumber-sandwich nibbling debutantes that swooned in the shade of the Pavilion. Even Hampton was enjoying himself. It seemed that nothing could spoil that mood... until the club valet shoved a note into Hampton's gloved hand.

Hampton's brow creased as he inspected the communication. The small envelope had the word 'urgent' scrawled across the front in thick black ink and was made of heavy, expensive paper. Turning it over, a sensation like a spider with frozen feet skittering down his spine made him shudder. It was sealed with crimson wax and embossed with a star-shaped design. Hampton had received a couple of similar missives over the years... they never ended well. Swallowing hard, he slipped the letter into his pocket and scanned the crowd for his master.

Eugene was over on the other side of the pavilion engaged in conversation with a striking young woman. *This isn't going to go down well.* Hampton thought as he started to thread himself through the crowd. He knew all the signs and could tell, even from that distance, that his employer was turning on the charm in an attempt to woo his companion. If Hampton had a shiny shilling for every time he'd seen his master try to unsuccessfully lure an attractive female to his hotel suite... he wouldn't have needed a job, he'd be loaded.

Taking a deep breath, Hampton stepped up behind Eugene and gently tapped him on the shoulder before whispering in his ear. "Excuse me, sir. You have an urgent communique."

276

"Not now, Hampton." Eugene barked drunkenly. "Can't you see, I'm busy. I was just telling Lady... um." He thought for a second. "Josephine, here about my time out East."

The bored-looking woman smiled unconvincingly.

"I'm sorry, sir... but, this can't wait. It's from *them*, sir." Hampton said gravely.

"*Them?* Who in blue blazes are you talking about, man?"

"You know, sir? *Them.* Your, ahem... *friends* from London."

Eugene swayed slightly as he fixed Hampton with a confused stare. "Hampton... you either stop being so bloody cryptic and spit it out or I'll have you scrubbing the latrines when we get back home."

Hampton sighed once again, retrieved the letter from his pocket, and jabbed a finger at the seal. Finally, the penny dropped.

Eugene's face darkened. All the gin-induced jollity evaporated in an instant. "I'm very sorry, Lady Josephine, but you'll have to excuse me a..." As he turned, he noticed that she had already scuttled away while he had been distracted. "Bugger!" He spat before rounding on his valet. "Dash it all, Hampton. She was that close to giving me her suite number." He held his tobacco-stained thumb and forefinger an inch apart.

Swallowing his scepticism, Hampton said sombrely: "I'm sure she was, sir... I'm very sorry, but..."

"I know. I know. It's not your fault. Very well,

open it up and read it for me, won't you? I'm far too drunk to focus."

"Very well, sir." Hampton purred deferentially, breaking the seal and taking out the note. "Do you think we should go somewhere private, sir?"

"Get on with it, man."

Hampton cleared his throat. "*Dear, Eugene. The brotherhood requires your attendance on a matter of utmost urgency. Meet me in the Rat and Raven public house in Hollowhills immediately. I have a car waiting for you outside.* It's signed with an S, sir. I assume that's Step..."

"Stephenson." Eugene spat. Finishing Hampton's sentence. "That blasted fellow just won't take *sod off* as an answer."

"Are you going to attend him, sir?"

Eugene thought for a minute before exhaling and puffing out his bewhiskered cheeks. "I'd better, I suppose... Damn the fellow!"

"Very well, sir. Should I collect our things from the cloakroom and meet you out the front, sir?"

Eugene didn't reply. His eye had been drawn by an attractive maid with a tray of drinks.

"Sir?" Hampton turned just in time to see Eugene take a flute of champagne from the tray and start engaging the maid in conversation. "Sir!" He shouted over the babble of conversation. "I thought we were leaving?"

Eugene smiled. "No rush, Hampton... no rush."

Hampton rolled his eyes before heading to the cloak-room. "Very good, sir."

It was dark by the time the Rolls Royce Silver Ghost crunched into the gravel car park next to the Rat and Raven. Hampton's nerves were jangling and Eugene Angove was so drunk that he'd been singing *The Good Ship Venus* for the entire journey. Mr Stephenson wasn't going to be happy. Their host was not known for his good humour at the best of times. After being kept waiting all afternoon, he would be positively belligerent.

Bringing the car to a halt in the shade of a large oak, the grizzled driver climbed out of the car and opened the door for his passengers. "Out." He grunted and doffed his peaked cap. This was only the second word that he had spoken since they stumbled out of the cricket pavilion; the other being, "In." Hampton slid out and assisted his master so he didn't fall flat on his face.

The jovial strains of W*e're Off to See the Wizard* being played on a scratchy gramophone record tumbled into the night on a cloud of cigarette smoke as Hampton opened the doors to let Eugene inside. The Rat and Raven was a dingy establishment almost entirely populated by grubby miners and bewhiskered farmers; so to say that the pair stuck out like a sore thumb would be a gross understatement. A hush fell over the tables as they took in Eugene and Hampton in their cricket-day formals. Hampton shuffled his feet nervously. Eugene flashed them all a big boozy grin.

"Good evening, chaps!" Eugene slurred. "I don't suppose you have seen a chap in a Homburg hat with a face like a smacked arse, have you?"

A smattering of sniggers accompanied all heads turning towards a table in a dimly lit corner of the bar. Hampton screwed his toes into his shoes and prayed that the floor would open up and swallow him.

"Ah, there you are, Stephenson!" Eugene waved, before turning to Hampton. "Could you get me a large Scotch, dear chap? I think I'm going to need it."

"Don't you think you've had enough, sir?"

Eugene scratched his chin thoughtfully. "Perhaps, you're right, Hampton. What would I do without you? ... Better make it another gin. I don't want to start mixing spirits now, do I?"

Leaving Hampton with his mouth wide open in disbelief, Eugene weaved across the room and plonked himself in a rickety chair opposite Stephenson. "Algernon, my dear fellow. I do hope I have not kept you waiting?" Eugene grinned, showing off the gap between his front two teeth.

Algernon Stephenson puffed cigar smoke into the air. "Not at all. I figured that you would try to irritate me, so I went for a hot bath and had a nice meal."

Eugene's smile dropped. Checkmate. "Right, so what do you want, Stephenson. I thought we were all square after the last *incident*. I know you saved my bacon in the Somme but I think we are more than even by now."

"Very true. We are." Stephenson nodded after a sip of his dark ale. "I come to you for a favour. I wouldn't have troubled you if it weren't of the utmost importance."

"I assume this is Brotherhood business?"

"It is." Stephenson offered Eugene a cigar, which he readily took.

"Then why don't you send one of your underlings? Why come and ruin my blessed cricket?"

Stephenson leaned forward and offered Eugene his lighter. "In case it has escaped your debauched attention, there is a bit of *trouble* brewing in Germany. All of our *underlings*, as you put it, are busy trying to fox the SS paranormal division. Besides, this requires a man of your, ahem, *talents*."

"*Talents*? What the devil do you mean, *talents*?"

"I mean..." Stephenson puffed smoke into Eugene's face. "I need someone who is used to inhospitable climates, and is somewhat *light-fingered*."

Eugene nearly choked on his Cuban. "What? ... I'll have you know, my business is wholly legitimate! I will not have you defame me in this manner!"

"Calm down, dear boy. I'm sure that the King's Customs and Excise, not to mention several of the world's police forces, don't need to know how you *acquired* some of your most sought after artefacts" Stephenson chuckled. After leaving the army after the war, Eugene became an adventurer and dealer in priceless artefacts. On paper it was a legitimate antique dealership... off-paper, however, Eugene could have been called a grave robber or tomb raider. He was known to swipe treasures out from under the noses of the world's most revered museums and institutions, then flog them at inflated prices to private collectors. "Look, here comes Hampton with your libation. Take a mouthful before you expire."

Hampton passed Eugene his drink and doffed his hat to Stephenson.

"Leave us, would you, Hampton? Go and get a drink on my tab. I fear this exchange is going to become somewhat heated." Stephenson smiled maliciously.

Hampton nodded, thanked the Lord, and scurried back to the bar. Never before had a light ale tasted so good.

Eugene drained half of his gin in one gulp, then sucked enthusiastically on his cigar. "You're a despicable bastard, Stephenson, you know that?"

"It has been mentioned on a couple of occasions, yes. It's a family trait, so I'm told. In any case, you will be very well paid for your efforts."

"Fine..." Eugene sighed after composing himself. "What do you want me to do?"

"A few days ago, Mr MacKinnon was contacted by this professor chap from the Miskatonic University in Arkham, Massachusetts. He was recently put in charge of the Innsmouth Collection, and..."

Eugene cut him off. "The what?"

"You must remember the Innsmouth raid back in the twenties? I told you about it several times."

"Oh, that weird little town with the mad fish cult?"

"The Esoteric Order of Dagon... yes." Stephenson's face darkened. "The Brotherhood has had *dealings* with them in the past so the FBI liaised with us on the raid and were obliged to keep us in the loop."

"Got you. Do continue."

"Anyway, the Innsmouth Collection was a haul of forbidden texts, strange jewellery and blasphemous idols. The jewellery and idols went to the Smithsonian while the books went to the Miskatonic. Professor Dudley was put in charge of the volumes in the restricted section of the library. While cleaning up a copy of the Livre d'Eibon from the Innsmouth Collection, he discovered a rolled parchment hidden in the bindings. He proceeded to fish it out using a hat-pin he borrowed from one of the librarians. Once unfurled, it appeared to contain what looked to be a map and a page of text in an ancient dialect. Dudley took the parchment to one of his colleagues, an old chap named Rice, who took one look at the thing and told him to contact us. You see, Rice, along with two colleagues named Armitage and Morgan, had endured certain *dealings* with things outside of human comprehension. Rice recognised some of the names and phrases mentioned in the passage almost immediately. Furthermore, the map appeared to show the resting place of an object of great power... the black stone of N'kai."

"As interesting as all this is, can you just get to the point?"

"The point, Eugene, is that after some research by our team at Cambridge, we have ascertained that the black stone is something that mustn't fall into the wrong hands... least of all those bounders in Berlin. We need you to accompany Dudley to Peru and retrieve the stone."

"That sounds easy enough." Eugene smiled. His natural arrogance bubbling to the surface. "Though, I don't understand why you need me. This sounds like the sort of thing any old adventurer could do."

Stephenson pursed his lips. "I wish that were the case, old friend. Unfortunately, it seems that the young Professor Dudley can't keep his trap shut. There have been six attempts on his life in the last week. Somebody wants that map... and we need to stop them getting it."

Eugene finished his drink and wiped his pencil moustache with his thumb and forefinger. "Oh, I do hate it when you use the royal we, Stephenson. It always means that I'm soon to be up to my ears in manure." He paused for a second. "Fine... How do I start?"

Stephenson drained his glass and stood up, pulling his greatcoat over his shoulders. "I have a plane chartered at RAF St Mawgan tomorrow evening that will take you to Massachusetts, where you will meet Professor Dudley and his team. I will send my car to pick you up. I suggest you call it a night and go sleep off the booze. It'll be a long flight and you will need your wits about you."

Eugene sighed and watched Stephenson begin to walk away.

"One more thing," Stephenson said, pausing in his exit. "If you handle the map, make sure you wash your hands before you eat."

"Why?"

Stephenson grinned ghoulishly. "Because dear chap. It is written on human skin."

Eugene shook his head. "Why is it always *human* skin with these occult weirdos? Why not rabbit or badger?" His pickled brain tried to put all of the information in order. It was a Herculean task, considering all the *refreshments* he had imbibed. As he sat and pondered, he watched Stephenson pay his bar tab and hand Hampton another envelope. Their itinerary, presumably.

Stephenson and Eugene had a strange relationship. They had been close friends and comrades in the great war, but this had soured after Stephenson joined the family business, so to speak. Despite having seen and heard things to the contrary, Eugene couldn't help thinking that the Brotherhood of Tamesis were a bunch of cranks.

Looking down at his hand, he realised he was still holding Stephenson's lighter. A mischievous glint appeared in his bloodshot eyes. He may have been bullied into taking the job, but there was one thing Stephenson couldn't make him do. Standing upright, he caught the attention of the landlord. "A large Scotch, if you please! And whatever my foot-man desires!”

MARCH 17TH, 1938. NEWBURYPORT, MASSACHUSETTS.

Vomiting up a hangover at thirty-thousand feet is an experience best avoided. Eugene Angove could attest to this statement by the time his plane touched down on the runway at Plum Island airport. Each stop for refuelling had been a nightmare, as Eugene had insisted on departing the plane each time in an unsuccessful search for a full English breakfast. By the time they landed, Eugene was like a bear with a sore backside.

“Blast that fellow, Stephenson. I can’t believe he’s found somewhere to send us that is wetter than England.” Eugene looked up at the glowering skies and shook his head. “What do we do now, Hampton? We appear to be in the middle of sodding nowhere.”

“According to our itinerary, we should have a hire car parked out front. A red 1937 Hudson Ter-raplane, apparently.” Hampton wrinkled his nose at this choice. He had been hoping to get behind the wheel of something a bit classier. A Cadillac, for ex-ample. “Then, we are to drive into Newburyport and meet Professor Dudley in the cafe across the street from the public library. Perhaps you will finally get your full English, sir.”

286

"I doubt it, Hampton. Though, you'd hope that a chap could get a decent breakfast in a place called New England, wouldn't you?"

Hampton nodded and rolled his eyes. "Indeed, sir. Shall we find this car and get out of the rain?"

"Lead the way, my good man. I have absolutely no idea what a Hudson Terraplane is. It sounds more like a knackered Spitfire than a car to me."

Hampton chuckled to himself as he led the way across the concourse towards the exit. The stalwart butler had a keen interest in motor vehicles, and his master's stunning lack of knowledge on the subject always made him smile. Eugene could shoot, hunt, ski, rock-climb, you name it, but the one thing he couldn't do was drive. Considering he was usually three-sheets-to-the-wind by lunchtime, this was probably a good thing.

Scanning the gravel car park, Hampton's heart sank a little when he spotted their car. Not only wasn't it a flashy model, but it was also caked in mud and had a number of dents in its bodywork. If the engine worked, it would be a miracle. "Stephenson has spared no expense, it seems." He muttered bitterly to himself as he opened the drivers-side door and saw that the keys were in the ignition and that there was a road map on the passenger seat with Eugene's name scrawled on the cover in smudged ink.

"I believe this is ours, sir."

Eugene sighed as Hampton loaded their luggage into the back seat. "Cheap bastard... I'm glad I pinched his lighter now. Have you seen it, Hampton?

The blessed thing is solid silver... must be worth a few bob!"

Slamming the rear door shut, Hampton moved to the passenger door and opened it for Eugene. "Here we go, sir. Newburyport isn't that far. We should be there in no time."

"Capital!" Eugene slid into his seat and scowled at the road map. "The sooner we find this blasted academic and get this over with, the better."

Surprisingly, considering the condition of the vehicle, the engine promptly roared into life. After a moment of figuring out which side of the road he should be driving on, Hampton steered them towards the exit.

"Sir, could you check the map, please? There doesn't seem to be a signpost."

"Certainly." Eugene started to unfold the map and squint at the lines and squiggles. "Aha!" He exclaimed after a moment of rustling and grumbling. "Here's the map, and here is Newburyport. I believe we turn right onto the Plum Island Turnpike. If we are going the right way, we will pass a turning for Newbury on Ocean Drive."

Hampton thanked Eugene and took a left at the exit. The road snaked through beautiful scenery on the bank of the Merrimack River. Hampton cracked the window to let some fresh air in and dampen the smell of old alcohol seeping from Eugene's pores.

"This turning up here should be Ocean Drive." Eugene dumped the map in the back seat and leaned forward to get a look. "It's looking good, Hampton...

Look out!”

As Eugene bellowed and grabbed the wheel, wrenching it to the left, a black Ford 7W shot out of Ocean Drive and attempted to ram them off the road. As they avoided impact and brought the car screeching to a halt. The Ford pulled a sharp U-Turn and came to a stop approximately fifty yards behind them.

“Bloody hell!” Hampton yelled in a mixture of shock and anger. “What does that bloody idiot think he’s doing? He could have killed us.” The normally unflappable manservant was one of those chaps born with a long fuse. When it burned down, however... “Excuse me, sir. Could you hold my bowler for a moment while I go and slap some sense into that damn ninnyhammer?”

Eugene slid the window open and peered at the black vehicle down the road. He sat in silence for a few moments, watching. The engine was still running, and he could hear it being revved. “I don’t think that would be wise, Hampton.”

“Nonsense, sir.” His butler replied as he rolled up his sleeves. “I was my regiment’s boxing champion during the war. I’ll give that fopdoodle a damn good thrashing.”

“No... you don’t understand, Hampton. I think you should put your foot down.”

“But, sir! The damn fellow needs to be taught some road manners! Why won’t you let me go and straighten him out?”

Eugene sighed. “Because, A, there are more

than a couple of chaps in that car, and, B... because one of them has just poked the barrel of what looks like a Thompson submachine gun out of the passenger window."

"What?"

"Drive, man!"

Smoke belched from the tyres of the black Ford as it came screeching towards them. Hampton slammed his boot to the deck and jammed the Hudson into gear. As they pulled away, the passenger of the Ford opened fire. A stream of hot lead raked the curved rear door, peppering the bodywork and smashing the rear window. Gritting his teeth, Hampton started to weave the car in an attempt to avoid the bullets.

Eugene fumbled in his pocket for his trusty revolver, turned over in his seat and returned fire through the shattered window, using the headrest to steady his aim. The shot went wide. "Blast! I can't get a decent shot with you snaking about the road."

"Would you rather I gave them a clear target?"

Eugene didn't reply, he just fired a couple of more rounds in anger at the situation.

"Who the devil do you think they are, sir? What do they want?" Hampton asked as he swung the car around a sweeping bend.

"I would hazard a guess that they are the same blackguards that have tried to off Professor Dudley; and I don't think they are here to say *welcome to America*, do you? Now stop asking questions and concentrate on the road."

290

Despite Hampton's heavy-footed driving, the Ford was gaining on them at an alarming rate. The gunman reloaded the Tommy-gun and opened fire again. They were sitting ducks. They would have both been goners had luck not played its hand. As the Ford came within ramming distance of the rear bumper, the gunman leaned out of the window to get a better shot. He was a bulky fellow in a wide-brimmed hat. The only feature of his face that Eugene could see was a wide, jagged-toothed grin. As he prepared to fire, Hampton weaved sharply to avoid a pot-hole. The Ford didn't see it and its front left tyre slammed into it, jolting the car. The gunman bellowed in fury as he slammed his head against the top of the open window and fumbled the Tommy-gun. It clattered to the road and bounced off into some bushes.

"Huzzah!" Eugene exclaimed. "Nice driving, old boy! ... Now, level off and let me see if I can't let some air out of this cad's tyres."

Hampton did as instructed and focused on keeping the car level as Eugene positioned himself to fire. As his finger squeezed the trigger, the Ford collided with the rear bumper in a shower of sparks and a screech of metal. The Hudson lurched and bucked. Eugene's shot slammed into the rear seat. The jolt of the impact slammed his elbow into the top of the seat, sending the revolver flying out of his hand and into the scrunched up map in the foot-well.

"Buggeration!" Eugene spat, as he tried to fish his revolver out from under his seat.

"Um... sir?" Hampton asked. "There appears to be a fork in the road ahead... which way am I going?"

Leaving his revolver for the moment, Eugene snatched up the map. The Ford was trying to edge alongside. It seemingly intended to run them off the road. As he tried to find the right part of the map, Eugene looked ahead and saw what the problem was. A sharp V of grass and trees suddenly loomed in the centre of the windscreen. To make matters worse, amongst the trees, with a pristine white gate, was a colonial-style home.

"Left!" Eugene shouted finally.

Hampton lined the car up for the left of the fork.

Just as they neared the tip of the verge, Eugene suddenly realised that he was looking at the wrong. Fork. "Shit! I meant right!" He grabbed the wheel and slammed the car to the right. The Hudson mounted the grass verge, sideswiping a danger sign and taking out a chunk of hedge and picket fence as it jumped and bounced onto the other road. They were lucky to be alive.

The much heavier Ford, however, wasn't so lucky. As it followed the other car onto the grass, it went wide, obliterating the gate and ploughing into the garden of the house. Unable to stop on the slick grass, the Ford hurtled between some trees and onto Water Street. Unfortunately for them, as it landed and careered forwards, its front tyres mounted the curb on the other side of the road. There was a loud *bang* as one of the tyres exploded. Suddenly the car was airborne as the bank fell away below it and with an almighty *splash,* it went nose-first into the Merrimack River.

Hampton brought the Hudson to a stop as he stared at the rear end of the black Ford sinking into the water. "Well, that'll teach the scoundrels, sir."

"Indeed it will, Hampton." He paused and looked at the commotion brewing by the house in the rear-view mirror. "I'd keep going if I were you, Hampton. I don't think we should be here when the owner of that house gets here. The poor chap looks fit to explode!"

Hampton looked, then nodded. "Agreed." Putting his foot to the floor once again. Hampton drove them safely into Newburyport.

The remainder of that fateful day went far smoother than the ride to town. Hampton parked the battered Hudson in a secluded corner of the library parking lot while Eugene retrieved his revolver from under the seat, reloaded it, and slipped it into his inside pocket. He was pretty sure they hadn't been followed after disposing of their attackers, but it was better to be safe than sorry.

By now, the dark rain-clouds had receded, and the sun was shining down on the quaint high street. Hampton had been praying that their rendezvous point wasn't one of those posh French-style affairs so his heart leapt a little when he spotted the sign for Bob's Cafe, it looked like a British greasy spoon.

His master would be pleased. Perhaps his quest for an English breakfast would finally be at an end? For Hampton's part. He would just be happy if he could get a decent pot of tea.

The day continued to improve when Eugene bid the proprietor, Bob, a good day and was replied to in flat Yorkshire vowels. It seemed they had found a fellow countryman. After a brief chat about *old Blighty*, Bob gave them a pot of hot sweet tea and went to prepare their breakfasts.

Aside from themselves, the cafe was empty apart from a young woman with a fashionable black Marcel hairdo and a scarlet neck-scarf pecking daintily at a cheese scone. Though he was pretty sure she wasn't hostile, Hampton made sure they were well out of earshot before engaging Eugene in conversation about their recent brush with death. Eugene was pensive. Despite his bluster and pretensions that it hadn't shaken him, it was obvious that something was bothering him about the whole situation. *Somebody* had told *them* that they were coming and obviously had access to their itinerary.

"You know, Hampton. I've been thinking. Maybe we should find our own way to Peru?"

"But, Mr Stevenson has flights planned out for us."

"Yes, and I'd wager that whoever knew about our arrival also knows about our departure. This operation has more blasted leaks than a cullender."

"That's true enough, sir. What did you have in mind?"

294

"I have more than enough cash on me to charter our own flights. I propose we drive down to Boston and get a flight from there... Not a word to our new *colleagues*. Let's keep this between ourselves. Trust nobody, especially this Dudley chap. Whether intentional or not, I'm pretty sure he is the source of our leak. It would be best if he knows nothing until it happens. Need to know basis, old chap."

Hampton nodded sombrely. It was rare for Eugene to talk so seriously. It was so rare that it had chilled his blood.

"Oh, look!" Eugene exclaimed joyfully, breaking the tension. "Here comes our breakfast!"

The portly cafe owner placed the gargantuan repasts in front of them and grinned. He knew he had just made the day for a couple of weary Englishmen. As soon as he walked away, Eugene attacked his feast with gusto. This was just what he had been craving. Yorkshire Bob was his new hero.

As soon as Eugene had dabbed up the remnants of his runny egg yolk with the final crust of fried bread, the bell above the door jangled. All heads turned as a furtive young man in a long dark coat, a pair of dark glasses and a fedora pulled down low entered the cafe flanked by two spotty youths in ill-fitting suits. The trio looked like they had just raided the local fancy dress shop.

"Professor Dudley, I presume." Eugene sniggered. "The clot couldn't be any more conspicuous if he was wearing a sandwich board proclaiming, 'Don't look at me, I'm undercover.'"

The bespectacled man caught Hampton's eye and nodded.

"For God's sake, man!" Eugene guffawed. "Come over here and stop making a spectacle of yourself."

Professor Dudley shuffled over to the table and introduced himself and his *team*. Eugene was nonplussed. When he had heard the word team, he had been expecting more than two young undergrads from the archaeology department. Dudley explained that the two men were the only people he trusted and that the plan was to hire some locals when they touched down in Peru. Eugene shook his head and sighed. This just kept getting better and better.

"There is one more member of the team, however... She should be here already."

"I'm right here, Prof." The woman from the window table had slinked up behind the two students and smiled at Eugene and Hampton. Her voice was low and husky, like she had been gargling neat bourbon and chain-smoking cigars. Along with the neck-scarf, she was wearing a figure-hugging pencil skirt and stockings. Eugene's eyes nearly popped out of his skull.

Professor Dudley introduced her as Sarah Green, a leading light of the Miskatonic anthropology department. She was going along to help with translations from the Book of Eibon, a text she had studied for many years along with other tomes on the *forbidden* list. It was clear from the way the two interacted that their relationship was more than simply professional. A realisation that took the wind out of Eugene's sails. For all his faults, he was never the sort of fellow that would "sugar another man's rhubarb." He may have been a rascal, but he wasn't a cad.

Once the introductions had been concluded, the group left the cafe. The two students, Ralph and Hank, had loaned the use of a university bus from the archaeology department. There were just enough free seats for the party, the rest had been stuffed with tents, shovels and other assorted expeditionary paraphernalia. Hampton transferred their luggage to the bus and left Mr Stephenson a scathing note tucked under the wiper. Eugene had used some rather colourful language.

As they climbed aboard, Eugene put Hank's nose out of joint by insisting that Hampton drive and he navigated. The Miskatonic team shrugged this behaviour off as pushy Brits. None of them guessed that they were up to anything... until they drove the wrong way out of town.

MARCH 25TH, 1938. THE PERUVIAN RAINFOREST.

Hampton's sleep had been invaded by increasingly bizarre dreams the closer the party had got to the temple. The journey had been surprisingly painless since flying out of Boston. Their pilot, a gruff Texan named Logan, had expertly navigated their journey to Peru, carefully avoiding the refuelling spots on the itinerary. Hampton had listened to Sarah and Dudley waffle on about the Book of Eibon and the Great Old Ones, while Eugene drank beer and played cards with Hank and Ralph.

Once they had touched down in Puerto Maldonado not far from the Bolivian border, Professor Dudley had set out trying to find a team of locals to accompany them on their quest. Unfortunately, the buttoned-up academic had failed miserably. Over coffee, Eugene had enquired as to exactly what he had said to the locals. It turned out that as soon as he'd mentioned the name of the deity that the temple was set up to worship, the locals had run a mile. It seemed that the name, Tsathoggua, instilled dread in the Peruvian populace.

Cursing Dudley's stupidity, Eugene had asked Sarah for a deity that *didn't* incite fear. Once they had refuelled with the local black bean, he had taken a wad of cash from Hampton, headed over to a nearby construction site and hired a group of stout-looking men to join them on a quest to the temple of Urcuchillay. It seemed that the llama god was in good favour. He would deal with their displeasure when they found the temple of Tsathoggua.

Dreams of a strange subterranean world lit with an eerie red glow had plagued not just Hampton but the whole expedition as they had followed the Rio Madre De Dios deeper into the rainforest. At a point indicated on the parchment of skin, they had ventured away from the river, picking up an ancient trail marked by sinister batrachian milestones. Eugene had somehow managed to steer the locals away from them before they could twig his deception. It seemed that with each passing effigy, the dreams would become more intense. Many of the team cried out in the night as they struggled against nightmare creatures in that hellish underworld that Sarah and Dudley had excitedly called N'kai.

Coming to in a cold sweat, Hampton sat upright on his bedroll. There was one hell of a commotion outside the tent. He rolled over to rouse Eugene, and was shocked to find that he'd already risen. Straining his ears as he hurriedly threw on his clothes, Hampton tried to hear what was going on. From what he could ascertain, it seemed that the natives had discovered their deception. They were currently raising Cain at Professor Dudley.

Poking his head out of the tent, he took in the scene. Dudley, Hank, and Ralph were doing their level best in broken Portuguese to calm the fellows down. It seemed that two of the bearers had awoken from awful dreams of a toad-like monstrosity and, after some discussion, had decided to scout the mile or so left to go to the temple. Less than a quarter of a mile out from camp, they had happened upon one of the milestones. The tarnished penny had dropped, and they had hurried back and confronted Professor Dudley.

Not seeing Eugene, he slipped out of the tent and looked around. His master was sitting over by the camp-fire scribbling in a notebook while Sarah enthused about some kind of discovery. She had the skin parchment in one hand and the Book of Eibon in the other and was waving her arms around like a demented windmill. She was immaculately coiffured despite the humidity and was adorned with her omnipresent neck scarf.

Shuffling over, he stopped at Eugene's shoulder. "Morning, sir, Miss Sarah. What the devil is going on?"

"Ah, what-ho, Hampton, my good man." Eugene grinned. From the ruddiness of his cheeks, he'd started on the booze early that morning. "Sarah here has cracked the gobbledygook on that vile bit of skin and as Dudley is busy with the mutiny over there, she has roped me in as her assistant."

Sarah frowned at Hampton. "Pay attention Eugene, this passage is crucial." She then spelt out a series of words that sounded more like rubbish than the original text. When she was finished, she turned to Hampton.

"It's an incantation, you see. It was written in Hyperborean, I have just translated it to the original Aklo."

Hampton looked at her like she had just dropped off the moon.

"Aklo is the language of the Great Old Ones. I think this incantation was written by a priest of Tsathoggua!"

"Incantation?"

"To channel the power of the black stone! To harness the energy of N'kai!"

Before Hampton could enquire as to why anyone would want to do that, all talk was silenced by the *crack* of a gunshot.

Sarah screamed as Ralph's head exploded in a mist of blood and grey matter. Eugene leapt to his feet, drawing his revolver. "Take cover!" He boomed as more shots rang out in the morning air. Professor Dudley and Hank scrambled back towards Eugene's position, covering their heads with their hands and ducking. Eugene crouched behind a large tree, taking Hampton with him. Peeking around the trunk, he addressed the natives. "Grab the rifles!" The Miskatonic team had brought five Winchester rifles that had seen better days to ward off animals.

The group of Peruvians had seen and heard enough. As a unit, they grabbed their packs and some rations and took off into the rainforest. This had been the final straw. Eugene, Hampton and the three academics were alone.

"I think those ruffians from America have caught up with us, sir!" Hampton shouted over the roar of the guns.

"I don't understand it... I simply don't understand it!" Eugene was furious. His face turning the colour of a baboon's rump. "How could they know we were here? We can't have been followed."

"Could it be that pilot chap, Logan?"

"I seriously doubt it, Hampton. I promised him Stephenson's lighter upon our return to the airfield. That and a wedge of cash is enough to guarantee his silence, I reckon. No... the only explanation is that they have seen the map."

"As distressing as this is, sir. I think we should figure a way out of here before launching our investigations on the matter."

"Well put, Hampton." Eugene thought for a moment. "Wait until they reload and I'll lay down some cover fire, then, Hampton, you and Hank run over to the rifles, take cover behind those trees over there and lay down fire when they reload again and we will come after you. Then we will race to the temple. We should be able to find some shelter there."

Nobody was particularly happy with this plan, but what choice did they have? When the firing stopped, Eugene darted from cover and started shooting in the direction of the gun-smoke. A pained *yelp* announced that he had scored a fluke hit. This made him smile. While he had the attackers on the back-foot, Hampton and Hank put their part of the plan into action.

Soon, the party was running for their lives down the overgrown trail, dodging branches and vaulting logs. From the commotion behind them. The attackers were in hot pursuit. Luck was smiling down favourably upon them as they avoided being cut down by flying lead, and soon, they were at the temple of Tsathoggua...

After Eugene's splendid demolition work on the temple entrance, he and Hampton descended deeper into the temple in search of Professor Dudley, Sara, and Hank. The flickering light from Eugene's torch made the roughly hewn walls come alive with dancing shadows. Hampton marvelled at the construction. It seemed to be carved out of solid rock which couldn't surely be the case. They were deep into the Amazon basin, after all. It had to be made of blocks but he was dashed if he could find any joins.

Once they had descended a certain distance, the plain stone walls suddenly became covered in strange carvings. It seemed to depict the history of some long-forgotten land. The most recent designs showed some kind of war. A monstrous toad with bat ears, sloth-like features and colossal wings was shown being forced into some kind of pit that was then sealed by a huge stone with an oddly warped star carved on it. Eugene's eyebrow raised as something struck him. Stephenson's lighter had the same design engraved on one side and a map of the rivers of London on the other.

Soon, the tunnel opened into a domed chamber with four horrific statues of the toad creature placed in a square in the centre. In the middle of these was some kind of font. Over to the far side was a door. Sarah and the Professor were examining the carvings on it while Hank sat and sobbed into a handkerchief. Ralf had been his best friend since they were boys. Eugene approached him and offered his deepest sympathies, declaring that not only had the world lost a fine man but a topping card player to boot.

"These figures here, the furry looking ones,"

Dudley said to Sarah. "What does the book call them, Voormi?"

"Yes, Professor. They were the earliest known worshippers of Tsathoggua. It is believed that they live on in the red caverns of N'kai."

"What do you think they are doing here?" Dudley pointed to a central carving.

"It appears that they are bleeding themselves into that font over there. It seems that is the way to open the door." Sarah took a small pocket-knife from her belt. "So, who's going to give it a try?" As she looked from face to face, nobody answered. "Anyone? I'm not doing it. I can't stand the sight of my own blood."

Finally, Hank sniffed. "I'll do it." The distraught young man snatched the blade and marched over to the font. "How much do we need?"

Sarah shrugged. "Just a slash across the palm should do it."

Taking a deep breath, Hank ran the blade across his skin, then clenched his fist and let his blood splash into the font.

For a second, nothing happened. Then the room started to rumble as a series of ancient pulleys and cogs turned to slide the doors slowly apart.

"It works!" Dudley whooped.

Boom!

Their elation was short-lived as a distant explosion announced that their pursuers had foregone delicacy and had decided to blast their way in.

"Quick, through the door," Eugene instructed.

"Come on, Hank!"

As the others rushed into the chamber beyond, Hank began to scream. It was deep and primal, borne of excruciating pain. Eugene watched as a boiling mass of black protoplasm rose up Hank's arm, liquidising his flesh and bone as it devoured him.

"The black stone!" Dudley yelled in joy as he raced towards a raised dais in front of a massive stone representation of Tsathoggua.

Eugene stumbled into the chamber, his mind in turmoil. Something was nagging at his brain. Spotting a brazier, he touched his torch to it and set it alight. Following Sarah and Dudley to the dais, he fingered the handle of his revolver in his pocket. "Did you two know that was going to happen?" He demanded. His blood boiling.

Dudley turned, his face ashen and eyes full of surprise. "N... no. I... I had no idea."

As Eugene went to round on Sarah, she snatched a lump of fallen masonry from the floor and used it to crack the Professor's skull open like a geode. As he fell to the floor, limp and lifeless, she reached into her ample cleavage and produced a loaded Derringer and pointed it at Eugene before he could draw his own weapon.

"Hands up, Limey." She sneered. Her voice revealing a hitherto hidden gurgle. "Toss the revolver in the corner."

Eugene, a sitting duck, did as he was told.

As she stepped forward, preparing to pistol-whip him, Hampton lunged out of the shadows and gripped her in a bear hug.

"The skin, Hampton!" Eugene cried. "Toss it into the fire."

Hampton was hesitant, it would mean letting her go. After thinking for a second. He wheeled her around and shoved her as hard as he could to the opposite side of the room. Next, he snatched the Book of Eibon from the late Professor's hand and took out the skin. As Eugene scrambled for his gun, he tossed it into the fire, where it started to *sizzle* and shrink.

Sarah roared in anger as she regained her footing. Her scarf had worked loose, revealing three slits on each side of her neck that opened and closed as she breathed. "Foolish human scum!" She screamed as she pointed her gun at Hampton and fired.

Hampton bellowed and spun like a top as the bullet slammed into his shoulder. Eugene let out a stream of foul language that turned the stale air blue and prepared to pump all six chambers into Sarah Green.

"Don't even think about it, Mr Angove."

Eugene turned his head and saw that four large men were pointing Mauser rifles at him. Each one looked almost identical. They had bulbous staring eyes and thick, rubbery lips. Each was in an ill-fitting suit. Eugene recognised them from descriptions that Stevenson had given him from the Innsmouth report. He was face to face with the fabled children of Dagon. They looked like a bunch of frogs in Al Capone's cast offs. It would have been funny had they not been pointing guns at him.

"Well done, niece." The leader grinned. "I see you have the black stone. Now, where is the incantation? Let's get this over with. Eugene here will be a fine tribute to the sleeping god."

"Niece?" Eugene snorted. "I knew there was something *fishy* about you the moment I clapped eyes on you."

Sarah shot across the room and slapped Eugene as hard as she possibly could.

"Sarah." Mr Green snapped. "There will be time for all of that later. Where is the incantation?"

"Gone!" Eugene grinned. "It's been turned into cracking, I'm afraid." He indicated the brazier.

Mr Green raged.

"Be calm, uncle." Sarah purred as she reached into Eugene's pocket and snatched his field notebook. "Mr Angove was kind enough to take dictation."

"Excellent!" Green smiled, revealing rows of jagged teeth. "Would you care to do the honours?"

"With pleasure!" Sarah stepped to the dais and started to chant the Aklo from the page. The room shook and buckled as, almost instantly, a red tear in the fabric of reality started to open in front of the effigy of Tsathoggua. The gateway to N'kai was opening. Mr Green snapped his fingers, and two of his goons grabbed Eugene and disarmed him.

As Sarah neared the end of the incantation, the rift widened, showing shimmering images of the land beyond. Cyclopean monoliths and twisted vegetation spread out towards a vast mountain in the centre. This was the nest of the sleeping god.

A frightful *crack* of lightning shot from the portal as Sarah read the final syllables of that guttural spiel. From the place it struck, a huge shimmering ball of black ooze started to grow. It shook and trembled with hunger. Whatever it was, it was alive.

"What is that thing?" Green cried in horror.

"I don't understand..." Sarah babbled. "It's the formless spawn of Tsathoggua! ... The final passage is supposed to stop it materialising and *cleansing* the temple." She scrutinised the page, then screamed at Eugene. "The final passage, where is it?"

"Do you think I just fell off a Christmas tree? I saw the look in your eye when you mentioned *harnessing* the power of N'kai. Nobody should have that power."

Sarah snarled and raised the gun to drill a hole between his eyes. Before she could fire, Hampton lunged from behind a supporting pillar and shoved her towards the spawn. With a hungry *slurp,* the spawn oozed forwards and engulfed the screeching Innsmouther.

Green cried in dismay as he ran to aid his relative. Eugene used the distraction to belt one of the goons in his bulbous belly with the point of his elbow then twist and knee the other one in the plums. Hampton, clutching his shoulder, grabbed the rifle from the one doubled over and swung it like a cricket bat at the skull of its fellow.

While this was transpiring, the other Innsmouth goon and Mr Green were being digested by the expanding spawn. It manifested pseudopods at will that shot out and ensnared them.

"Out!" Eugene cried as he grabbed a rifle off the floor, then snatched the black stone from the dais. It was only a tiny object, but Eugene could feel the power it contained surging through his fingers.

Hampton and Eugene raced back up the tunnel and out of the temple, leaving the spawn of Tsathoggua to *cleanse* his temple. Once they had caught their breath, they scouted for the Innsmouth camp and retrieved all of the explosives they could find, then loaded the atrium and let it blow. Before leaving, Eugene took Stevenson's lighter and tossed it amongst the rubble in the hope that the star-like symbol would keep the horrors of N'kai within.

"So, what now, sir?"

"Well, Hampton. I suggest we secure some supplies and a small tent, then hike back to the airfield. I can't wait to get back to Blighty and hand this damn stone over to Stevenson."

"He's going to be dashed upset about his lighter... and that book. I think the Miskatonic want it back."

Eugene smiled. "To be honest, Hampton. I couldn't give two toffees what that jackanape thinks. He'll be lucky if he escapes our meeting with his nose intact."

Hampton chuckled and followed his master into the rainforest. One thing was for certain. After seeing the horrific spawn of Tsathoggua, he'd never look at a bowl of jelly in the same way ever again.

The Authors

CHARLOTTE LANGTREE

Charlotte Langtree is a poet, aspiring novelist, and writer of short fiction. Raised in West Yorkshire, she has a deep love of hills, berry-picking, and her unique accent. She's been creating stories for almost as long as she has been alive, and has a profound respect for the magic of the written word. She has been published in several magazines and anthologies. In December 2020, she was named 'Author of the Month' by Paper Djinn Press. You can find her online by following the links below:

Website: www.charlottelangtree.wordpress.com

Facebook: www.facebook.com/CharlotteLangtreeAuthor

Twitter: www.twitter.com/CharlotteLangt5

GORDON LINZNER

Gordon Linzner is founder and former editor of Space and Time Magazine, and author of three published novels and dozens of short stories appearing in Fantasy & Science Fiction, Twilight Zone, Sherlock Holmes Mystery Magazine, and numerous other magazines and anthologies. He is also a copy editor, a licensed New York City tour guide, a sound technician, and lead singer for the Saboteur Tiger Blues band, among other odd jobs.

312

He is a member of the Horror Writers Association and a lifetime member of the Science Fiction & Fantasy Writers of America. His short story "Show and Zeller" was nominated for a 2021 Shamus Award.

ALANNA ROBERSTON-WEBB

Alanna Robertson-Webb is an author and editor who enjoys long weekends of LARPing, is terrified of sharks and finds immense fun in being the editor-in-chief at Eerie River Publishing. She one day aspires to run her own nerd-themed restaurant, as well as her own LARP game.

She has edited over ten books, such as Infected by Blair Daniels, A Cure for Chaos: Horror Stories from Hospitals and Psych Wards by Haunted House Publishing, The Deliverer by Tara Devlin and the 2020 to mid 2021 Eerie River Publishing anthologies. Alanna's writing has been published in over eighty different collections, and more information about her work can be found at:

https://arwauthor.wixsite.com/arwauthor

DECLAN FLETCHER

Declan Fletcher in his boring everyday life is an IT project manager. A long time reader particularly of sci fi and fantasy he finally decided to try his hand at writing himself. Still new to writing he has stories in Lost Lore and Legends a collection of drabbles andis excited to write more. Outside of writing he'll basically watch any sport that someone is willing to televise from his couch in West London.

DAVID BOWMORE

David was born in gypsy caravan, on a wintery night with the sound of thunder and the flash of lightning welcoming him into the world.Forty-five years later, he started writing fiction.

True to his coming into the world, he has lived here, there and everywhere, but now lives in Yorkshire with his wonderful wife and a small white poodle.

In his time, he has worn many hats; head chef, teacher and landscape gardener.

His award winning book of connected short stories 'The Magic of Deben Market' was enacted by BookStreamz in December 2020.

Discover more about David's writing at

www.davidbowmore.co.uk

DONOVAN 'MONSTER' SMITH

Monster Smith is an author, writer, film producer, director, podcast host, cryptozoologist, and mixed martial artist from Chandler, Arizona.

NEEN COHEN

Neen Cohen is an Australian Sapphic Speculative Fiction author, and lives in Brisbane with her partner, son and fur babies. She has a Bachelor of Creative Industries from Queensland University of Technology and is a member of the Springfield Writer's Group. She's had a multitude of 'day jobs' to pay the bills but her heart has always been in the art of marking dead trees with squiggles of ink and graphite.

When she's not running after her son, spending time with her partner or working at the current 'day job', she can often be found writing while sitting against a tombstone or tree in any number of graveyards. She's also discovered a new found passion for throwing sharp objects at thick pieces of wood (knife throwing and axe throwing) and tries to squeeze at least 30 hours in to each day because sleep is for the weak.

To keep up to date with all of Neen's misadventures you can find all her links in one convenient location: https://linktr.ee/neencohen

C. MARRY HULTMAN

C. Marry Hultman is a teacher, writer and sometimes podcaster who is equal parts Swede and Wisconsinite. He lives with his wife and two daughters and runs W.A.R.G –The Guild podcast dedicated to interviewing authors about their creative process. In addition to that, he runs the website Wisconsin Noir – Cosmic Horror set in the Dairy State where he collects short fiction and general thoughts.

Find out more about him at

https://linktr.ee/C.MarryHultman

CHISTO HEALY

Chisto has been writing full-time for one year and in that year he has had almost 200 published works. He lives in NC with his equally wacky fiancee, her mom, his two brilliant teenage daughters who have proven to be incredible muses, and his son Boe who keeps them all on their toes.

You can check his badly maintained blog at

https://chistohealy.blogspot.com

TIM MENDEES

Tim Mendees is a horror writer from Macclesfield in the North-West of England that specialises in cosmic horror and weird fiction. A lifelong fan of classic weird tales, Tim set out to bring the pulp horror of yesteryear into the 21 st Century and give it a distinctly British flavour. His work has been described as the love-child of H.P. Lovecraft and P.G. Wodehouse and is often peppered with a wry sense of humour that acts as a counterpoint to the unnerving, and often disturbing, narratives.

Tim has had over seventy published stories in anthologies and magazines with publishers all over the world. His novellas, Burning Reflection, Spiffing, and The Creeping Void are out now.

When he is not arguing with the spellchecker, Tim is a goth DJ, crustacean and cephalopod enthusiast, and the presenter of a popular web series of live video readings of his material and interviews with fellow authors. He currently lives in Brighton &H ove with his pet crab, Gerald, and an army of stuffed octopods.

https://timmendeeswriter.wordpress.com/

https://tinyurl.com/timmendeesyoutube

MORE FROM
BREAKING RULES EUROPE

- o Face of Fear by C. Marry Hultman
  e-book:books2read.com/u/49lVg0
  Paperback: mybook.to/Face-of-Fear

- o Dawson Junior G3 by Brian Wagstaff
  e-book:books2read.com/u/4EP99E
  Paperback: mybook.to/Dawson

- o Boy in the Wardrobe by Esther Jacoby
  e-book: mybook.to/Boy-Wardrobe

- o New Life Cottage by Esther Jacoby
  e-book:books2read.com/u/m0wAzW
  Paperback: mybook.to/New-Life-Cottage

- o The Wait by Esther Jacoby
  e-book:https://books2read.com/u/4Dgz8Q

- o Liebe ist Warten by Esther Jacoby
  e-book:https://books2read.com/u/mZaVD2
  Paperback: mybook.to/Liebe

- o Musing on Death & Dying by Esther Jacoby
  e-book:books2read.com/u/49lVg0
  Paperback: mybook.to/Musings

- o Earth Door by Cye Thomas
  e-book:books2read.com/u/mKyXKv
  Paperback: mybook.to/Earth-Door

o Graffiti Stories by Nick Gerrard
  e-book:books2read.com/u/m2MQOR
  Paperback: mybook.to/Grafitti-Stories

o Punk Novelette by Nick Gerrard
  e-book:books2read.com/u/4jLpqv
  Paperback: mybook.to/Punk-Novelette

o Struggle and Strife by Nick Gerrard
  e-book:books2read.com/u/4DRyqr
  Paperback: mybook.to/struggle-strife

o Fake Escape by Natalie Hughes
  e-book:https://books2read.com/u/bMXL5X

o Murder Planet by Adam Carpenter
  e-book:books2read.com/u/bMXllV
  Paperback: mybook.to/Murder-Planet

o Generation Ship by Adam Carpenter
  e-book:books2read.com/u/49Nk8M
  Paperback: mybook.to/generation

o Cold as Hell by Neen Cohen
  e-book:https://books2read.com/u/bxennv
  Paperback: mybook.to/Grafitti-Stories

o Six Days to Hell by E.L. Giles
  e-book:https://books2read.com/u/bWrLyq
  Paperback: mybook.to/SixDaystoHell

o Just 13 anthology
   e-book: https://books2read.com/u/mKy1B9

o Lost Lore & Legends Anthology
   e-book: books2read.com/u/m2RrwG
   Paperback: mybook.to/Lost-Lore-Legends-pbk

Find us at:
www.breakingrulespublishingeuro.com

9 789198 684124